THE FLAME OF BATTLE

THE FLAME OF BATTLE

THE FLAME OF BATTLE

By Melinda R. Cordell

THE DRAGONRIDERS OF SKALA BOOK 1

THE FLAME OF BATTLE

Rosefiend Publishing.

THE FLAME OF BATTLE

Ordering information: For details, contact the publisher at
hello@melindacordell.com
Cover design by We Got You Covered.

Amazon ISBN: 978-1-953196-42-2

Second Edition: December 2022

Note: Some parts of this book were originally published in the first one-third of THE FLAME OF BATTLE, 2018 edition.

10 9 8 7 6 5 4 3 2 1 blast off!

Subscribe to my newsletter and get a free dragon book!
https://melindacordell.com/subscribe/

THE FLAME OF BATTLE

Dyrfinna and her sword-friends only want to mourn their friend Thora, the Queen's daughter, after she died after visiting her husband-to-be, King Varinn. But when, after her burial, Thora walks into the banquet hall and starts killing men, all Hel breaks loose. Only Dyrfinna is able to return her dead friend to her eternal rest – but not before hearing a terrifying story from her lips.

The only recourse for this awful deed is revenge. Dyrfinna is more than ready.

Dyrfinna is thrilled for a chance to prove herself as a warrior and as a commander of her ship and the warriors on board. She is proud to go to war for her friend's sake. But a death that Dyrfinna herself caused comes back home to roost. Whatever she does, she can never escape a great wrong she did ... nor will she be forgiven for it. Or forgive herself.

But as they sail to battle, everything goes wrong. And, unbeknownst to her, she's about to meet her worst enemy.

TABLE OF CONTENTS

THE FLAME OF BATTLE

About 1000 AD

THE CARNELIAN RING

The sound of thunder travels fast in a Norse settlement.

It had been a cold, drizzly afternoon in Skala, the town upon the sea named for the small queendom that stretched across the barren fjords and rocky peaks of the land.

In the harbor, the great Viking ships sat sullen under a steady drizzle, while the eternal waves shushed across the rocks of the shore.

On the side of the mountain, at the Queen's keep, the dragons grumbled as the stablers built a great bonfire in the mouth of their cave, and they huddled close to it.

Until, out of nowhere, a horrifying flash of lightning speared the ground from the low clouds, drowning everything in white light, followed instantly by a crash that shook the ground.

The dragons jumped. Several spread their wings, startled, and a number of them hissed.

But a garnet dragon, whose name was Serja, turned watchfully, their eyes blazing.

Serja gazed at the place where the lightning had struck for a time without a word. A light scrim of smoke and ions drifted up and faded. After a time, the dragon spoke.

"It has begun," they said.

*

The crack of thunder still echoed against the craggy mountains when the screams began.

Dyrfinna, a girl of seventeen years, crouched over her brother's unmoving body, frantically shaking his shoulder. A thin wisp of smoke drifted up from his open mouth.

"Please. Please," she whispered, smoothing back his tousled hair. A shadow of a memory: how, when he was a little boy, she'd combed his thick hair so it stood on end, and they'd laughed and laughed. "Eirik, *no.* Please. I'm sorry. Don't go. Don't …"

A loud cry from behind her made her jump.

It was their father in his fine cloak, straight from the Queen's court, his eyes going wider and wider, his face melting into a kind of grief she'd never seen before in her life.

Dyrfinna scrambled back. "I'm sorry … I'm sorry … Papa, please … I didn't mean to …"

His broad hand cracked her across the face.

"You monster! I should have realized it would come to this," he hissed. "I should have sent you off to be a fosterling as soon as my son was born. I should have known there would be no end to your jealousy!"

She felt herself dissolve into tears. *You raised him up over me. But I wasn't jealous!* "Papa, no…"

"You are no longer a part of the Corae Guard," Egill hissed, spit flying. "You are banned from the dragons, banned from warfare. I will give you away in marriage just so I can be done with you. Is that clear?"

"But Papa …"

"No more! Get out of my sight, you monster!" her father screamed, raw with grief.

She blindly fled from where her dead brother lay.

"Ah, my son, my son," her father said, and his voice cracked, followed by bitter sobbing.

"I didn't mean to. I'm sorry. I'm sorry," she whispered as she ran on wobbly legs, head still ringing from the explosion of lightning and magic she had created. She pulled her hands and arms tightly against her sides, certain that the magic she'd let loose during their argument was still crackling and fizzing along her fingers – overflowing with fear that she might accidentally loose it again.

This was not supposed to happen. She didn't even know where this power came from. Her magic consisted of simple charms and spells for warfare and dragonflight – mostly spells that would shield her from fire, or sustain her when she was exhausted in battle. She'd never called down anything of this magnitude before.

Now her mother came running toward the place where Eirik lay dead, led by several of her neighbors.

Dyrfinna's heart dropped hard in her chest. She flung herself behind a gnarled oak and pressed against the bark as she raced past.

Don't look, Mama. Don't look. I'm sorry. I'm sorry.

Her mama's agonized scream. Her broken cries. The worst sounds that Dyrfinna had ever heard a person make. She sank to the ground, her back to the oak, and buried her face in her hands.

Word spread fast through Skala. More people ran past. She huddled by the oak for a long time, praying that nobody would see her, trying to make sense of it in her mind, trying to understand how it had all happened.

"Did you kill him?" someone snapped. "Did you do it on purpose?"

A gossipmonger stood there, sneering at Dyrfinna.

Dyrfinna felt the magic flare, felt it fizz into life in her hands again. *Odin's eye, not again!*

She fled without replying, arms and hands still alive with magic. People who saw her go by hissed and drew back.

She went to the only refuge she could think of: back home. There was no use in running away. She'd face her punishment. She just wanted to weep before they took her away to be put on trial.

Dyrfinna collapsed on the bed, her breath shuddering, trying to tamp down the magic.

Aesa, her little sister, peeped in. "Sissy?"

"No!" Dyrfinna cried, starting up from her bed. "Stay away from me! Stay back! I don't want to hurt you, too!"

"You're not going to hurt me. Eirik was being mean," Aesa informed her. Apparently she had not left the house after Dyrfinna had run off after Eirik, yelling at him, some time ago.

"You don't know what just happened after we left. And it doesn't matter what he was doing," Dyrfinna cried. "Please, just get back!"

"Aesa. Do as your sister says," came a new voice.

At the voice, Dyrfinna gasped.

In an instant she was kneeling, pressing her forehead to the floor to the visitor amid a new flood of tears. "Don't come near me," she pleaded. "I'm sorry. I can't control it. I didn't mean to do it, I didn't mean to."

For it was Thora who stood in the doorway – the Queen's daughter.

Her golden hair, tightly braided around her head, nearly brushed the top of the door frame. A deep red carnelian gleamed in the simple golden circlet she wore in her hair.

"Yes. I can still see the magic on you," Thora said. "Aesa, please step back."

"You can't tell me what to do." Aesa stubbornly folded her arms.

"Yes, I can," Thora said. "Your sissy is scared. You need to give her some space so I can help her." She gently put her hands on Aesa's shoulders, scooted her aside, then came in. "Gather yourself, Finna. Tell me what happened."

Dyrfinna recoiled in shame but pulled herself together as she got to her feet, and told Thora everything that had happened.

Aesa gasped at what Dyrfinna said and started to sob.

"Mama! No!" her little sister cried, running blindly out of the room.

"Your mama's by the docks," Thora said before the door slammed behind Aesa. Her sobbing faded out of hearing.

And now Dyrfinna burst out with a sob she couldn't control. "I'm sorry." She took off her brooch, the beautiful silver brooch that Thora had given her emblazoned with the dragon Corae, who had given her life for Dyrfinna and her friends. "Take this," Dyrfinna said as grief constricted her throat. "I cannot be part of the Corae Guard anymore."

Thora shook her head. "I will not accept your resignation. I need you at my side."

"Not anymore," Dyrfinna insisted, still trying to give Thora the silver brooch. "This brooch I value over gold and riches, but after what I did today, I cannot wear it any longer. I am too much of a danger to all of you."

"How?" Thora asked.

"I don't know where these powers came from. I've k … I struck down my younger brother," she said, choking on the words.

Thora pulled a ring off her finger, a golden band with a gleaming red carnelian in it, and held it up to Dyrfinna.

"Put this on your finger," she said. "It will restrain your magic so it hurts nobody. It works just the same as the dragon collars."

Dyrfinna slipped on the ring, still warm from Thora's finger. The fizz of magic instantly dissipated from her fingers.

Relief rushed over her and she slumped, touching her hands, her arms, making sure the magic was really gone. "I didn't mean to," she said, stupidly, though she had already said it over again over again.

"I've lost an older sister," Thora said sympathetically. "Grief … does things to you. And I know you didn't mean to call the thunder. It was an accident."

Dyrfinna shook her head, unable to speak.

"Many a young mage has been taken aback when their powers awaken," Thora continued. "Though their powers seldom manifest the way yours have …"

"I am not a mage," Dyrfinna said angrily, starting up.

"All the same, your powers need to be tamed."

"No. I mean that I'm never going to use this magic. I'll just wear this carnelian until I die," Dyrfinna added, holding up the ring. "I'll be bound like a dragon. I don't care. I never want this to happen again."

"Dragons require different bindings." Thora took Dyrfinna's hand and examined the ring she'd just given her. She murmured something and passed her hand over the carnelian, which began to glow softly, and squinted at it for a long moment.

Finally, the carnelian's glow faded, and Thora set down Dyrfinna's hand. "I had this ring made for other purposes. This has some of the bindings you need to suppress your magic, but not all of them. I'll have a ring specially made for you, that locks into your magic and holds it steady … until you can be trained," she added, leveling a gaze at Dyrfinna. "The training is not optional."

Dyrfinna looked down. "But Papa says I am no longer a part of the Corae Guard. He forbade me from having anything to do with dragons, or weapons training."

"Finna. He actually *said* that?"

Dyrfinna nodded, a knot tightening in her throat. "He said I don't deserve to lead armies into battle. That I don't deserve to fly dragons, or handle glittering swords. He said he will marry me off as quickly as possible, and that will be the end of it."

Dyrfinna buried her face in her hands, crushed with grief and remorse. "He said that he should have sent me off to be a fosterling when Eirik was born."

Thora's face had that stubborn frown that was, in better times, adorable. "He thinks he can kick you out of *my* personal guard, that I chose myself? The personal guard who I trust daily with my life?" she asked, incredulous. "No, he most certainly cannot. That's nonsense." Thora took Dyrfinna's hand. "Chieftain he may be, but this changes nothing. You are still a member of my personal guard."

"But … but my father said that I was not deserving. And … he's right," she said. "I'm not. I … killed my brother." She could barely manage to speak those words – those words that made her horrifying act real. "Please. He's right. I must be cut off from my people, now. Exiled. What I did …." She could no longer speak.

The queen's daughter stared at Dyrfinna for a moment, then did something extraordinary. She took off her golden circlet, then sighed and sat down next to Dyrfinna on her small bed.

Dyrfinna hid her amazement. Thora, though a friend, always remembered that she was royalty. To see her unbend like this and act like a normal person boggled the mind.

Thora turned her circlet in her hands. It was still slightly bent from where her dragon had stepped on it — she'd said at the time that she was going to get it fixed, but clearly she'd never gotten around to it. "Finna. I need to tell you something. You probably already understand this. But your father is not your friend. He is not even your ally," Thora continued, "so it doesn't matter what he says."

But it does, Dyrfinna thought, bowing her head. She'd tried for so many years to get him to love her the way he'd loved her brother. Now he never would.

"Finna, I trust you with my life. I will always protect you, just as you have always protected me. This time will be no different."

But her brother's dead eyes, half-open, floated between Dyrfinna and the memory.

"I am not worthy of the confidence you place in me," Dyrfinna mumbled.

"You are," Thora said warmly. "And someday, when I am queen, *you* will be my second-in-command — not your father."

"I think he knows that." *And it pisses him off,* she thought.

"Retirement will do your father good. Perhaps he will learn to be a little less … unbending."

"Ha."

Thora nodded. Now she got to her feet and put the circlet back on. "You are still a member of my guard, but you will have to go before a conclave."

"I'm fine with that," she said. "Let them do what they will to me. I accept their punishment."

"I will talk to the völva, but I think your punishment will be different than what you expect. She will likely agree with me about how your powers need nurturing, not punishment."

Dyrfinna's mouth tightened. She shook her head, hard. "I only want to pay the blood-price for what I've done – preferably in my own blood. I want to atone for what I've done. Please."

"Not in your blood. No. Give yourself time to mourn."

Dyrfinna's shame – her disgust with herself – those words her papa had said – all of it went in circles in her mind, so much so that she almost wanted to rip herself out of her body and be free of them.

"I will be a blot on your reputation if I stay with the Corae Guard. My brother's blood is on my soul."

"I can deal with my reputation," Thora said. "In the meanwhile, I will let your sword-friends know what happened. I'll send the völva to you, and call the conclave, and once they have made their judgement, I'll have your ring made."

Dyrfinna's eyes filled again. She could barely speak around the tightness in her throat. "I do not deserve your kindness. But, thank you."

Thora paused in the doorway, her clear blue eyes meeting hers. "Do not tear yourself down. The guilt will be agonizing. But I will help you through it because you are my friend."

Dyrfinna bowed her head. "Thank you."

That was Thora, the best of all the Vikings of Skala.

She should have been Queen.

But the Norn had spun out a different fate for her.

One year later

A FINAL GOODBYE

A cold wind gusted in from the sea. Fine spray fell over Dyrfinna's arms and back as she and her friends each carried a heavy-laden chest to Thora's funeral ship. The scent of her friend's room, of the lavender and rose petals she always added to the linen, floated off the chest, soon to be devoured by fire.

Dyrfinna's heart was too full of pain for her to speak.

Today, she'd lost everything.

She squinted against the wind, the late afternoon sun burning her eyes. Or maybe those were tears. At this point, she could not tell.

The pyre for the Queen's daughter had been raised on the shoreline for her journey to Helgafjell, the holy mountain, to join the kinfolk who had gone before her. Thora's great funerary boat sat upon the pebbly shore, surrounded by silent crowds of Vikings.

The dragons stood over them, waiting to accompany Thora on her final voyage, their gemlike scales glittering like garnets and gold from their internal fires. Each of them wore a golden collar set with large carnelians, gleaming red in the fiery sun.

Once aboard, Dyrfinna set down the heavy chest next to the prow. How many times had Dyrfinna stood balanced here in the old days with her sword, her unbound hair blowing in the breeze, enjoying the feeling of flight as the ship leapt through the waves.

This sturdy ship had been Thora's favorite. She used to take her friends – her Corae Guard – on excursions along the coast. Skeggi would recite poetry. Rjupa would sit next to Thora, singing along. Thora would try to ignore the book that she'd brought along – she could never go anywhere without a book – but she'd end up reading it anyway. Dyrfinna would stand balanced next to the prow doing sword exercises while Gefjun and Ostryg leaned over the sides, annoying the fishes.

But now the ship was prepared for burning, with dry peat and tarred wood filling the upper deck up to the oaken gunnels.

Thora's dragon, Serja, puffed hot air over Thora's body, trying to keep the flies at bay as they gathered around her face and tried to crawl into her mouth and nostrils.

Dyrfinna climbed up to the rail and walked to them, balancing on the rail.

"Our poor girl," Serja said softly. Thora's dragon had long horns and thin, hairlike feathers behind the horns and around their ears. Their face was narrow, like a deer's, with smooth scales that gleamed like embers when the wind blew on them.

Dyrfinna stroked Serja's feathers as she gazed on Thora. Her thigh accidentally got too close to one of the carnelians on Serja's golden collar, and a small spark of magic popped against her leg. She moved without thinking.

"We cannot believe that Thora's gone," Serja said with a shiver through their great wings, folded neatly at their sides. "She just flicked out of life so quickly, like a mayfly."

"I know." Dyrfinna laid her head on the dragon's nose, feeling the warmth of their internal fires, and the quiet song the dragon was humming to itself.

Serja gently rested their head against Dyrfinna. She leaned back, feeling that bond, that friendship they'd grown into through the years. Though Serja was Thora's dragon, Dyrfinna often rode her, too.

If Thora had lived, she would have become Queen, and Dyrfinna would had been the chieftain of Skala, Thora's second-in-command. Dyrfinna would have flown into battle at her side on dragonback.

But now, the life that Dyrfinna loved was over. No more dragons. No more glorious flights, laughing with her friends on dragonback over the ocean. No more weapons training with the best instructors. No more training in the magical arts.

Her father had come to her before Thora's body had lost its warmth. "You are out of the Corae Guard," he said. "There is no Corae Guard now. After Thora's funeral and burning, you will be barred from the dragon stables. Permanently."

Serja should have been mine! Dyrfinna thought, gazing into the dragon's eyes. *We're bonded!*

"Remember your place, Finna," her friend Rjupa said in a sad voice from behind her.

Dyrfinna breathed deeply. *This is not about me,* she reminded herself. *Today our nation is in mourning. I can weep and bemoan my fate tomorrow.*

Dyrfinna kissed the dragon's nose and hopped down, turning to face what she didn't want to see.

Thora had been laid upon the kindling, wearing her green dress of thick wool lavishly embroidered with gold, and a wide belt of exquisitely tooled leather around her waist. Dyrfinna, along with her friends, adjusted her dress so it lay beautifully around Thora's body, set her long, golden braids over her shoulders, and lay gold coins to cover her half-open eyes. They adorned her neck with a necklace with beads of gold and amber.

Upon her brow they set her golden crown, a delicate band with a single gleaming carnelian.

Rjupa set Thora's well-worn books that only a few in the land could read – some written in Latin, some in runes. The calfskin covers were soft from all the times Thora's hands had held them.

Finally, Dyrfinna knelt at Thora's side and laid her hnefatafl game, king's table, next to her body, with the amber game pieces in a small drawskin bag.

Yielding to an impulse, she opened the bag and poured out the pieces to look at them one last time. The amber markers clicked in her hand – half of them a rich, dark orange, the other half of them a lighter orange. The king's piece, with its small crown, stood above the other pieces, translucent, glowing in the afternoon sun. Like Thora's books, this, too, had been worn smooth by constant use.

How many times had Dyrfinna and Thora bent their heads over these pieces on the hnefatafl board, mulling through different strategies to capture the king? How many long afternoons like this one had flowed past until the sun hung low in the window of the keep, and Thora's servant appeared in the doorway to say, "The Queen would like you to come to dinner one of these days. She has called you at least fifty times." Her servant had a knack for overstatement.

But Thora would frown, her eyes never leaving the board, and say, "Wait a moment, I'm about to capture Finna's king." The poor servant would have to wait, hoping that the Queen wouldn't have to call her fifty more times.

Now Dyrfinna looked for a long moment at her friend's bluish face, the smell of decay filling her nostrils.

"This isn't right," she said, and gently poured the pieces back into their bag.

"I know," Gefjun said, gazing fiercely down at their friend's corpse. Her hair was twisted up in a loose bun, though many red tendrils had escaped, through which the sun blazed. "It's not right. She was too young to die." Gefjun always became sharp when she was deeply upset, and often when she wasn't.

"Sometimes it happens," Rjupa said quietly, joining them, tears shimmering in her eyes. She was a small woman with delicate features, but today she wore the war-prize she had earned: The gigantic helmet of Iron Skull, pitted with the marks of many swords and axes. It dwarfed her face, but she wore it with deserved pride. "Many people die young."

"But it doesn't make sense," Gefjun said. "She wasn't even that sick when she came home from King Varinn's. I checked her myself! She seemed fine, only tired and sneezy. Then the next day she collapsed in the garden and died."

"I don't know," Rjupa said softly. "It seems wrong. But nobody knows why the Nornir choose to cut the thread of somebody's life."

"Oh, I'll tell the Norns what I think of that," Gefjun snapped.

"Take care what you say about the deathless gods," Dyrfinna warned.

"Oh, stop, Finna. Even if they did come for me, you'd fight the Fates themselves just to be belligerent."

Dyrfinna wasn't sure if this was a complaint or a compliment, so she let it go. "Rjupa's right. But …" She blew out a hard gust of air, gazing again at Thora. "If there had been any way that I could have died in her place, I would have. I would have much rather died in her place."

Those words had surprised Dyrfinna as soon as they came out, and she felt the full weight of them. So did her friends. Now they were both quiet, gazing at her, worried.

She instantly looked down and her heart convulsed. "I didn't mean it like that," she added, low.

Gefjun and Rjupa exchanged a glance. Then Rjupa laid a small hand on Dyrfinna's back. "There's no use in second-guessing yourself," she said gently. "This can't be easy, coming so soon after your brother's … death."

If that what you choose to call it. "I know," Dyrfinna said, low.

"Yeah, everybody's talking about it. I mean, how Thora died," Gefjun said roughly as Dyrfinna turned back. "Because you don't die of a *cold.* You just don't. She didn't even have a fever." Gefjun was a healer, dedicated to her work, her old burgundy tunic always smelling of sage and thyme and other herbs. "It doesn't make sense."

"But as the head of her Corae Guard, I should have gone with her to King Varinn's."

"She said we didn't need to. Said it a half-million times," Gefjun reminded her.

It would have been different if I'd gone with her. A huge, nameless anguish fell over Dyrfinna, and she turned away.

"The dwellers at Helgafjell will see how much we loved her," Rjupa said in her small, broken voice, "when she comes sailing up to their holy mountain with all these riches."

"I only wish we had more books to send with her," Dyrfinna said.

The other girls laughed, despite their tears.

Now Dyrfinna smiled. She imagined what it would be like when Thora sailed to the holy mountain. Thora would sail out of the mist of life into the next world on her ship, her riches ranged about her, her horse whickering at her back. The residents of the holy mountain, the dead of the ages before, would gather on the shore to receive the young queen and greet her – and she'd take no notice of them because she would be sitting on a bench on the boat with her feet up, reading a book.

So where did your brother end up when you killed him? Dyrfinna asked herself. *Which shore did his ship carry him to? You denied him entry into Valhalla, for he was not killed in battle or in defending himself.*

Would he have gone to Hel instead?

"The tide is coming in," somebody called from the shore, breaking her out of these dark thoughts.

One of the men lay a pair of open scissors on Thora's chest, and her feet were tied together to keep her from walking after death. Dyrfinna shook her head at their worries. This was Thora, who would have been queen. What an insult, to think of Thora coming back as a draugr.

The young women climbed back down from the funeral pyre and hopped off the side of the ship. The tide was well in by now, and they splashed into ankle-deep water to walk to dry sand.

The sun was setting in glory, reds and oranges suffusing the sky across the great expanse of salt water. The great mountains of the fjords stood in silent grandeur under the changing sky.

Hundreds of Vikings that stood along the shore, gathered on the green meadows that led to the ocean, the gleam of torches from hundreds more in their ships on the ocean.

Dyrfinna glanced over her shoulder. There, faces ruddy in the light of the sunset and the faint glow of the garnet dragons, came the rest of her sword-friends – Ostryg and Skeggi.

The sword-friends had also been Thora's guard, defending her in all things. They wore matching black cloaks that were clasped with a silver brooch that represented Corae, the dragon who had died defending them and Thora.

Dyrfinna was to lead them in the sky dance of the dragons.

This is going to be the last time I can ride a dragon, she thought, and nearly felt the tears come on.

Which turned to anger. *I should be mourning Thora, not what my father has taken away from me!*

She cleared her throat, pushed her grief away.

A HIGH HOLY PLACE

The hiss of the waves on the shore blended with the soft sniffles from the watchers.

Now the völva came through the crowd with her great wrought-iron staff in the shape of a snake covered in runes. The woman, who was about her mother's age, wore a headdress topped with owl feathers and the skull of a fox who had once been her familiar. A fringe hung down over the völva's eyes, obscuring them, and glass beads made an otherworldly clicking sound when she moved.

She was followed by a flock of girls in ceremonial dress, preparing the next part of the ritual as the incoming tide swirled around their ankles. The rising waves hissed against the sides of the funerary ship as she sang her holy chant over Thora's remains.

The stone that filled Dyrfinna's chest grew heavier. Breathing deeply of the ocean air, she smelled the scorch of the dragons that stood by the water.

The jeweled scales of Thora's dragon, Serja, gleamed as they finally turned away from the ship. An errant spark from their breath drifted into the kindling, which began to smolder.

"Not yet, not yet," the dragon murmured, and stuck out their forked tongue to quench the spark.

Dyrfinna went to Serja and patted them on their gleaming flank.

"I am sorry," she said in a low voice.

"We try not to tie our heart to you short-lives," said Serja, breathing over Thora's body, chasing away the flies. "But this farewell is especially hard for us."

Serja generally referred to themselves in the royal "we," as if they were a plurality instead of a single being. Dyrfinna did not understand how that worked, but she was not about to argue with a dragon.

"Me too." Dyrfinna and the dragon leaned their heads together.

The bond they shared tugged at her heart.

The question of who would be Serja's next rider was not going to be up to Dyrfinna to decide – nor would it be up to Serja. Bitterness sprouted in her heart like stinging nettles.

"We don't want to be separated from you," Serja said, "even though it is what your father has ordained. We feel as if we mourn more than the loss of Thora – we are mourning your loss, too, Dyrfinna." Their wings opened slightly in their agitation.

The carnelians in Serja's collar glowed. After a moment, Serja calmed. "However, patience is best," they added. "Nobody knows what the future holds in store."

"That is true," Dyrfinna said – though in her heart, she gazed at a bleak future where she was trapped at home, bearing children for some rough husband, bitterly watching him leave for war and glittering swords and battles on dragonback – *her* world.

I can't live like that. I just can't.

The booming of a drum came from the shoreline. The völva nodded at Dyrfinna. The next part of the ceremony was beginning.

Behind her, Rjupa took a deep breath, her face a mask of tears under Iron Skull's helmet. Thora had been kindest to her when she was a thrall who had escaped from and killed the cruel warrior, so Thora's death had hit her especially hard.

"Here we go," Dyrfinna murmured.

"We will walk with you," Serja murmured, looking around, concerned to find themselves out of place during an important ritual.

Dyrfinna placed a hand on the dragon's side. Despite the seriousness of the event, her heart lifted to be walking at her beloved dragon's side.

The crowd parted before her, opening a path to where the völva stood next to the rest of the dragons, the waves washing around her bare feet under her long gown.

"Come," she sang, a cascade of notes.

Dyrfinna came forward now, Serja at her side, her friends following behind.

The five sword-friends walked toward the dragons past the great chieftains, jarls, and petty kings and queens that ruled the small kingdoms around them. All stood in respectful silence.

But one man towered over them all – or seemed to tower, in Dyrfinna's mind. He wore no ornaments, no cloak, no crown. His blonde-red beard was tidy on his chest, his long hair sleek down his back and curling naturally on his broad shoulders. His bearing was of a man of rank and true nobility, one who had seen much over his life of traveling to the highest courts of every land.

This was Dyrfinna's father in name only, Egill. His disapproving eyes lay heavily on her from where he stood at the Queen's side, her second-in-command.

This was the man who would make certain that Dyrfinna would never ride Serja – or indeed, any other dragon – ever again.

Dyrfinna looked only at the völva, but in her peripheral vision she could see the anger that drew a line down her father's brow.

As second-in-command to the queen, as chieftain to the town of Skala, Egill had argued loudly against her flying in the ceremony.

The Queen had the final say, of course.

An angry snort from her father as she walked past, head high. She felt his breath on her arm.

When Dyrfinna was a little girl, Papa called her his little warrior. They'd play-fight with toy swords, and he'd let Dyrfinna trounce him. He'd bounce every time she swatted him with her sword, shouting "Ow! Ow! Ow! Ow!" as she chased him in circles.

Her eyes prickled.

Why couldn't he love her the way he used to? Didn't he know that, down in her heart, she was still the same little girl she used to be?

Dyrfinna could hear somebody whispering about her. Even here, at Thora's ceremony, she could hear some gossip whispering maliciously how Dyrfinna didn't deserve to be there. "There's nobody to protect her now," they hissed.

Her father had a lot of friends that supported him, people who agreed that Dyrfinna had killed her brother out of spite. But they only said this when her back was turned.

Dyrfinna straightened and rolled her neck, looking across the small Viking city of Skala toward the great mountains of the fjords and the endless ocean. The smell of wood smoke from many chimneys came to her. Even this far down on the shore, she could hear the complaints of the sheep on the hills, a dog barking at the city's edge, the rush of waves on the shore, the mewling of a seagull – all the sounds of home.

Surrounded as she was by this beauty, Dyrfinna felt desperately unfulfilled.

They had now reached the place where the rest of the dragons had gathered, waiting for the sword-friends to ride. Each of the dragons wore a jeweled collar, glimmering with carnelians, which they were fitted with as soon as they hatched.

"There you are," said Shriken, a silver-scaled racing dragon, nudging Rjupa. She threw her arms around the dragon's neck.

Dyrfinna's father had, only a few days ago, awarded Rjupa with the only open position of dragonrider, giving Shriken to her as her own personal dragon. "As befitting one of Thora's *personal* guards," he'd said with a fond smile to Rjupa.

That had hurt more than words could express.

Dyrfinna climbed onto Serja's back as they stood majestically still, their wings slightly open. Ostryg vaulted aboard her father's glittering black mica dragon named Krekkaq, while Gefjun rode the Queen's golden dragon, Tandryss, the calm one.

Skeggi was riding Old Red, a gigantic blood-red drake. He was talking about a ship funeral he had witnessed about a hundred years ago, while Skeggi was frantically trying to hush the old dragon before he said something embarrassing.

"We were trying to flame a ship," Old Red rambled, "but the skies opened up into a downpour. I tell you, it was like being in a waterfall! None of us could see past our assholes, if you know what I mean."

"Too late," Dyrfinna murmured to herself.

Poor Skeggi went bright red to match the dragon, while the watching crowds of Vikings were chuckling.

"No, we don't know what you mean," Serja said aloud.

Old Red seemed to remember where he was. "Oh! Well. Skies are clear tonight," he said, looking around at the crowd as if surprised to see them there, and stopped talking.

Just then the voice of an old friend rang out from Thora's ship. The old steersman, Hakr, had climbed aboard to guide her ship out to sea.

"Now the tide is high," he said, for now Thora's ship was afloat. The crowd turned to him as he hoisted the sail on Thora's ship with sure hands. The old Viking's beard was gray, and his blue eyes were set in a permanent squint against the weather and the sun from his many years on board ships as he traveled the world.

"Come, my friends. We go now to sea," he proclaimed to Dyrfinna and the sword-friends. The wind blew sweetly from the shore – the gods were smiling upon them, to have the wind blowing in the right direction – and the ship slid through the waves toward the deep.

With one hard, calloused hand upon the tiller, Hakr turned his face toward the sun, low in the west, steering Thora true on her last voyage.

Dyrfinna laid her hands on Serja's neck, the dragon's scales so warm under her hands, watching the black ship sail away.

Who are you, Dyrfinna? a voice had asked in the dream. *What do you want?*

"I want to fly," she murmured as the sea wind blew strands of hair into her face. "It's all I've ever wanted."

But if she lost her ability to fly dragons and fight … if she was to be separated from the dragon that loved her most … who was she then? What did that make her? A demoted dragonrider, forced to marry, separated from her friends and family, trapped in a world she despised.

Singing an old song to the dead at sea, Hakr steered the ship between the many rocky islands that speckled the coastline, guiding the funerary ship and its precious burden out to sea.

The ship glided on the brilliant orange sea-road of sunset as if it would sail in a holy voyage to the sun itself.

The sight wrung Dyrfinna's heart.

"I have to leave." Dyrfinna looked out over the ocean. "I have to go someplace where I can live as a shieldmaiden and warrior."

She looked up at Serja, grieving. Leaving her sword-friends, her little sister, her mother, and grandmother would be hard. But leaving Serja would be the hardest blow to bear.

THE BLAZING SHIP

"This is the last flight of the Corae Guard," Dyrfinna said quietly.

"I doubt it," Ostryg said, straightening the bearskin that he wore around his broad shoulders. "Egill isn't going to do anything that stupid."

"Well, if Egill is marrying Finna off, then where does that leave the rest of us?" Gefjun said in a low voice. "I'm telling you, he's splitting us up."

"I don't believe it. You're being paranoid, sweetie." Ostryg blew her a kiss.

Dyrfinna stretched her back, then gently patted Serja's neck. "Are you ready?"

"Aye, we are." The dragon's enormous wings came storming out, deep garnet wings that could have encompassed Thora's ship. The four other dragons did likewise. Then, with a running start and a great sweep of their wings, Serja sprang. Their wings labored to be free of the pull of the earth, and they were airborne.

A burst of wind, and the dragon soared upward, their wing beats growing easier. The shoreline shrank, while the distant mountains to their left expanded their ranges as the world revealed itself more and more.

Dyrfinna's heart lifted. She loved the sweep of the dragon's wings, the cold wind in her face, Serja's easy grace as they leaned into a turn. The sea under the sun's glare was orange with small rocky islands. When she turned her face away from the glare, the islands were rough peaks of rocks, softened with the green of grass and sedges. Sea birds whirled around the cliffs further down the coast.

"I never want to be separated from you," Dyrfinna said fiercely.

"Nor I from you," Serja said, and Dyrfinna's heart felt the dragon's burning heart nested inside hers.

Now, as the dragons drew closer to Thora's ship, threads of the völva's song from the water's edge traveled to them, the young girls around her singing a faint chorus that made Dyrfinna think of the sweeping flakes of snow in the wind.

"Here we go," Dyrfinna called across to her friends. She pulled her head together to concentrate on the ceremony.

Dyrfinna guided her dragon in the sacred ceremony, the flights of the five dragons braiding around each other in the air, looping and curving around each other with grace. Her heart swelled as Serja easily followed her guides, singing as she flew.

As they swung back toward shore, still in their braided flight, she could see the gleam of lanterns from around the barrow, the crowd of Vikings standing solemn and still. Behind them, a small spectator climbed the hillside to get a better view.

Dyrfinna took in the beauty of the rough, mountainous land from the dragon's back. Far away on the edge of the horizon, three other dragons flew, glittering like emeralds though the sun was dimmed by clouds. She recognized the dragons as a few that often traveled the fjords with messages between the high-born jarls and the queens.

Below their braided flight, Hakr guided the ship through the islands, its final voyage smooth and sweet on the gentle water. But soon the waves grew higher, for the open sea grew closer and closer. Finally, the ship rounded the final island, and swung on the waves of the open sea. She could hear faint words floating up from Hakr, who was praying aloud to the gods for a good voyage for the sturdy ship.

Dyrfinna led her friends in. Serja backwinged down, the other three dragons following.

Dyrfinna's throat tightened. She was close enough to see Thora lying, in her green ceremonial robes, upon the pyre.

"You should have had a chance to grow old, my friend," Dyrfinna said, her voice catching. "You helped me during … the worst time of my life, as you've helped so many others. You would have grown into the best Queen we'd ever known."

Now Serja spoke, her voice like the hiss of the breakers on the shore. "Your life was like that of a mayfly's, so short. I watched you grow as I carried you on my back. You read me so many old stories and poems, passing on the wisdom that you discovered in your books. It breaks my heart that you have gone, so young."

With an easy expertise brought by years of practice, Hakr lashed the tiller in place to hold it steady. Then he unlashed his small faering from the side of Thora's ship, climbed into it, and rowed until he was out of fireshot.

Dyrfinna circled with Serja, carefully leading her friends into position.

"There now, young one, I'm well away," Hakr called up, leaving the oars slack in the oarlocks.

"Young one? I'm twenty years old," she said.

"You're still a wee lass to me," he said fondly.

Old Red, flying low over the water, said, "While you're no more than a dragon chick to me, small man."

"That affords me some measure of comfort, you scaly old lizard." Hakr leaned back in his boat, a smile cracking through his beard.

"Lizard? Lizard? I'll have you know that I'm more lizard than you'll ever be," Old Red sang out.

"I believe I am perfectly fine with that," Hakr said.

As the dragons rose, Dyrfinna took one last look at the face of her friend, the last glimpse of Thora she'd ever get to see in this world. She lay on the tarred, oaken ship with her earthly goods glittering around her.

The thought of what she had to do next hurt. Thora lay there, patient even in death, saying, *It's going to be all right, Finna. Don't worry.* Then she'd put an arm around Finna's shoulder and they'd tip their heads so they touched, leaning on each other, and stand like that for a moment. A sweet, affectionate gesture. Now she lay on her ship with her hands crossed over her chest, waiting patiently for what was fated to come.

"Fire," Dyrfinna commanded in a voice with no air behind it.

Fire blazed down from Serja's mouth, wild billows directed down at the pyre.

Thora vanished among the flames inside a great crackling, and heat billowed up. The other three dragons came drifting down, one at each corner of the pyre, and added their flames.

"Hold steady," Dyrfinna called in a clear voice, even while tears fell unchecked from her eyes. "Hold your fires steady."

The flames licked and caught the tarred wood. Blazes roiled up, greedily devouring the ship, black smoke rising. Still the dragons blazed.

"Stop," Dyrfinna called, and each dragon followed suit. The fires that the dragons had kindled in the wooden ship now blazed. They backwinged to get away from the worst of the fire.

The leaping flames rivaled the brilliant sunset in the west, and cast a long track of light on the rippling sea. The sky swallowed the smoke.

Her throat tight, her eyes aching, she restrained herself as she flew Serja away from Thora's ship.

They flew back in silence. Hakr kept pace far below on the ocean's face as he raised a small sail on the faering, tacking the fleet boat into the wind.

Serja began to bugle, and the other dragons joined in, a wild chorus that echoed from the mountains.

"Look at the ship," Skeggi said, low, as if he could not trust his voice.

The ship blazed upon the sea. By now the sail had completely burned into tatters. Presently both sail and mast fell over with a crash that could be clearly heard on shore, and a whirlwind of fiery sparks rose high into the sky.

"Goodbye, Thora," Dyrfinna said in a small voice.

Far away, a gout of flame blazed up on Thora's ship, then died down. But by its light, she could make out the outline of the other ship that was sailing near Thora's ship. It hadn't gone away – they seemed to be just drifting.

Dyrfinna turned and kissed Serja's nose. "My beautiful dragon," she said quietly, her heart breaking. "I don't want to be parted from you."

"Nor I from you," Serja said, gently pressing their face against Dyrfinna.

She embraced the dragon lightly to keep her arms from burning, filled with grief.

"I am losing two friends today," Dyrfinna told Serja, her voice breaking. "Both Thora and you. And I don't know what I'm supposed to do now with my life without you with me."

"I will not be far from you," Serja said. "We can still talk with each other, can't we?"

"Dyrfinna, enough," came a man's voice.

She startled and turned. *Odin's tears, not again!*

Egill, her papa, came striding up and seized Serja's bridle. Serja jerked their head back in surprise, but said nothing as the carnelians on their golden collar gleamed.

Egill shook the dragon's bridle, looking only at Dyrfinna. "You are finished with dragons and with Thora's guard. You no longer authorized to ride this, or any other, dragon. Thora's dragon is now the property of the queen. Your training is over. Finished. Do you understand?"

The dragons looked at one another, but obediently said nothing.

Dyrfinna tried to push back her despair, locking eyes with Serja. "Could I visit my friends in the dragon stables?"

Even though she knew what he was going to say, Egill's words cut her even deeper. "No. You are barred from the dragon stables. Permanently."

It was all she could do to keep standing in the face of that edict.

The sword-friends burst out in protests.

Skeggi said, "Now, hold on, sir. That's a little harsh, don't you think?"

"Egill, just give her a moment," Gefjun added, her voice sharp. "We're all feeling some things right now."

"Yes, and it's cruel to say this to Finna," Rjupa said, hurt.

Egill turned on the friends with a sharp look. Even at this moment, Dyrfinna couldn't help but be proud of how they looked flanking her, all five of them wearing the matching capes and the silver brooches of the Corae Guard.

If only Thora could have seen them.

Egill lowered his voice. "I am in charge of the Queen's stables – and I have every right to choose who rides my dragons," he said. "Dyrfinna, unhand Thora's dragon immediately. As for the rest of you, there is no more guard for Thora. You're still esteemed warriors, but you can rise in the ranks just like any of the regular warriors. We won't be showing favoritism toward anybody from now on."

A long, shocked moment from the sword-friends.

"So … are you telling us that the Corae Guard is *finished?*" Skeggi said.

Rjupa's hand flew to the brooch of Corae that she wore. "No!"

"Don't say that," Gefjun gasped.

Ostryg's hand reflexively dropped to where he stored a dagger in his tunic, but he said, "You can't do that, sire."

All Dyrfinna could think was *It's all because of me. If they weren't associated with me, this never would have happened.*

"Not entirely. You can still wear your cloaks and brooches that Thora gave you," Egill explained kindly, as if he was doing them a favor. "But you can't make yourselves at home in the Queen's keep or dragon stables the way you have in the past. None of you will be given a permanent dragon the way the senior dragonriders have."

Several of her friends gasped.

Egill went on. "However, you four are certainly eligible to earn the right to fly your own dragons. Good evening. I'll see you at the Queen's banquet later."

Stunned, the sword-friends watched Egill lead Serja away.

Dyrfinna could not breathe.

"Favoritism?" Ostryg hissed beneath his breath.

"*Earn* a dragon?" Gefjun's red hair was nearly uncoiling from its twist from the force of her indignation. "After all we've done for Skala, this is what that rotten heap of headcheese tells us?"

Old Red leaned his long neck down to the sword-friends. "Well, in all my born years I have never seen anything like this," the dragon grumbled. "Such contempt! Pardon my language, but that sucked ass through a straw."

THE OUTSIDER

Earlier, while Thora's ship was being put out to sea, something else had been happening.

At the foot of one of the stark, rocky cliffs, out of sight of the Vikings on the shore and the dragons in the air, a young woman stood on a large, flat-topped rock that jutted out from the foot of the cliffs. It was about ten paces wide, but now that the tide was rising, the briny water was creeping up the sides and threatening to make the distance much less.

By the light of the setting sun, the light glinting off the seithr staff she held, her hair and dress washed in red. She had been crouched here during this whole display, watching it with contempt.

"Stupid bitch," she muttered as Thora's ship set out to sea and the dragons launched into the air, slowly following the ship as it cut through the waves. "All that gold. What a fucking *waste*."

The dragons began weaving their flight paths as they followed the ship out to sea. Leaning on the staff, the young woman pulled herself to her feet at last, then turned her attention to the chalk lines she'd drawn on the rock just above the high-tide line, making certain everything was just so. This was going to be the most important incantation she'd ever made. It had to work.

Everything depended on this. If she could set this in motion, the leviathan's vile eyes would turn to her from under the earth. At this time, it was in too much of a weakened state than do more than direct its attention to her.

But with her help, it would do so much more.

Out at sea, the dragons began blasting the ship with fire.

She laughed aloud. "Finally! How do you like it, bitch? Does it feel good?"

Laughing in satisfaction, watching the flames, she waited for the dragons to turn away from the blazing ship and fly toward shore – waited for them to swoop past the edge of the cliff that hid her from view from the rest of the shoreline, where all the other accursed people had congregated.

Now everybody was out of sight, unable to see what she was about to do.

She knew that handling this much power could possibly kill her.

But she intended to survive.

"Enjoy your party," she sneered, staring at the blazing ship.

Then, holding the seithr staff, she opened her arms in silent appeal and marshaled her strength, breathing deeply, letting her hatred and disdain build like an ocean within her, an unstoppable force.

She spoke a word of command, and the magic blazed through her like a star, burning her in agony. But she only smiled, blood flecking her teeth, and she reached toward the blazing ship on the ocean.

FIRE ON THE FLOOD

"I've got to leave," Dyrfinna said.

An hour had passed, and she, like the rest of the Corae Guard, had changed out of her dragonriding outfit – *for the last time,* she thought – washed off the smell of smoke – *for the last time* – and put on fine clothes before she met Gefjun.

"I've got to leave," she said again, her voice sounding hollowed-out.

"You're not leaving," Gefjun snapped as they walked through the houses of Skala toward the Queen's hall. "Just because your papa can't get over himself."

"Can't get over what happened to Eirik, you mean," Dyrfinna said without thinking, then wished she hadn't said anything.

Behind them, the night gleamed with stars, and a cold wind blew in from the sea. Dark clouds were coming in, scudding before the moon, making her look like a swimmer in dangerous waters.

The other Skalans of the town were also walking in the same direction that Dyrfinna and Gefjun were going. Ahead, the queen's banquet hall loomed imposingly from its perch on the side of Mount Pyrr. Tonight it was lit with torches and lanterns, looking festive, though the villagers' mood was anything but. The murmur of conversation was thick and a skald was playing his harp.

This great hall, one of the oldest in the area, was the pride of Skala, for it was there that the Queen met her honored guests and gave sumptuous feasts. Tonight they would be dining with all those kings and jarls and chieftains who had stood on the shoreline with the rest of the people of Skala to see Thora off on her last journey. And they would be with the queen to comfort her in her grief.

And here came Skeggi and Rjupa. Dyrfinna was pleased to see everybody was wearing their matching cloak and silver brooches of the Corae Guard, despite what Egill had said.

Rjupa looked lovely in her gray dress. This time she left Iron Skull's helmet at home, skillfully braiding her dark chestnut hair in a crown around her head. Skeggi … he wasn't conventionally attractive. He had dark brown eyes, wavy brown hair that he kept braided, and a neatly-trimmed beard on his chest. His little owl slept on his shoulder, occasionally opening her yellow eyes then closing them again after deeming the going-ons as beneath her notice.

"Are you all right?" he asked Dyrfinna, and an electric thrill went through her when she met his eyes.

"No, she's not," Gefjun said, gesturing at Dyrfinna. "She wants to leave this place."

"Can you blame her?" Skeggi asked. "After what Egill said to us, I would be half-inclined to follow her."

I wish you would!

Just then Ostryg came strolling up, also wearing the cloak and broach, and carrying a gigantic caribou antler in one hand. "Follow who? Where are we going?"

"I'm leaving this place," Dyrfinna said as they all stood in the middle of the stairs, people walking around them. "There's no point in me staying here."

"Speak for yourself," Ostryg said. "We can still rise in the ranks if we do everything right."

"She can't," Rjupa said sadly, raising a hand to Dyrfinna. "It's not right if we're not all in it together."

The words warmed her. Rjupa always had such a good heart…

Just then, something caught Dyrfinna's eye. She looked over her shoulder … and froze.

"Everybody," she breathed. "Look. Look at the sky."

Strange flames were rising from the sea.

These weren't northern lights. These were guttering orange flames, though with an odd, fuzzy quality. They slowly rose from far out at sea, drifting into the night sky with a weird, sickly glimmering, then snapped out of existence.

"What is that?" Skeggi breathed.

Dyrfinna counted nine flames rising into the sky, but after the ninth, the flames stopped and there were no more.

The wind picked up, smelling of smoke … and death. Everybody recoiled. Then another breeze blew, more softly this time, and the stink was gone.

"That fire might indicate treasure," Ostryg muttered, resting the caribou antler on his shoulder.

"Or the presence of the dead," Dyrfinna said.

Her words landed in a deadly silence.

"Not Thora," Gefjun said. "No."

"But her ship went in that direction," Ostryg said.

Another deadly silence.

"I could take Serja," Dyrfinna whispered. "Fly her out there and see what those flames are, then fly back before anybody notices she's gone."

"No," said Ostryg. "Even if your papa's acting like a complete dick, you still can't sneak off with his dragons. I'm sure he's ready with any excuse to have you whipped or at least publically humiliated. Don't sulk at me like that, you know it's true."

It always pissed her off when Ostryg was right.

"Besides, Thora can't come back," he continued to the group at large, gesturing with his antler. "She's out at sea. Her whole ship's been burned. What's Thora going to do, anyway? Run across the water? Call her dead relatives and set them on us? Personally, I think the lights are from her treasure, showing us where it's located, *if* you want to fly out there and dive that deep and piss off her ghost."

Now they reached the top of the stairs, where the great hall stood before them, an awe-inspiring sight. From inside came singing and the sounds of a harp and the sounds of many voices.

Two superb doors stood before them, made of solid oak and richly adorned with carvings that told the history of the gods. Yggdrasil, the mystic ash tree, was carved on each door. At its roots, tending it, were the three Norns -- Urðr, Verðandi, and Skuld – spinning the fates of all people. In its branches hung Odin, wounded by his own spear, sacrificing himself to himself to gain wisdom. At the roots of the tree gnawed the dragon Níðhoggr.

Skeggi went in through the man's door with Ostryg, while Gefjun and Rjupa walked with Dyrfinna through the women's door.

Dyrfinna always paused as she walked in, gazing with wonder at the grand, vaulted ceiling above her, and the incredible scenes carved into the wooden walls, showing the many expeditions and daring deeds of their Skalan ancestors – pillaging monasteries, fighting chieftains, exploring new lands. There was a scene in which the wild dragons were tamed and collared, which had helped make it possible for their people to travel almost all over the known world.

The carvings glowed in the light of the fires, and their colors had darkened to rich reds and browns through the centuries since the hall was first built. Shields of bright colors, ornamented with silver and gold, hung below the woodwork.

But tonight, the walls were covered with black and grey cloth to drape the great hall in mourning, so that all knew of the great sorrow and loss that Skala had undergone.

Running along the long northern wall were the tables where the important guests sat eating their food and drinking great horns of mead. In the middle of these tables sat the high seat of the Queen, which was beautifully carved with tableaus from the old stories. Old weapons from the Romans, with Latin inscriptions, hung on the walls. Over the queen's high seat hung her many weapons – including her best double-edged sword, all ornamented with gold. The sword was sheathed and wrapped in bands of peace. No one but Queen Saehildr could break those holy bands that held her sword in its scabbard, and she could only do this when war had been declared.

The Queen sat in this high seat now, her head drooped on her hand, wearing a lovely robe with fur that her other hand stroked as if it were a cat. Great grief gazed out through her eyes.

In a slightly lower seat facing her, in a place of honor, sat Egill.

Dyrfinna's heart thumped as soon as she saw him.

The other high seat, the throne that matched the Queen's, was empty. This would have been Thora's chair, and it now was left empty in her memory, to do honor to her.

In the old days, Dyrfinna and the sword-friends would have stood at attention next to Thora's throne. Now they didn't need to.

"But ... should we still stand by her seat?" Dyrfinna asked.

"It would be the honorable thing to do," Skeggi murmured.

"We should just do it," Ostryg said fiercely.

Egill ignored them, and the Queen was lost in her grief.

Dyrfinna took her regular place at the right side of Thora's old seat, and her friends swiftly joined her in a final show of respect for Thora, standing at attention.

Now the people in the room were looking at them, nodding in approval. Maybe Thora wasn't here, but certainly her spirit was.

Egill looked at them. "That's enough. Go sit down. You're embarrassing yourself by making a spectacle."

The air pressure in the room could have dropped from the collective inhale that the sword-friends made.

"Enough," Egill said. "Don't make the Queen upset."

Dyrfinna turned toward Thora's seat and bowed low. This was the beginning of a presentation they used to do to pay Thora honor when one of the big kings was in attendance. They flicked out their swords and shields, dropped to one knee with their swords upraised toward her high seat, then leapt up with a great shout, swords across their chest, and with a final sharp, military turn, faced front and stood motionless.

One final shout from Dyrfinna, and all sheathed their swords in one smooth motion.

Applause and cheers at the performance.

Egill grimaced slightly.

Once the applause died away, he leaned forward. "There's no place for you up here anymore. Please, go."

Dyrfinna shot an appealing look at the Queen, but she was lost in her own thoughts of grief and offered no indication that she'd noticed what had just happened.

The sword-friends broke up their ranks and went to sit down with the rest of the people.

Ostryg said, "Now that Thora's gone, we're just … we're just like everybody else."

"That doesn't matter. We swore an oath," Dyrfinna said hotly.

"Nobody denies that," Skeggi said in a low voice. "Our oath still holds, always. Upon her bones."

"Upon her bones," they echoed back.

"Let's go sit with the others. Please." Rjupa took a deep, shuddering breath, but didn't weep.

But Dyrfinna went to her father, and stood at attention before him, and waited for a long, long moment until he finally deigned to look at her.

"Papa. Is there any way I can make it up to you for the damage I've done?" she asked. "It isn't right that my friends have to suffer because of me. They didn't do anything wrong."

"Nobody is suffering," he said as if he were exhausted by the subject. "You are making a big deal over nothing. You act like you're under attack when you're not. Could you please just stop with the hysterics for one day? Just one day?"

"Nobody is being hysterical here," Dyrfinna said sternly.

"Go sit down." Egill turned away.

The sword-friends found a place to sit among the other Vikings and said little, staring at their hands or moodily eating. Dyrfinna sipped from a horn filled with mead, barely tasting it.

"After that, I'm half-inclined to think that we should all leave with you," Gefjun grumbled.

Dyrfinna snorted. "But you've sworn an oath of loyalty to the Queen."

"So have you," Ostryg pointed out, spearing a cut of meat with his assassin's dagger.

"Besides, where would we all go?" Dyrfinna asked. "I don't even know."

Just then, a little pair of hands went over Dyrfinna's eyes. "Guess who?"

"Loki!" Dyrfinna reached behind her and grabbed her little sister, who squealed and tried to wriggle free. "Loki, you rat, I've got you now!"

Gefjun leaned in. "I know of one person who would be upset if you left," she murmured as Dyrfinna's sister, Aesa, popped out of her grasp, giggling.

Aesa was just ten years old, and Dyrfinna loved her more than anything. Aesa also considered Dyrfinna her hero. When she wasn't playing involved games with her friends, which involved elaborate stories about how things *really* were in Asgard, she followed Dyrfinna and the rest of the sword-friends around.

Aesa demanded to learn swords and fighting, which Dyrfinna was happy to teach her, and tried to keep up with Dyrfinna's extensive exercise regimen. Dyrfinna allowed this, though she forbade her sister from scaling the side of Mount Pyrr as she did several times a week. Only safe activities for her little sister. She was not going to lose another sibling. That was non-negotiable.

Aesa was going to make a great shieldmaiden someday, she was sure of it.

Dyrfinna turned and caught Aesa. "Loki, you troublemaker, how dare you take my sister's shape! I'm going to eat all your food. Then you'll be sorry."

Aesa stuck out her tongue. "Go ahead and eat all my food. I'm Loki, so I can make any food I want. You can't stop me."

She'd been a Valkyrie for several moons but lately she had been switching over to Loki. She was probably going to travel through the whole pantheon at this rate.

"Oh, yes, I can." Dyrfinna held a honey cake toward Aesa, then pulled it away when she reached for it. "Sit down next to me and I'll give this to you."

"Don't let her sit on me," Gefjun squawked in mock indignation.

"Sit on her! Sit on her!" Ostryg cried.

Aesa squeezed in between the two friends and primly sat on Gefjun.

"Ugh, stop, you're crushing me!" Gefjun pretended to die.

"You're just playing, I'm not heavy. Scoot over." Aesa grabbed the honey cake out of Dyrfinna's hand and started eating it. "I liked how you were flying Thora's dragon earlier. I waved at you. Did you see me?"

"I saw you," Dyrfinna said, which was not entirely true.

"I was surprised that Papa even let you go up there at all."

Dyrfinna grimaced. At least Aesa had missed that scene.

Just then, Queen Saehildr rose to speak, and the room hushed as she did. Aesa motioned for Dyrfinna to be quiet, though she hadn't been speaking.

Queen Saehildr wore a lavishly embroidered dress made with red cloth that had come from the Caspian. The long train of the dress swept the floor as she walked. Her slender body and regal bearing was made more graceful by a belt of gold that encircled her waist. Her arms were graced by two spiral bracelets of gold, and on one of her right fingers was a spiral ring that ended with a snake's head.

"My people," she said, her voice ringing against the ancient walls, "I have lost the best and most beloved part of myself. When my husband, King Hjalmar, died six years ago, I thought my pain was beyond enduring. But now I suffer more than I ever thought possible."

Queen Saehildr blinked rapidly, gazing up at the high rafters of the hall, taking a moment to compose herself before she continued. "I thank all of you for coming here tonight, and keeping me company during my most grievous loss. And I thank you for remembering my beautiful daughter, whom I love. My heart has been carved out of my chest. I have no more to say. Eat now, drink; feast, my people, and remember Thora."

She slowly turned and fumbled her way back to her high seat as if blinded by grief, and bent her head into her hands, as her close friends and allies gathered around and gave her comfort.

The mood in the dining hall was muted. Vikings sat quietly, gazing sadly into their drinking horns or speaking in hushed whispers.

Aesa sniffled.

"Are you crying?" Dyrfinna asked.

"Loki never cries," she said stubbornly.

"Yes, he does." Dyrfinna put an arm around her shoulders. Aesa stiffened for a moment, but then she leaned in with another sniffle.

Dyrfinna squeezed her. "I miss Thora, too."

"It's not just that," Aesa protested. "I don't know. I hate everything."

"Me too, Chickybug."

Aesa was quiet for a moment.

Then Aesa said, "I thought I was going to be done crying. I keep thinking about Eirik. And I keep on being sad. I hate it."

That broke her heart all over again. Dyrfinna squeezed her sister. "I know. Me too."

"That's dumb. I don't like it."

Skeggi was watching Aesa with compassionate eyes. He was well-versed in children, having raised all of his brothers after his parents died. He lifted his sleepy owl off his shoulder, who complained with a little owl grumble, and set her on the table in front of Aesa.

"Oh!" Aesa said through her tears, and gently petted Smoke with one finger, watching as her big golden eyes slowly closed again.

"Watch my owl for a moment," Skeggi said, getting up.

He went over to the skald, talked to him, and then was handed the ancient harp that the old man played.

"Oh, look," Rjupa breathed as Skeggi sat down, placed the harp on his knee, and struck a chord that rang over the quiet conversation of the people.

"Queen Saehildr, thank you for this feast that you are giving us tonight. And thank you for the friendship of your only child," Skeggi said. "Her loss is hard, and I wanted to sing tonight."

Dyrfinna took a long drink of mead. His wavy, long hair hung in his eyes, beautiful in the glow of the heavy wax candles that lit the tables, as he struck a new chord on the harp. With strong, skillful fingers, began to play as he sang "The Ballad of Skar" in his sweet baritone voice, thrilling her down to the marrow.

As Skeggi sang in his warm voice, Dyrfinna thought of Thora's body sinking deep into the ocean, her wealth glittering to its grave around her, even as her spirit sailed on in triumph to the holy mountain.

By the end of the poem, gasps and sniffles were heard from all around the hall, and Dyrfinna had to rub the tears from her eyes.

"But we must not grieve forever," Skeggi said, though tears stood in his eyes. "Let us remember Thora, for we all loved her. We have food here to dine upon, and sweet drinks. Let us enjoy each others' company tonight, here in this beautiful hall."

Now he played a livelier tune called "Sweet Honey in the Tree" that rang from the rafters, and some of his musician friends joined in. An old Viking kept time on the spoons, playing a snappy rhythm as an accompaniment.

The mood in the hall improved. When Skeggi finished and handed the harp back to the skald, he began playing a dance tune. Conversation became louder, and laughter was heard.

Skeggi joined them back at the table, where his friends congratulated him and Ostryg slapped him on the back so hard he choked. Rjupa leaned on him and he smiled, putting an arm around her. Aesa handed back his owl, her tears gone.

Why do I love him so? There were so many reasons. It was the nobility of his spirit that drew her. The way he greeted everybody in a courtly manner. His beautiful voice when he sang, and how he could break your heart in an instant with that voice. His burning passion for music, for song, how his face lit at the sunrise, how fervently he prayed to the eternal gods.

Dyrfinna looked down at her horn of mead to hide her love-starred eyes.

Ale, beer, and mead were plentiful. Dyrfinna had gotten some roast pork and rye bread, along with that drinking horn of mead she'd been longing for. The banqueters were beginning to become merry now as the drinks warmed their bellies. The fire burned on the hearthstones, cheerfully crackling, blazing and casting its light over the people in the hall and making all warm and comfortable.

There, many warriors and berserkers in the hall were telling stories about their exploits, each competing with the others and trying to be the bravest of all the number.

Dyrfinna was listening to all these stories, and enjoying her mead, though she was getting drowsy. She rested her chin on her hand, her mind drifting, singing Skeggi's song to herself.

Just then she heard a whining sound next to her feet.

She leaned to one side to look under the table. A number of dogs generally walked under the table of the hall sniffing for scraps of meat or bread, or looking for a friendly Viking to beg food off of – and Dyrfinna was no exception, for she and Aesa had been dropping scraps for them all through the meal.

But now the dogs were whining, looking toward the great doors at the front of the hall.

Several dogs that had been lying under the table now pulled themselves up, looking around, ears pricked in confusion.

"What's the matter, puppies?" Aesa got to her feet, standing on her tiptoes to try and figure out what the dogs were seeing. "There's nothing there."

Dyrfinna tore off a piece of bread and tried to give it to the whining wolfhound, but instead of delicately accepting it as he usually did, he turned his head away, looked to the north, ears up. Except ... there was nobody in that direction, only the thick stone wall and the women's door.

A muttering growl rose from the wolfhound's throat. He licked his lips and turned aside as if afraid.

One of the hounds started howling. Most of the other dogs joined in. Those that didn't kept looking toward the north wall of the hall, whining or growling deep in their throats.

The singing died away. Several men yelled at the dogs to shut up, making more noise than the dogs had been.

"Sissy, what's going on?" Aesa pressed to Dyrfinna's side.

"I don't know," she said quietly, putting an arm around her, all her senses on high alert.

Ostryg made a rude noise. "It's only the ghost of my ass, come back for revenge." He threw back another drink of ale.

"Stop that," Gefjun told him, also getting to her feet behind Aesa. "Dogs know things that we don't."

"So do owls," Skeggi said as his owl, now wide awake, flew into the rafters where she perched, moving her head side to side and staring at the north wall with huge yellow eyes. She was slowly poofing up, each feather rising, her wings opening, until she looked twice her size.

Rjupa looked toward the door that the dogs were howling at. "Do you want to go outside with me and check?"

"Aesa, stay here with Gefjun," Dyrfinna said, loosening her sword in its scabbard.

"I'll go with you," Ostryg said, dagger in hand.

Just then, a servant, who had gone outside to bring in another barrel of ale, burst through the north door screaming, and slammed the door behind him.

"What happened?" somebody asked.

With a strangled sound, the boy staggered toward Dyrfinna, then fainted dead away, striking his head on the table's edge as he went down.

Dyrfinna knelt next to him. Gefjun knelt at her side, for she was a medic, and immediately began treating the bleeding gash on top of his head.

He groaned as he slowly came to.

"What happened to you?" Dyrfinna asked.

"Thora," he groaned in a broken voice, tears in his eyes. "I saw Thora."

DRAUGR

Vikings looked at each other in confusion, though a few scoffed and rolled their eyes.

"Some people simply can't hold their liquor," somebody muttered.

Gefjun knelt next to the servant and checked the boy's head for injuries, gently touching the giant goose egg that was forming where he'd struck the table.

His eyes were only on Dyrfinna, though. "Thora's face," the boy said, his voice trembling. "It looked at me out of the forest. And it hissed." He gasped for breath.

Ostryg shook his head. "The servant is a child. I believe he's been drinking from that casket of ale he was supposed to have brought in."

"I'll be beaten if I drink," the boy said, almost angrily. "But I know what I saw."

"Leave the boy alone," Rjupa said. "You have no right to treat him so rudely." Ostryg looked affronted but took another drink of ale, saying no more.

There came from outside a heavy tread from around the hall. Dyrfinna felt the vibrations of the footfalls through the table. She got to her feet, her hand on her sword hilt.

The dogs around her feet were growling in earnest now, also rising to their feet, hackles up, tails straight out behind them or tucked between their legs, their lips curled in snarls.

A hand burst in through the window, smashing the shutter in with a sound like a small explosion. The moon was veiled with a watery cloud, and by its dim light, a bloated hand reached in, grabbed the broken pieces, and ripped them off their hinges as if they were birch bark and not aged black oak.

The hand vanished, replaced by the glimmer of a malicious eye in a bruised-looking, discolored face that peered through the broken shutter and glowered at them. A guttural noise, almost a moan, from the creature.

Several of the dogs around Dyrfinna's feet went silent and slinked away. The great wolfhound stayed with her, the hound who reminded her of Thyra, her childhood companion. The wolfhound pressed against her leg, and she felt her shivering.

"What is that?" a woman screamed.

Dyrfinna stared in horror. "The question is, *who* is that?" she asked in a whisper.

The bruised-looking face vanished. The next moment, the door to the hall was violently shaken.

Dyrfinna tried to speak. She wet her lips and tried again. "Warriors," she said, her voice echoing around the nearly-silent hall, sounding almost conversational

– not the shout she'd intended to make. "Warriors, arm yourselves, lest we die."

The sound of steel being drawn by half the Vikings in the hall nearly covered the noise of the door being shaken again.

Great fists banged against the thick, oaken wood until the door was pushed inward off the frame. It gave way too slowly, but then a panel of the door snapped off. A dark blue, swollen hand, oozing congealed blood, reached in through the hole and broke off another piece of wood, easy as snapping a chicken bone, and the gap became larger.

Screams came from around the hall; a servant boy collapsed in a fit in fear.

With a berserker's shout, Ostryg flung himself forward and swung a sword at the exposed arm. Enraged, roaring, the creature grabbed the bare blade in mid-swing in its swollen hand. Ostryg struggled against the hand's grip, trying to wrench the blade free, but the beast was stronger. Still holding the blade in her hand, the monster ripped it from his grip, snapped it in half, then flung it back at him.

Ostryg dodged the flying shards, but one pierced his shoulder. He leapt back and grabbed a spear out of Skeggi's hands to protect himself, then spun, pulling his assassin's knife and throwing it dead at the draugr's throat. But the knife, though thrown true, only bounced off its skin and went spinning away.

"That should have brought her down!" he yelped.

The draugr shambled toward him. He flung the spear true at its chest, but instead of piercing the draugr through, it merely bounced off.

But now his wound from the large shard of sword was bleeding heavily, and he was forced to retreat.

"Fix me up," he panted, running back behind the tables to where Gefjun had her arms outstretched to him. "Fix me so I can fight her again."

She tore off his shirt over his shoulder, yanked out the piece of sword, pressed a folded piece of cloth over it to hold back the blood, and began quietly chanting. A glow came from her hand – healing magic that Thora herself had taught her, long ago.

"Archers!" Egill cried, having already lined up an impromptu force at the back of the hall. "Prepare arrows!"

Vikings shouted, "No arrows! No arrows!" for many of them, now shaken out of their initial shock, were running to the front of the room to test their valor against this creature, grabbing weapons and shields from where they were displayed on the wall.

In the meanwhile, Dyrfinna grabbed frightened people and children and herded them toward the back of the room, trying to get everybody out of danger before the draugr attacked them.

"Get back! Get back!" somebody shouted, and the war-ready Vikings moved back – only slightly, their forged steel gleaming in the light from the moon before dark clouds scudded across its face.

"Don't let it bite you," somebody else warned. "It will devour you. And even if you're lucky enough to break away from its grip, you will become one of these walking dead before our eyes. Beware."

The monster, half-seen in this obscured light, heaved itself over the wreckage of the door frame like a shadow of Hel, then drew itself up. It sniffed the air with what remained of its nose like some wild creature, seeming to wince at the light of the hearth and the torches. Then the creature burst out with a high-pitched keening noise that drilled into Dyrfinna's ears and made her knees into water.

The clouds slid away from the moon, revealing a form that was much more familiar. The creature turned its face from left to right as it looked upon the people in the hall. The creature stepped into the light of the torches, the firelight upon it at last, revealing its face and body.

Shrieks and cries went up from the revelers in the hall. Horror grabbed Dyrfinna by the throat.

"How did she return?" Dyrfinna whispered. "Who has done this to her?"

For it was Thora standing there, a bloated, blackened creature.

All of her golden finery was gone – her crown, her rings, her necklaces. Half of her golden hair had been burned down to the blistered, red scalp, while the rest of it had grown long and matted. Her nails were long and sharp, like claws; her skin looked bruised with patches of yellow and dark bluish-purple on her face and arms, her hands and face swollen. Seaweed and algae hung from her sodden dress that had been burned black, the trim torn away, all her golden jewelry gone. Her wandering, vacant eyes, whitened with the glaze of death, glimmered with hate.

"She's a draugr," somebody cried. "An unhallowed revenant!"

The Queen staggered up from her high chair at the front of the hall, eyes wild. "Oh, Thora, no! My child! My sweet baby!" Egill sprang down from his chair and supported her as she sagged, keening, against his chest.

Gefjun's shaking hand was over her mouth; Skeggi leaned forward, eyes wide. "This is impossible," he whispered.

The Vikings who had been so hungry for battle against a faceless monster now shuffled back slowly when faced with Thora's animated corpse.

As she turned her sightless eyes upon the room, she groaned, a deep, heartrending sound that brought renewed sobbing from her mother next to the thrones.

In an instant, Rjupa stood at Dyrfinna's side. "We need to call the ! Does anybody know where she is?" she cried in a shaking voice, quick tears rising in her eyes.

"No," somebody else said. "Do you want to sneak past this monster and fetch her?"

"She's not a monster," Rjupa cried indignantly. "She's never been a monster. How is this possible!"

"I'll fetch the völva," Skeggi said, catching Rjupa by the shoulders. "You alert the dragons and bring them here."

"Good idea," Dyrfinna said.

Skeggi caught Rjupa's hand and they ran to the back of the building, darting into the open past Thora's draugr to run out the door farthest from her. A moment later, from outside, Rjupa's horn sounded, two loud blasts, signaling danger.

Thora's revenant groaned again at the sound – and roared. With frightening swiftness, she lunged and threw her arms around a Viking who wasn't able to scramble out of her reach in time. A collective cry rose up from the people in the hall.

"Stop her!"

"Save Heidrek!"

"Help me!" her captive shrieked. He struggled to escape, trying to draw his axe. With supernatural strength, her bruised blue arms tightened like steel bands around her victim. Thora dug her teeth into the side of his neck, tore out a huge gobbet of flesh, and wolfed it down. He screamed as his blood spurted.

The draugr mauled the young man like a wolf ravaging a dying deer. Her angry teeth bit through his flesh of his shoulder and neck, crunching through tendons and bones, as he went into convulsions, his eyes rolling back in his head.

"Great Allfather!"

"Save Heidrek!"

Several men rushed her, axes and spears upraised, and the other Vikings leapt in, striking at her with bare steel. She flung the dying man aside and turned on them, blood pouring from her mouth. She caught an axe as it fell on her, tore it out of the attacker's hand, and flung it back at him, striking him between the eyes and cleaving his skull in two with a great spray of blood.

The other Vikings tried to strike her with spears and swords, but the edges of the blades didn't cut her, glancing off her as if her skin were made of iron.

Ravening, she lunged at the men who were attacking her, and lumbered across the patterned floor toward the thrones of the Queen and her second-in-command, Egill, maddened for blood.

Egill caught the Queen's arm, shouting to his friends, "Quickly! Throw the tables down on their sides to create a barricade! Then we can defend ourselves from her attacks behind them."

The Skalans sprang to work. Silver platters of roast pork and delicious fowls crashed to the ground; drinking horns and silver cups of mead and ale splashed as the tables were upended and flung on their sides.

Egill, who stood in guard position between the distraught Queen and her dead daughter's walking corpse, quickly directed Queen Saehildr toward the barricades.

Other mourners fled for refuge behind the tables, herding the older people and maidens to safety, bringing the kings and jarls and chieftains with them.

But a new group of young men refused to join them. Grabbing shields and spears from off the wall, they laughed mockingly at the people behind the barricades, and sneered at the ones who had already tried to fight Thora.

"You sniveling cowards," one laughed as Thora's revenant lumbered toward them. "See how slowly this one moves! We'll show you what true courage is. We'll win our glory and subdue this monster."

One of their spears plunged into Thora's side. The warriors cheered. "We've got it now!"

With a roar that rattled the rafters, Thora grabbed the shaft of the spear and ripped it out of her body, the man holding it striving to keep his feet. He released it to stagger back.

With one powerful motion, she spun the spear in her hand, plunged it into his guts, and yanked the man to her, flopping like a fish. Then she grabbed his chin and ripped out his throat with her teeth.

"Restrain my daughter!" the queen cried, rising up, eyes flowing with tears, arms open. "Somebody restrain her."

Gefjun knelt over Ostryg. She had staunched the bleeding with her spell and now was busily sewing up the wound as he endured the pain, watching the draugr carefully.

Dyrfinna turned to Gefjun. “You can heal with the magic Thora taught you. Are you able to use this magic to return a person back to their right mind?”

“A person, yes.” Gefjun’s voice cracked as she threw a look over her shoulder at Thora devouring the warrior, then instantly returned to stitching Ostryg’s wound. “Thora taught me how to do that. But … is she a person anymore?”

Thora gnawed like a starving dog on the dying Viking, who made awful, shaking wails … which ended when she bit down with a skin-crawling crunch, and ripped out his larynx.

Dyrfinna, gritting her teeth, pulled her sword. Her hands, her whole body was shaking at the sight of her dearest friend cruelly killing men. “All I can say is that Thora’s body walks and she is out of her mind. It’s not right that she’s like this now. It’s not right.” That shook tears out of her eyes. “We are going to make this stop, now.”

A HORRIFYING REVELATION

But then Dyrfinna gasped.

"Aesa!" she hissed.

Aesa had sneaked out from behind the tables and was standing alone in the middle of the floor facing Thora. The draugr's back was to her as it devoured its victim.

"I know I can help her," Aesa whispered, and though she was agitated, she spoke with seriousness. Then she raised her hands toward Thora. "Loki, help me," she whispered.

"Aesa, no!" whispered Mama, stretching her arms out over the barricades.

"My daughter! Come back here! Now!" Egill hissed his command, his voice filled with agony. He roughly grabbed several warriors and shoved them forward. "Rescue my daughter!"

Dyrfinna vaulted over the barricades and stealthily ran to Aesa, sword out, trying to keep her running footsteps quiet so the draugr wouldn't raise its head and notice them.

Dyrfinna only seen draugrs from a distance, shambling across the winter landscape on a night too bitterly cold for words. Even that sighting, from a distance, led to the whole of Skala being evacuated to the Queen's stone keep, while Dyrfinna and her friends flew up on dragonback, searching for them to burn them into harmless ashes.

Everybody knew of their horrifying strength, and their thirst for living flesh.

Thora crouched over the gob of blood and flesh that used to be a warrior, cracking bones in her teeth.

Dyrfinna's knees felt like water as she took her place in front of Aesa, sword in the guard position, but she filled her body with breath to defend her sister.

"Aesa. Get back to the barricades, now," she whispered.

Aesa made no sign that she'd heard. Her face was drawn up into a little frown of concentration as she whispered her spells, manipulating the magic with deft movements of her hands before letting the spell go, filled with little hooks to snag Thora's mind out from the draugrs.

Dyrfinna knew enough of magic to see that the spell was very good. The carnelian ring that Thora had given her glowed brightly in response as the latent magic came to life in her heart.

She stood still, as she always did when the magic took an interest in what was going on around her, carefully watching. But then the carnelian in her ring glowed a little brighter, and a soothing feeling floated down over her heart. After a moment, the dangerous magic quieted.

But Thora's draugr whipped its head around, blood flung from its teeth, and stared at Aesa.

Her sister's little hands, which were suspended in the air to cast her spell, began to shake.

"Back away, Chickybug." Dyrfinna's voice was low as she raised her sword to guard.

Thora's draugr watched the motion of her sword, unmoving.

Dyrfinna did not jump. "Thora. Remember who you are," she said to the draugr, gently moving Aesa behind her with her elbow, then backing up.

The draugr rose from the corpse it had been devouring and stalked toward them, moving in a sidewise, crablike motion that Thora had never used when she was alive.

The carnelian ring warmed on her finger. She could remove it, and allow the magic within her to awaken …

Dyrfinna's mind filled with all the things that could go wrong – that *had* gone wrong for her before.

No. She would not allow herself to speak that magic into being. She would not make that mistake a second time.

Unbidden, the memory of her brother came to her. How the lightning had cracked with an explosion that threw her back, momentarily blind and deaf. Even now she could smell the scorch. She could feel the sickening disbelief that struck her as she crawled along the ground, groping her way across the grass with trembling hands, until her hands met burned cloth and flesh that lay as still in death.

Dyrfinna shook her head hard to rid herself of the memory. This was not the time, especially with Aesa behind her, her shaking hands still trying to cast a new spell to call the real Thora forth out of whatever possessed her.

Dyrfinna's heart pounded against her ribs. "Aesa, get back, get back."

Now Aesa took one step back, then another, still concentrating on the spell.

But Dyrfinna stepped toward the draugr. *If I die today, let it be because I gave my life to keep my sister safe.*

Out of nowhere she felt a great rush of relief.

She'd never understood until that moment how much she wanted to redeem herself for having killed her brother.

To your keeping I commit my spirit, great Odin. Only let my sister live.

Thora's ruined body smiled in a way that Thora never would have smiled when she was alive. As if it knew of ways to kill her that she had never imagined.

The draugr's mouth came open and it burst at her like an explosion.

Dyrfinna shouted, the cords on her neck standing out, and sprang aside, intensely aware of those snapping teeth and the horrible risk she was taking. The draugr staggered past. She shoved it to throw it off balance and kept shoving it every time it tried to get to its feet.

It screeched, turning to look at her with a savage fury.

"Back, Aesa!" Dyrfinna cried again, praying that she'd gotten over the barricades. The monster ran at her again, and Dyrfinna leapt out of its reach.

Dyrfinna had trained every day of her life with weights and endurance work, considering it part of her warrior's training. But the strength of this draugr was beyond anything she'd ever fought. It was all she could do to keep out of the reach of its claws.

Crazed with fear, she stared into Thora's filmy blue eyes – and let the monster seize her.

"Thora," she gasped, using all her strength to resist her friend's unrelenting arms as they grabbed her.

Their claws dug deep into Dyrfinna's flesh as it tried to pull her close, its jaw working. She threw her head back slightly in agony, but said, "Thora. Come back to yourself. It's me, Finna. Your friend."

She could hear Aesa murmuring behind her. She sensed Gefjun running toward them, trying to stay out of Thora's line of vision.

"Thora. Wake up," Dyrfinna pleaded, her arm shaking from holding those angry teeth away, from resisting those tearing claws.

In that moment, Thora's eyes seemed to shift – her dead eyes seemed to focus on her. Those cruel, talon-fingered hands loosened slightly.

"Thora?" Dyrfinna asked.

Just then Ostryg came running in from behind the draugr. He flung his arms around it, pinning its arms to its side, and with an eye-bulging, berserker's roar he hauled it up off her feet.

There came a frightening moment of struggle. Everything happened too fast. Thora's draugr was too powerful, and bucked so hard that Ostryg was nearly flung off his feet. It thrashed, trying to tear any part of him that it could reach with her clashing teeth.

They crashed through a table, benches and food flying, Ostryg's face and neck going redder and redder with exertion.

Staggering, Dyrfinna saw the chain mail shirt on the ground where she'd dropped it. She snatched it up and tried to throw it over the draugr's head. It threw it off.

"I can't hold her!" Ostryg cried in a strained voice.

But suddenly the dragur flung Ostryg aside. It shrieked, its filmy eyes turning straight toward Gefjun, catching her sneaking up on her. Gefjun's eyes went huge.

It lunged at her, as fast as thought.

"No!" Dyrfinna flung herself at the draugr, sword out, and crashed into it before it could grab Gefjun.

"I need you to distract it!" Gefjun cried.

Dyrfinna and the draugr tumbled to one side. The draugr's steely arms grabbed her, its sharp nails piercing her arms, and it tried to pull her close, its slathering jaw wide, teeth snapping.

Dyrfinna brought her leg up, bracing her foot against the draugr's chest so it couldn't pull her into the reach of its jaws, then shoved.

Its claws tore loose from her arms and it went sprawling back, and Dyrfinna fell to the ground. She rolled under a table to get out of reach of its claws.

"Someone get the chain mail!" she cried. "We need to pin its arms!"

The table exploded over Dyrfinna's head as Thora's corpse smashed it into splinters.

"Fire!" Egill shouted, and a burst of arrows clattered into Thora – and rattled to the floor without making a mark on her.

The nightmarish corpse of her best friend turned and shrieked at them. Dyrfinna grabbed a table leg from the wrecked table to shove Thora back.

But when Thora's dead eyes met hers, the memories of all the old times with her friend came back to her, and she wavered.

Thora took that instant to crush the wooden table leg in her hands and yank it, along with Dyrfinna to herself – but Dyrfinna released it, sending Thora staggering backwards and crashing to the floor.

As soon as Thora was down, Gefjun darted in from the other side, pressed her hand hard against the draugr's burned and blistered scalp, and spoke three words from one of Thora's own spells.

A faint glow came from Gefjun's hand. For some odd reason, the residue of the spell left the taste of radishes in Dyrfinna's mouth.

Thora's head suddenly lolled to one side, and her arms and legs went slack, though she still struggled.

Gefjun staggered aside, about to vomit from the backlash of her spell. Dyrfinna opened the chain mail shirt and yanked it down over its arms with Ostryg's assistance, pinning them to the draugr's sides.

The draugr sprang up from the ground, slamming its burned skull into Dyrfinna's cheekbone. Stars flashed in her vision and she tumbled back.

But she'd succeeded, she realized dimly through the blinding pain in her face and eye. The draugr's head and torso were covered by the chain mail shirt, its head shoved partway inside a sleeve. Its arms were partially pinioned inside the chain mail, though it strove to wriggle out. Its teeth struck sparks on the inside of the metal shirt as it staggered around the floor.

Barely able to see through the pain in her face and arm, Dyrfinna lunged, grabbed a fallen war axe with her good hand, and slammed the flat of the heavy blade against the draugr's head, pitching it to the ground.

Ostryg pounced and pressed it to the floor. The draugr bucked and twisted like a monster of the deep trapped on dry land.

"Now, Gefjun! Now!"

Gefjun wiped her mouth and knelt at the draugr's side.

"What happened to you?" she softly asked as she placed her hand on the corpse's head. Light glowed out from under her hand as she closed her eyes. Sweat beaded on her forehead as she worked the magic.

Suddenly, the corpse went limp.

The room fell silent. Ostryg, breathing heavily, kept the draugr pressed against the floor. Dyrfinna slumped next to Gefjun, who was swaying.

"I had to work out the spell on the fly," Gefjun croaked. "I've never used anything like this on somebody who's dead before. I didn't think I could make it work."

"Where am I?" came a strange, gravelly voice – from Thora.

Gefjun and Dyrfinna stared at each other, their mouths open.

"You did it, Gefjun," Dyrfinna whispered.

"Your sister helped," she panted, "but once this is over, I am going to have a talk with her about not doing dumb things that could get her killed!"

The smell of rotten flesh and putrefaction rose into Dyrfinna's face as Thora worked her teeth, inexorably, against the inside of the chain mail. She concentrated on trying to breathe, trying not to choke.

Thora, what happened to you?

Gefjun's voice was gentle, her hand on the back of her head, holding the spell steady. "Thora, you are dead. Your body attacked our fighters here in the queen's banquet hall. Why are you here? Why did you come back?"

The whole hall became quiet. That was the all-important question. If somebody had done something to incur the wrath of the dead, they needed to find out how to atone so there would be peace.

The voice that came out of Thora was distorted, strange. "King Varinn killed me."

If the hall had been quiet before, now it was dead silent.

Horrified, Dyrfinna and Gefjun exchanged glances before Gefjun spoke again. "He killed you? How?"

"Poison," Thora said. "A flask of poison. I drank his wine and returned home. I drank and returned home...."

An outcry. Queen Saehildr rose from behind the barricades, wailing, clutching her hair.

"Thora, is this true?" Dyrfinna asked.

"She says it is!" Gefjun cried, her face reddening with anger. "Didn't you hear her? She was murdered!"

"But can we really trust the word of a revenant?" Dyrfinna asked aloud.

"Why would Thora lie to us?"

Dyrfinna didn't have an answer to that besides, "But is this really Thora?"

"Poison," Thora said again. "It was poison."

"But why? Why did he kill you?" Dyrfinna asked.

No reply. Thora went back to gnawing on the inside of the chain mail, struggling against her bonds.

"Thora, what must we do to give you peace?" Dyrfinna asked.

"You must burn my body to ash. Bury me in honor," she said. "Then … avenge this wrong that has been done to me. Avenge me." Thora began gnawing fiercely on the inside of the chain mail.

"How did you come back to this place?" Dyrfinna asked. "We sailed you out into the sea and burned your ship. How did you come back?"

The draugr said nothing, now beginning to struggle again. The little spark of Thora had apparently sunk back into the chaos of death.

"Wrap her body in unbreakable chains, the kind we use on captive dragons," Dyrfinna said. "Then one of us must remove the chain mail that binds her head so … so we can give her peace again. Bring one of the dragons here, to burn her body to ash."

"I will get the dragons and bring the chains," Rjupa said, tears in her eyes. "Hold her for just a moment longer." She chose several armed warriors to accompany her, just in case more monsters were walking in the night, and they rushed out.

A great cry came from the front of the room. Dyrfinna looked up. Queen Saehildr was now standing over her revenant daughter, her face a stern mask though tears welled up in her eyes.

The queen took out her knife and cut the palm of her hand. Blood welled up, dripping down on Thora's draugr.

The draugr shrieked as the blood dripped upon its face, gnashing its teeth against the chain mail and writhing anew. But now it seemed fixed to the ground, unable to rise.

"See me now in my distress, eternal gods!" the queen called, her vibrant voice filling the hall. "See what has been done to my daughter, whom I loved so dearly. I vow before all of you that the person who did this will come to grief. See to it!"

Then she stooped over the draugr. Her tears fell thick and fast, dripping from her face down onto Thora.

As her tears fell upon the draugr's burned and swollen face, puffs of steam rose up. With the first tear, the monster stopped struggling and its swollen face went slack. With the second and third tear, its mouth and eyes closed. With the fourth tear, the monster rolled onto its side and curled up. In that position, it looked human again, as if it she were just a girl, a tired girl who only wanted to rest. She lay there, no longer struggling, no longer a monster, but a dead girl at last.

A sigh of relief moved through the hall.

"Her mother's tears, her mother's blood," Gefjun said softly. "This is powerful magic."

Queen Saehildr took a moment to regain her regal poise, standing with her head bowed, wrapping her hand with a bandage that Gefjun gave to her from the pouch at her waist.

"Thank you," the queen said softly to Ostryg, Gefjun, and Dyrfinna, as a tear flashed from her eye. "Thank you for helping to bring my daughter back to herself. You have saved the lives of many warriors tonight."

The queen went striding to the wall where the great sword hung, bound in the bands of peace. As she walked there, she took up a great drinking horn, filled to the brim, from one of the tables that had survived the fight intact. There, before the sword, she faced her people. Her wounded palm left some of her blood on the side of the drinking horn as she held it.

Now the queen spoke. "It has been customary at great feasts as this one that we should make vows to perform great deeds of valor, in order to make our names shine forth through the ages with renown. I do so now before all of you who have loved my beautiful daughter, whose heart was bold and brave."

Queen Saehildr now lifted the drinking horn high, as silence fell over the hall.

"I vow that I will, by next year, have exacted my revenge against King Varinn of Ravndal, whether it be that I have driven him out of his realm, or slain him. I vow to have my revenge, and I vow to take his kingdom as my own!"

With that, she drank the contents of the horn in one draught. Then, with a shout, she flung the horn into the fire so it could never be used for any base purpose. The hall rang in cheers.

That done, the queen turned to the wall and brought down the sword with its bands of peace on it, bands which were not meant to be broken. She burst the bands, one after the other, pulled the sword free of the scabbard, and lifted it over her head, where its brilliant blade flashed in the torchlight.

The whole hall erupted in cheering. She leapt up next to her high seat, still hoisting the sword into the air.

"Do as the draugr bade us," the Queen commanded. "Follow her directions to the letter. Bring peace to her spirit, once and for all. As soon as my beloved daughter is at peace again … then shall we prepare for war."

"Revenge! Revenge!" somebody shouted. More cheering. "Revenge! Revenge for the Queen's daughter!" People grabbed drinks and lifted them to the success of their new mission.

There came a shout, and the cheering died down. Two of the kings and their retinue were gathering at the front of the room to address her.

"Queen Saehildr, we regret to say that we take no joy in seeing this," said one of the old kings. Instead of the hammer of Thor around his neck, he wore one of the cross symbols that the monks were forever foisting on the Skalans. "We will not be joining you."

"I take no joy in your fleeing from the fight," said Queen Saehildr. "I have witnessed your heroic deeds on the fields of battle, and you have never backed down from a fight. I would never have counted you as a coward, without honor."

The old king raised his bearded head. "We are afraid, but not of the enemy, dear Queen – we fear the peril of our souls if we blindly follow this course. We are shocked by what the draugr said, for this flies in the face of everything we know about King Varinn. He truly loved your daughter. He never would have done anything like this to her."

The Queen slowly shook her head. "Did you not hear my daughter tell us what happened? My daughter would not lie."

The bearded king pressed his palms together. "I merely ask you to consider, Queen Saehildr, that the creature that was speaking is not your daughter."

The Queen raised her head, pressing her lips together.

The bearded king continued. "That is a draugr – not the sweet girl we all knew and loved. Ghosts, demons, draugrs – these are fallen creatures in service of the devil. They lie to make you follow the paths of sin just to see you cast to hell. Draugrs are also among the damned, and they are no different."

"You have been led astray by fools," the queen replied. "Like Odin, we prefer to seek wisdom and understanding, instead of listening to stories spread by drunken monks."

Dyrfinna grimaced slightly. Though she considered the new mythologies to be a pale imitation of Odin's saga, she wished that the queen had kept that particular statement to herself, especially since the old king had come all this way to pay his respects to Thora.

A low murmur spread through the hall.

The king, pretending to take no notice of it, took a final drink from his drinking horn, then bowed to the Queen. "We will be leaving. We will take no part in this. Good night, your majesty."

While this was been going on, Dyrfinna realized she was growing woozy. She looked at her arm … and was shocked to see that it was covered with blood, as if she'd slaughtered a hog. Blood slowly welled up from a bite mark she didn't notice on her shoulder.

The draugr had bitten her.

A DEADLY TRANSFORMATION

Ostryg shook his head. "Those Christian kings are out of their minds," he grumbled, wiping off his hands. "Why are they so upset over the words of a draugr? Their god is a draugr, too, isn't he?"

"Yes," Skeggi said, frowning at Ostryg's disrespect.

"And he let himself get killed without a fight. By *Romans*," Ostryg added scornfully.

A flash of cold fear seized her, and she staggered to her feet. "I … I'm going to be sick," she murmured in explanation to Gefjun as she turned and headed toward the door. Gefjun half-nodded, her attention turned toward the discussion between the Christian king and Queen Saehildr.

Not knowing what she was doing, she staggered out the door, her heart pounding in a frightening, sideways motion, as if caught in a vice.

Outside, torches burned around the front of the queen's banquet hall, but beyond loomed the dark forest prickly with spruce and fir trees. The night air was cold on her blood-covered arm, and stung in the wound on her upper shoulder.

Her body started shaking against her will.

"I was bitten by a draugr," she whispered to herself, the cold fear now piercing her through.

Bone-deep despair came to her then.

This was not how she wanted to die.

She felt as if she were going mad with fury. Once bitten by a draugr, there was no cure for it. Only the awful transformation … and after that, bloodlust.

A wild thought came to her: to run into the hall and drag her father out, and take him away, and bite him, too, so he knew how it felt to be so deeply betrayed …

"That's enough!" she told herself. "This isn't about how I feel. This is about saving lives."

Her throat closed up.

She had to take herself away from here – fast.

Dyrfinna began running through the dark forest, racing through the needle-covered branches, running up the lower slope of Mount Pyrr.

If she transformed into a draugr, she wasn't going to do it at the Queen's hall, where innocent people like her little sister were. Her heart trembled at the thought of Aesa in her clutches…

No. That was not going to happen. She was going to go up as high as possible on the mountain. When the transformation came on, she didn't want to know what was happening to her, and she wanted to be as far away from everybody as she could. And once she knew she was out of hope, once her mind began to be eclipsed by that of the draugr's, then she would perch at the edge of a cliff over a deadly drop. She would perch there until she was certain that all hope was gone, until the last bit of her consciousness was about to be pinched out like a candle by the draugr's hunger … and then she would step off.

Maybe it's not going to happen like that, she thought as she reached the edge of the forest, where the steep rocky path began. *Maybe I won't transform. It doesn't seem possible – doesn't seem fair.*

A horrible, itchy sweat, like nothing she'd ever experienced before, popped out all over her skin. It felt like thick oil.

A spasm locked Dyrfinna's legs, and she fell hard against the rocks. The spasm passed over her, tightening every muscle in agony before it released her.

Gasping, retching, she pulled herself to her feet again, smelling the rancid sweat all over her body, on the edge of vomiting.

I'm going to have less time than I bargained for, she thought.

She could hardly keep her feet, but she began clambering up the steep, rocky trail, stones slipping out from under her feet and cutting her hands, her body racked with pain and sickness, trembling.

This was a trail she climbed up at least once a week, and she was usually able to trot up this part of it. But the slow transformation kept wracking her body with spasms, and she could only manage a crawl.

She wished she could tell her little sister why she had to leave. Wanted to tell her sword-friends that she loved them, that they would now be safe from her father.

Maybe Egill would give them dragons, once she was out of the way.

Not fair, she thought, but there was no help for it now.

She fought up the trail, groaning deep in her throat, shaking. *I'm doing this for Aesa. For Skeggi. For Mama and Grandmama. For all my friends.*

Her sight blurred, she was gasping for breath as she fell again. She shook her head, crawling on hands and knees. Her breath was bubbling, as if there were fluid in her windpipe. Her muscles jittered and spasmed, and a vile taste rose in her mouth.

At this point, she was done. If she was going to die, let her. Ahead was the first cliff.

She whispered a prayer to Freyja, asking her to watch over her family, to care for her friends, and asking her to let Thora rest in peace. Her tongue grew thick in her mouth, and the words she was saying turned foreign and strange in her mind.

She thought of Skeggi … and she gnashed her teeth. To seize him and bite into his throat, drinking hot blood, that metallic taste of life. She stopped and turned. Blood, people, they was down the rocks, not up. Could almost smell them from here. Want to taste blood. Turned and shuffled down the rocks, going back. A big place there, ahead. Much blood there, many people to scream and run from her. Fingers twitched.

A red gleam fell over her from behind.

"Eh?" she snarled in the voice of some slathering beast.

Serja was flying up to her, their garnet body and great wings glowing with their internal fires, casting garnet-red light over the rocks.

She snarled at the dragon. This blood she could not drink, though she lusted for it. Too much hot, like fire. The foul beast cast hurtful light on her. She threw up an arm to shadow her eyes. Screeched a warning to the foul serpent, get back!

"Take off your ring," Serja commanded as they backwinged in for a landing. "Take off your ring at once!"

Hateful dragon needed to shut up. Needed to die! She screeched at it, louder.

"Thora's ring," the foul dragon said. "Remove the ring that Thora gave you."

Dyrfinna's mind drifted to the surface briefly, and she raised her hands, staring at them, her draugr-addled mind trying to make sense of the words. The red jewel on her finger gleamed like bad fire, and it was hot. It hurt.

"Slide it off your finger before I bite your finger off!" the bad dragon shouted.

Dyrfinna pulled the ring off – and yelped as a wave of awful heat roared through her body.

She dropped to her hands and knees on rocks. Her heart burned with bad flames. Fire roared through her veins, scouring her, and she wailed in pain.

Serja drew her head back slightly. "Finna, I don't know if you can hear me in there, but your latent magic is the only thing keeping you alive – though at this point, this late, I don't know how effective it will be at stopping your transformation."

Red light coming out of arms, her body. The bad magic raged in her. It tumbled her like the fierce surf. Wave after wave slamming her down. Cruel magic sweeping her feet out from under her.

She turned on the bad dragon, snarling. Hot blood would burn her, but she didn't care. Fierce lust for dragon blood. Made her ravenous, wanted to rip dragon with claws and teeth …

"Why did you come up here, so far up the mountain?" bad dragon asked. Big wings picked dragon up, lifted it over her grabbing claws. "Why did you not send for help?"

She snarled, hissing, before she was able to control herself. She stepped back, shaking her head. "Who would help me?" she asked. "I'm transforming into a … a monster! I was bitten by a draugr. So I took myself away so I wouldn't hurt my loved ones again. Serja, help ..."

A fog filled her head. A moment later, Dyrfinna woke up, standing a few feet away from where she'd been a moment ago. Serja had moved back out of her reach. Dyrfinna's throat hurt as if she'd been screaming.

"I need to die," she said. "Before my father learns how pathetically I've fallen … before I turn into the monster he always said I was."

Dyrfinna had not meant to say those words – and she sagged beneath their truth, making a whining sound like a dog. But now she walked straight to the cliff.

Woozily, Dyrfinna looked down at herself. Her tunic and her arm were a shiny scarlet. She snarled and gibbered like a beast. Her arms grew thicker. Her fingernails extended, grew long and sharp.

She pointed at the bad ring.

"Bad ring here," Dyrfinna barely managed before her words devolved into gibberish and snarling. Her body convulsed, hurting all over. She struck a rock.

"Your magic was released too late," Serja said quietly. "I tried to get to you quickly, but I didn't realize what was happening in time."

"Not! Afraid!" She crawled to the cliff's edge. Far down were many people, tasty blood. Didn't want to fall. Wanted to hurt them, eat.

Serja was now looming over her, sniffing at her wound.

Serja lowered their head to gaze into Dyrfinna's eyes. The ringing in her head intensified, and she felt as if the earth heaved. She wasn't sure if that was smoke rising around her from the dragon's breath, or if she were just on the verge of passing out. Or both.

"We do this because of your courage and selflessness," the dragon said.

"What are you doing?" Dyrfinna slurred, hardly able to form the words.

"Understand that we do not take this step lightly," Serja said. "It will lead to complications, and we will be breaking a rule we have sworn to uphold with our life. But if we don't do this, you will die, and dragonkind will need you in the upcoming battle."

Dyrfinna blinked. Had she heard that correctly, or did she just dream it?

Serja snuffled at Dyrfinna's wounded arm – and then licked the wound.

Burning pain consumed her arm, even worse than what the draugr had inflicted on her, burning hotter than her own magic.

With a snarl, Dyrfinna curled reflexively. A hissing rolled through her head as she tried to clutch at her arm without touching it, racked with pain.

The burning moved from her arm to her heart and met the magic there. Pain coursed through her veins as if her blood had turned to fire. She struggled, racked with agony, eyes wide. *What have you done to me?* she tried to say to the dragon's watchful golden eyes, but her mouth and throat refused to work.

Dyrfinna tried to fight to her feet, could not, and went crawling across the ground like an insect, crazed with pain, gnashing her teeth

Serja lowered their nose to block Dyrfinna before she could crawl any further. "We need you to breathe," they said in a low rumble. "Breathe."

Dyrfinna sucked in a breath, then another. The world steadied. She leaned against Serja's nose breathed again, more slowly.

"That's it," the dragon said in a low voice. "Keep breathing. Relax."

As she did, the burning through her body became less intense, more endurable.

Shakily, she sat up and clutched her chest with her left hand, breathing slowly, trying to regain control.

Her arms were still more muscular, her fingernails still long and sharp, but they now looked somewhat normal – didn't look monstrous as they had a moment ago. When she looked at her bloody arm, she wasn't possessed by blood-lust, and the snarls and growls that she's been uttering had now stopped.

But the fire went on raging in her blood, racking her with pain.

"What did you do to me?" she asked the dragon, half-choking.

We have cauterized your wound, Serja's voice sounded in her mind, though they did not speak aloud. *We have added our feeble powers to the power that already lives inside of you, to counteract what*

plagued you, but there will be other aftereffects; do not be afraid of what you will feel.

Dyrfinna went agape with amazement, but made no sound.

Was that you? Did you speak into my mind? she asked Serja.

Yes. Serja's eyes glittered with pride. *In saving your life, in tasting your blood, in healing you, we chose to create a bond with you. Having this link is one manifestation of it.*

Dyrfinna looked into Serja's golden eyes – and was filled with a wave of warmth, of blissful peace, that she'd never experienced before.

The burning magic subsided when she met the dragon's eyes, much to her relief.

Dyrfinna took a moment to catch her breath before she spoke. "So … what happened now? Am I still turning into a draugr?"

Serja snuffled at her like a dog with overheated breath. "No," she said aloud. "The transformation has stopped. You have been restored to yourself. Though you seem to have held on to the extra strength that your body as draugr used to defend me."

"So … I'm not turning into a draugr?" Dyrfinna asked, confused. "I don't have to destroy myself?"

No. In fact, you can put your ring back on now. Your magic and my magic both put an end to the draugr's attack.

"I'm not an abomination any more?" she whispered, feeling her face.

No. You are not. You are a little changed, but our magic together overcame it.

"Thank you. Thank you," Dyrfinna whispered.

Serja chuckled inwardly. *I have made a good choice,* they said, returning Dyrfinna's gaze. *I have known you for most of your young life, have watched you grow up with my dear friend, have witnessed your loyalty and strength. As a result, your magic has also been powerful.*

Dyrfinna froze now. "My magic?"

You will need to be trained in how to use it, Serja said. *It is essential that you learn – instead of trying to block it with your carnelian ring.*

Dyrfinna was still woozy, so she wasn't entirely sure that she was actually having this conversation. Still, she said, "I don't want to learn. Nobody wants to teach me, anyway."

Serja gleamed a dark garnet under the starry sky, gazing at Dyrfinna. *I will teach you,* they said.

"You? Teach me?" Disbelief, excitement – and fear – all bubbled in Dyrfinna's heart. "But I've been barred from the stables – from you." And I'm going to leave this place, soon.

Magic finds a way. Serja gazed at Dyrfinna, her eyes never wavering.

Fighting her wooziness, Dyrfinna looked at her arm. While the rest of her arm was still wet and red with blood, the wound itself, where the dragon had licked it, had already scabbed over and was no longer bleeding. She stared in disbelief, trying to make sure that she wasn't dreaming it.

I didn't know dragons could do this, Dyrfinna said.

We are not allowed to, Serja said. *Please, do not tell anybody – whether human or dragon – what we have done here. Not a word.*

"I swear it upon my life, which you have saved." Dyrfinna got up and threw her arms around Serja's neck. She pressed her cheek against the dragon's burning scales, still shaking from all that had just happened.

Then she shook more when she realized that Thora had felt that way … the last bit of Thora left inside her draugr-infested mind had been forced to endure that degradation, had been forced under the black waters of the draugr-mind.

"How did Thora become a draugr, anyway?" she cried to the dragon. "We performed the rituals. We honored the blessed gods. She was buried under silver to keep her from walking. She was a blameless woman, and I loved her, and she didn't deserve any of this!"

"I don't know," said Serja. "I am as confused and enraged by this as you are. It's possible somebody raised her – a necromancer, perhaps."

Dyrfinna leapt to attention. "Did you see anybody standing alone when we were flying over the ocean earlier?"

"Not that I recall."

"Nor I. If only I'd looked around me!" Dyrfinna cried, striking her hands together angrily. "But we can try to find this person now. Serja, fly me to where a necromancer could have cast such a spell. A point near the ship, where such a caster could have been hidden from our view, and their cursed power could have reached our ship."

"Gladly," Serja said, crouching so Dyrfinna could leap aboard.

They flew up and down along the coast, landing on the small, rocky islands that peeped through the ocean waves, looking through the cliffs that fronted the sea. Dyrfinna realized that she could see more clearly in the dark, and asked Serja why.

"It's likely that you still have the heightened senses of the draugr," the dragon explained as Dyrfinna investigated one of these islands for traces of a necromancer.

Dyrfinna nodded, though this troubled her. Though there was no moon, she could see as clearly as if it were twilight.

I hate draugrs, she thought, and now I … might be one. She stared at her hands, which were larger and more muscular, her nails looking thick and yellowed. *Will I have to wear gloves now?* She wondered. *What other changes had this transformation wrought that I don't know about?*

Father was right. Now I really **am** *a monster.*

She sighed, straightening up from her investigation of the island. "Even if somebody had been out here," she said to Serja, "all traces of them would have been wiped out. The high tide that carried Thora's ship out to sea would have also washed over this island, and many others like it."

"No." Serja said, snuffling at the ground. She blew out a wisp of flame, sustaining it against the surface of the rock. Under the flame, Dyrfinna could now see the faint remains of runes and sigils that had been scratched into the thin layer of black algae that coated the rock.

"It was here," Dyrfinna breathed, trying make sense of the faint symbols, though she could barely read. "What do they mean?"

"I'm a dragon," said Serja.

"Fair enough. I'll ask the völva to look at these."

"Come," said Serja, crouching again so Dyrfinna could mount. "Perhaps there's some trace of … something on Thora's ship."

They found what was left of it further out to sea. It had burned completely down to the waterline, and the waves had overwhelmed it. Now it bobbed underwater, a blackened shadow just below the heaving waves, barely buoyant enough to float, but not enough to break the surface. It wouldn't be long before it finally sank to the ocean floor.

They looked at it for a while, Serja circling the wreck. Dyrfinna felt how the dragon's heart was too heavy for words – just as hers was.

None of this should have happened to Thora, Dyrfinna thought.

We agree, Serja replied.

Finally, the dragon began flying back to shore.

It's late, Serja said into Dyrfinna's mind. *We'll bring you back secretly, so nobody will be the wiser for my having flown you around the shoreline.*

"I want to find who did this to Thora," Dyrfinna said as she leaned into the wind.

"We will help you in any way we can," Serja said.

THORA'S RETURN

Rjupa had been awakened very early by a rap on her door – Egill's knock.

She rolled out of bed, fully clothed, groggy from having slept very little since she'd been informed of the mission on the previous evening.

"We are leaving," Egill said outside the door. "Come to the stables and saddle up."

She threw on her heavy overcoat, caught up her traveling bag, and hastily complied.

In a very short time, Rjupa was airborne on her small-winged racer dragon, following Egill and the Queen on their dragons as they traveled slowly down the coastline of the country.

The journey was uncomfortably silent. The Queen was mostly silent, and Egill was friendly enough though distant, more interested in talking to the Queen if he talked to anybody.

Rjupa spent her time talking to her dragon, who was named Shriken, and adored her. She was a swift, small-winged dragon, and silver-scaled so she glittered everywhere she went. Most dragons had gemlike scales which could be rough on the hands, but Shriken was smooth, almost like a salamander – and like the salamander, and all the other dragons, she had an affinity for fire. Heat always rose from her skin from her internal fires, making a ride in the high altitudes more comfortable.

Hairlike strands, something like thin feathers, grew from Shriken's birdlike head and streamed in the breeze, and her body was snakelike without the spikes and horns that most dragons had. Her wings were cut in a way similar to falcons – if falcons had ended up with membranous wings, like bats. Her long and sharp wings allowed Shriken to fly swiftly when the mood struck her.

Shriken whistled softly, her long silver tail making circular loops in the air behind her.

Her heart always thrilled to be flying so high over the land. The coast rolled past below them. Little green and brown islands dotted the sea. From this height, the mountains looked soft and moss-covered, with deep folds and dark valleys. Far inland, a group of low mountains sat in majesty, a dark blue against the horizon. The wrinkled sea crawled below. They glided over a cliff where flocks of puffins were flying over the waters, thick as bees.

Rjupa sighed. "I wish I could share this with you," she murmured to Skeggi, though he was far away.

Ahead, a single mountain, a sharp-edged flint that looked ragged as a tooth, stuck out of the ocean with a light scrim of vegetation clinging to its base. Some men were rowing a boat around its coves, a fishing net trailing behind them as they pulled at the oars. They waved at the dragons as soon as they appeared in their sights, and never stopped until they were nearly out of sight.

Rjupa waved back. She always did. Even now, after all these years, it still amazed her how lucky she'd been in her life. In her old life, she had been a thrall to a cruel man, and he had set a spell upon her that did not allow her to remember her old name. When she'd escaped, Skeggi had given her a name – Rjupa, ptarmigan, a white bird with a black eye stripe that lived among the rocks, fanning their tails and keeping their territories, unobtrusive and quiet in the snow but always beautiful.

The story of how Rjupa, a former thrall, had come into the confidence of the queen and her daughter was a strange one. Rjupa had killed the famous warrior, Iron Skull, while his army was invading Skala. To reward her bravery, and because she had no other place to go, Thora asked Rjupa if she would like to live at the place. Rjupa had accepted. After Rjupa had settled in, Thora had flown her on dragonback to her old home to see if any of her old family had survived, but their old home and her old village had been burned to the ground. Heartbroken, Rjupa had returned to Skala with Thora to stay.

So Rjupa had served Thora and the Queen for all those years, acting as something more than a servant – closer to an advisor or friend. It was a privileged position to be in, but serving them helped Rjupa work through some of her past damage that had been inflicted her life. She did her best to make herself worthy of their trust.

And there was the fact that, like it or not, she wanted to show Dyrfinna up. She tried not to acknowledge it when it appeared in her mind. But it was there.

Not that she hated Finna; quite the opposite. But sometimes Finna started thinking of herself as the be-all-end-all of humanity, and Rjupa wasn't having any of that.

Rjupa's dragon looked over her shoulder. "Are you drifting off back there?"

Rjupa shook herself out of her thoughts. "No. I mean … well, yes, I am."

"I hope that we will land soon," the dragon replied, her long wings gliding on the chilly air blowing in from the ocean. "I'm so hungry. I keep dreaming of a nice, plump goat."

Queen Saehildr, flying ahead of them, sat silently on her golden dragon Tandryss, unmoving, saying nothing. Egill flew wingtip to wingtip with the queen on his black dragon, Krekkaq, whose scales glittered in the sun like bits of mica.

Both of them had recently lost their children.

Egill had long blonde hair and a crinkly golden beard to match. He was a square-faced man, stiff-necked, wearing a great bear's fur cape over his shoulders. He had smiled little since his son had died, a tragedy that had left Dyrfinna utterly distraught and Egill silent and furious at her. But he had become more tender, more gentle to everybody else, and especially the Queen after Thora had failed and died.

It was as if grief had hollowed him out, left him understanding how vulnerable all of us truly are, Rjupa thought.

Queen Saehildr, on the other hand, had been silent for most of the journey. Her dark brown hair had been braided into complex designs around her head, leaving her neck white and bare in the cold wind at these altitudes. She wore a woolen black traveling cloak, edged with patterned gold that covered her body, and her golden earrings sparked in the sunlight. Her grey eyes were blank with weariness, with heart's-hurt. Her head drooped slightly over the golden dragon's neck, as if heavy with dark thoughts.

It had been a long flight. Bored, Rjupa lay forward across the dragon's neck like a squirrel lying on a limb, despite her straps pulling on her middle – those were designed to hold her in the saddle if the dragon had to suddenly veer hard to one direction or another.

She wished she could have had one of Thora's books to look at on the flight, not that the words in it meant anything to her. But the illuminations in the margins, the tiny illustrations inside the letters and along the margins, were incredible.

Thinking of Thora on dragonback with her book brought back a deep ache of grief.

Rjupa had been there two weeks ago when Thora had returned home from her visit to King Varinn's.

Rjupa remembered how she and Skeggi had been cuddling in a dark corner of the hayloft in the dragon stables, well out of sight of prying eyes. Here, in the dark, they had given themselves over to enjoying the afternoon together, their bodies entangled, kissing each other's eyes and faces, progressing leisurely through the phases of love.

Suddenly, cries from outside made them start up in quick terror at being discovered – but it was not that, much to Rjupa's relief. A man's voice called, from outside the stables, "Ho! The Queen's daughter is on her way in! She will be here within the half-hour!"

This call was generally given out as soon as the Thora's dragon had been spotted, a gleaming garnet mite on the distant horizon.

Rjupa had shakily blown out her breath as she began to put her dress back in order. "I'm glad that's all it is. Let's go meet her," she said in a quiet voice to Skeggi so nobody outside would hear.

Skeggi laughed low next to her ear, so close that his voice gave her shivers. "Not right away. We have time. Just a little longer?" He kissed her again, nipped gently at her earlobe.

"Oh, stop. I want to look normal when she arrives." Rjupa brushed off the skirts of her dress.

"We'll have plenty of time later. I want to see Thora, anyway – ask her about her new husband-to-be," she purred.

Skeggi flopped over on his back in the hay, rolling his eyes. "Plenty of time? Do you know how hard it is for me to escape the prying eyes of five little brothers?"

"They're not *that* little," she said, standing up and shaking out her dress.

"They've certainly become a lot more devious since they've been growing up. I remember when they were small, and they'd play a game called, 'Punch 'em in the Nuts.' Well, technically, I guess they still play it," he added.

Reluctantly, Skeggi sat up. They checked each others' hair for bits of hay, put their clothes in order, and sneaked out of the hayloft while everybody's back was turned.

"See? They never notice," Rjupa whispered.

"Well, I suppose," Skeggi added, sneaking around a corner – and he tripped over a wooden bucket and went down with a crash.

A dragon's guard peeped out of a nearby doorway and looked from Skeggi to Rjupa. "Did your sweet lover lose the use of his legs again?" she asked.

"I *meant* to do this," Skeggi cried from the ground.

"Tidy up so Thora doesn't tease you for snogging," the guard added before vanishing again.

"They're wise to us, Honeybee," Skeggi groaned.

Rjupa laughed as she helped Skeggi to his feet, brushed another bit of hay out of his brown beard. "Is your mind elsewhere?" she teased.

"No. Yes. Maybe." Skeggi wrapped his arms around her for a moment. She hummed happily, leaning back into his embrace. He hummed back, his beard tickling the side of her face, his smell of musk and wood smoke pungent and sweet to her. Even in little moments like this, they fit together so well. It always made her happy. Then she grabbed his hand and led him to where Thora would be landing.

The dragon landing over the city of Skala was a broad plateau above the mead hall and the Queen's grand hall with home.

Among the usual busy dragon guards and stablers, a stranger was hanging around the landing, a new girl that Rjupa had never seen before, a blonde girl with a hood.

The dragon landing was where the dragons were kept when they weren't being flown. A corral was kept nearby for the cattle and goats, and these were brought out to feed the dragons. At the back of the level area were stone stables, partly built with stones, and the rest cut out of the solid rock. The floor sloped toward the front to allow water to drain out, and a broad sill made a protected walkway in front of the stables and kept the rain, snow, and wind out. There were thirty stables for all the dragons.

But these days, many of those stables stood empty.

The Queen now had only ten dragons in the stables, though in the olden days, fifty years ago, thirty dragons had served the previous king. Slowly, over the years, many had died off, whether of natural causes or in war. A few had been given as gifts or dowries. One had escaped its collar and had gone on a rampage, blazing fire everywhere and killing several of the dragonguard. It had flown away to parts unknown before it could be captured and killed.

Though the dragons had been allowed to go on mating flights, the females, except for a rare instance, had stopped laying eggs. And the wild dragons were extremely mean and untamable.

Nobody could figure out why this was happening. It wasn't only the Queen's dragons that were suffering – other domesticated dragons around the land, in other kingdoms or jarldoms, were also dwindling out and dying away. The dragons didn't seem to be suffering or miserable – they seemed placid enough in their roles. Magicians and völvas alike had tried to increase the dragons' fertility through spells. Dragon farriers and stablers alike tried giving them different foods, attempted different health practices. Monks had been going through old texts to see if perhaps they could find answers in the histories. No human seemed to have a good answer.

By now Thora's dragon was close enough for them to see Thora swaying in the saddle as if drowsing off. One of the dragonguards shouted "Hullo there!" to her, waving wildly. She startled slightly, looked up, then smiled brightly and waved back. Several people on the landing cheered.

"But if she got married, then she'd have to go away to live with Varinn," Rjupa said softly to Skeggi. "Then we'd hardly ever see her."

"Maybe they could both rule both kingdoms," Skeggi said. "They'd rule over our land and Varinn's. That's why these marriages are made, you know."

Then Queen Saehildr came walking up, and more people cheered. She bowed slightly to them, looking regal, glowing with joy.

"My little girl is home again," she said softly.

Rjupa smiled. "Thora is no little girl, your majesty."

Queen Saehildr watched Thora's dragon fly in. "She is not," she agreed, "but I still remember when she was a little apple-cheeked child clambering into my lap and winding her arms around my neck. However old she gets, she'll always be my little girl."

Rjupa and three other people said "Aww" at the same time, and they all laughed, including the Queen.

"I can't help but be so proud of Thora," the Queen continued. "I hate to let her go, but she will do such good things as she grows. She builds alliances and cares for her subjects. She will go far."

The garnet dragon, Serja, swept in with the guardian dragons at their side, then backwinged, slowly descending until their hind feet touched the stone pavement and they landed, taking a few steps forward. Heat shimmered off the dragon, and the wings flung a gale of heat at Rjupa and Skeggi as they stormed shut.

Immediately upon landing, Serja swung her head back, snuffling at Thora. "We are so glad to see you still upright, our liege," her dragon said.

"I'm fine, sweetie," Thora said gently, patting the dragon on the neck. "All the same, I could use some help to get down. I feel wobbly after that long flight."

The Queen came forward, followed by Skeggi. Thora took Skeggi's hand and climbed down. She seemed shaky, as if on the verge of shivering. One of her servants unfastened the case from the dragon's back and brought down her mochila, a large leather bag with her other supplies.

Once Thora was on the ground again, to everybody's surprise, she carelessly flopped into her mother's arms as if she were a mere peasant, not a queen's daughter. Queen Saehildr looked surprised, but didn't say a word about her lack of decorum, because Thora was snuggling up against the Queen like a little girl.

"How was your visit with King Varinn?" the queen asked.

"Oh, lovely." Thora lowered her head with a smile and blush as she raised herself upright again. "He is kind – very courtly and generous."

"Is he handsome?" somebody in the crowd piped up, and they all laughed, including Thora and the Queen.

"Yes, he is handsome," Thora said. "But, ever better yet…" Her voice hushed as if she were telling a salacious secret. *"He also loves to read books!"*

"Well, might as well marry them now, there's nothing that can top this match," somebody stated.

Thora's face glowed. "I don't want to jinx this. But … I'm very happy right now."

A flurry of joy came from the group all around. "We can make sacrifices to the gods tomorrow," Thora continued. "I need some time to talk to the völva about this, but I must do this later, after I recover."

"So are you tired from the long trip?" Skeggi asked graciously.

Thora smiled, but her face looked stretched and wan. "I confess I don't feel too well. Right now, all I want to do is sleep."

"Is there anything else you need, my daughter?" the queen asked. "A light meal, perhaps?"

"Rest. I'll feel better once I've had a nap," Thora murmured.

When Thora began to walk up to her room with her mother, Rjupa and Skeggi followed, as well as some others, including a young woman with blonde hair wearing a hood. She nudged Skeggi, but he was watching the queen and her daughter.

"Do you know that girl?" Rjupa asked, pointing. "I haven't seen her before. The blonde."

He looked into the group of Thora's friends, toward the blonde.

"A blonde?" Skeggi asked, confused. "There's no blonde girl there."

Confused, Rjupa said nothing more. But when she looked back, the blonde girl was gone – completely vanished.

They came to the women's side of the hall. Skeggi had to cool his heels outside the door, because the men were not allowed.

"Good-bye! I'll miss you!" Rjupa joked to Skeggi as they left him behind.

"I'll wait for you outside," Skeggi said, wandering off.

Rjupa followed the Queen and Thora up to her room in the Queen's palace.

Thora flopped down on her bed without removing her shoes. "Ugh, the only good thing about traveling so far on dragonback is that I have time to read," she said. "Though reading on dragonback makes me sick at my stomach after a while. Where's my book? Did they bring it in?"

One of the servant girls, who had brought her things into her room, lay the book next to her hand on the blankets.

"Thank you," Thora said, placing it on the table next to the bed. She sat on the side of her bed, kicking off her shoes. "And now, I really must sleep. I don't mean to chase everybody off, but oh, sweet sleep sounds so wonderful right now."

At this hint, Rjupa, along with the other friends, left Thora's room.

How could Rjupa have known how things would end for Thora only a few days later?

But now, as Rjupa flew behind the Queen and Egill on her long dragon flight, there was something that Rjupa was trying to figure out … something that, now that she was thinking back over the day, didn't sit right, something that felt odd about the situation. But she couldn't figure out what it was. She knew now that Thora was already under the effect of the poison that would eventually kill her – hence her tiredness. If only somebody had realized it at the time!

But it broke Rjupa's heart, thinking of how happy Thora had been about Varinn, even while she was dying from the poison he'd given her.

The Queen broke her long silence, startling Rjupa out of her memories.

"Varinn's keep is there," came the Queen's voice, quivering with suppressed emotion.

Far ahead, against the side of a mountain, blue in the distance, was a fortress built into the side of the mountain, walls and buttresses thrusting out, almost as if they were part of the stone and had grown there naturally.

Rjupa looked back at the Queen. Her face had turned to stone, except for her eyes, which burned as they took in the sight.

A BARE DAGGER

They landed some distance away from the keep, in a forest on the side of a mountain. Egill led their dragons under the cover of the evergreens which grew so thickly, hiding them from the skies.

The Queen said nothing, but sat apart from them, so still, wrapped in her great cloak. From under the hood of her cloak, her eyes burned like embers. Rjupa had never seen her like this, and it alarmed her.

Egill laid his hand on the Queen's, but she didn't seem to notice.

Rjupa took a sausage out of her pack and put it on a stick. "Warm this up for me," she told Shriken, who breathed a small flame on the sausage until it began to hiss and sizzle. She placed it on a small clay plate, added some bread and cheese, and carried it to Queen Saehildr.

Egill hastily removed his hand from hers, though it didn't bother Rjupa to see him like that. He was merely trying to comfort her.

"Your Majesty, do you need anything else to …?" she asked softly, holding out the food.

"No," Queen Saehildr said, almost before Rjupa had finished speaking.

"I apologize," Rjupa said, standing there awkwardly with her plate of food, hoping that her stomach wouldn't growl because that cooked sausage really smelled good.

Egill shook his head. "No need to apologize. You have done nothing wrong. You are acting out of kindness." He stole a glance at the Queen, who still would not look at either of them. He lowered his voice. "It is hard to lose a child," he added to Rjupa. "It ... changes you. You can never go back to who you were before. It changes you forever."

Rjupa realized that Egill was also talking about himself – for he had lost a son when Dyrfinna had accidentally killed him.

"I'm sorry, sir," Rjupa stammered.

With another look at the queen, Egill got to his feet and walked a short distance off, beckoning her to follow. Rjupa set down the plate and did so.

Once they were out of earshot, he bent down to speak to Rjupa, his blue eyes concerned. "In some ways, I am saying this only because you might not understand my situation," he told her. "What I've seen and experienced, over the last year, I wouldn't wish on anybody, however deep my hatred is for them. It takes a toll on every aspect of your life." He sighed. "I don't know if any of this surprises you, because I'm sure that my daughter has been telling you a different story."

Now Rjupa paused, not certain how to proceed.

She instantly understood that he was saying this to her for a reason – the same reason that he'd chosen her over Dyrfinna to be in the dragon corps. He wanted her as his ally. He wanted her cooperation. And he wanted to get back at Finna for killing his son in the most hurtful ways possible … but she walked right past that reason, pretending it wasn't there.

"She hasn't told me any of the story," Rjupa said. "Even now, I'm not clear on what happened. The only times she mentions what happened is when it comes up unexpectedly in conversation. Otherwise, she doesn't talk about it."

Rjupa moved closer, wondering if he would tell her what exactly had happened on that awful night.

He gazed out toward the water, the dark face of the ocean. "You have to understand that Finna acts like she's suffering when she doesn't have to. A lot of people have to suffer the same kind of pain. She's not the only one who has lost loved ones."

Rjupa nodded, listening, not sure what he was getting at.

"I brought you here with us, Rjupa, because you're level-headed and clear," he said. "You are not pushed around by your emotions the way she is."

Now, even though Rjupa was friends with Dyrfinna, and even though she would have done most anything for her, she had her limits.

Rjupa had watched her family die at the hands of Iron Skull so long ago, had been forced into captivity by him, had endured horror that she shouldn't have survived as a thrall girl.

She had only been able to kill Iron Skull because she'd witnessed Dyrfinna standing in battle, keeping her head while everybody else was losing theirs. Because she and her friends were trying to help Rjupa. If Dyrfinna and her friends had not been there to help her, she would have likely given herself up and been murdered at his hands.

But there was a little space for her pride in herself. Dyrfinna considered herself the best at everything, but Rjupa was a good dragonrider, too. Not so likely to pull crazy stunts the way Dyrfinna did – which was the reason she had been brought along on this mission. And maybe to rub it in to Dyrfinna a bit.

So their friendship was also, in a deeply buried kind of way, a competition.

Egill continued. "My daughter has changed over the years. She's demonstrated that she's not worthy to be a dragonrider. She lost her temper enough to kill my son."

He might have a point, she thought. *He grieves his son. He truly does.*

That night Rjupa couldn't sleep, missing Skeggi, as always, but something else prickled at the edge of her mind. She picked up her blankets and moved close to Shriken, who was stretched out full length on the ground, down to the tip of her toes, her long silvery tail twitching behind her. Shriken lifted her head and snuffled at Rjupa. Good thing she wasn't as superheated as some of the other dragons.

"Can't sleep?" the dragon asked drowsily.

Rjupa ran her hand over Shriken's nose, and the dragon closed its eyes in contentment, like a cat. Rjupa rolled herself up in her blanket and cuddled up next to its legs, using one of them as a pillow for her head.

She was beginning to drift off, finally, when a small scuff woke her up again. She cursed inwardly and rolled onto her side. Somebody had gotten up to take a piss, likely. *They could have waited until I'd fallen asleep,* she grumbled, with all the logic of a half-asleep person.

But when she opened her eyes partly … they sprang open the rest of the way.

A dark figure, wrapped in a cloak, slipped through the forest, a knife glimmering in her hand.

Rjupa tensed. It was Queen Saehildr herself who was carrying that knife and sneaking out of the campsite, moving as softly as a moth in the air.

What is she doing? Rjupa, now awake, unrolled herself from her blanket and followed. Her dragon opened one golden eye and then closed it again.

Rjupa was worried. More than worried, as the Queen's heart-hurt had been especially deep as any mother's grief she'd seen. Thora would have wanted her friends to care for her mother after her death. To see Queen Saehildr walking out of the campsite into the dark forest with a bare dagger in her hand made Rjupa immediately fear the worst.

Into the dark woods they went. The shadows closed in overhead, and Rjupa was on full alert for every sound.

Suddenly the Queen stopped. Rjupa tried to make herself small, but it was too late – the Queen turned, eyes wide, and saw Rjupa. She made a terrifying sight, there in the faint starlight that drifted through the leaves, her upraised dagger gleaming.

"Come out, you who follows me, if you dare." The Queen's voice, low, was like the voice of a feral animal, ready to fight the hounds that held it at bay.

Rjupa took a breath and, pushing her courage to the sticking point, stepped into a patch of starlight so the Queen could see her. "Please, your majesty. Skala needs you. We all grieve for your daughter, but we still need a queen to lead us. Don't do this."

The Queen's eyes grew cold. "My mind is made up. Do not turn me from this path."

A frisson of fear made cold sweat pop out over Rjupa's body. "Your majesty, please," she whispered, walking to the queen, though not close enough to touch her. "Listen. I wanted to end my miserable existence many times when I was Iron Skull's thrall, when he used me to his own sickening ends. I stayed my hand, and then some kind goddess showed mercy on me by bringing me to you and Thora. I could not live with myself if I did not stay your hand, even in the depths of your grief."

The Queen frowned in puzzlement for a long moment, but then her gaze turned down to the dagger she held. She half-laughed, then, as if surprised by an understanding, then sheathed it.

"Self-slaughter never entered my mind, child. I apologize for the confusion. I have a different mission, one of revenge, and I cannot tarry here."

Relieved, Rjupa said, "Let us carry out your mission for you. That's why we're here, isn't it?"

The Queen shook her head. "You have a different purpose. My mission tonight is personal. Do not tell Egill that I have gone. I will be back before dawn." With that, she turned and was done.

Rjupa went back to her blanket and dragon, shaking from the encounter, and it was a long time before she could go to sleep.

The next morning, however, Rjupa found Queen Saehildr sleeping next to her dragon as if she'd never left her blanket. Nothing on her face betrayed the anguish that she'd been showing only hours ago.

IN THE KING'S HALL

Rjupa was certain the Queen couldn't've gotten much sleep, but as soon as she unwrapped herself from her blanket she sat up, awake, still wearing the same skirts and kirtle she'd been wearing yesterday. The Queen only took a moment to rebraid some of her hair that had gotten loose during the night. She sat down next to a small cookfire that Rjupa had asked Shriken to kindle.

"Today I would be glad to accept your food," she said, picking up a piece of hot pan bread, and juggling it in her hands as she waited for it to cool. "I apologize for my shortness yesterday."

"I accept your apology, your Majesty," Rjupa said, pleased and relieved. She seemed to be in much better spirits today.

She ate the pan bread as the others gathered around.

Rjupa noticed that the Queen was wearing some new gemstone. What was odd was that she'd had a carnelian on a gold band for years. But this one was a slightly different shape and luster. It seemed to gleam at Rjupa, as if it winked. The Queen's ring had never done that before.

"Where'd you get that ring?" Rjupa asks.

"Egill gave it to me, long ago," the Queen said, distant.

Rjupa had seen the carnelian ring that Egill had given to her a long time ago, had seen it a million times, but this ring was different.

Rjupa brought her some fresh, cool water to drink, adding a bit of wild mint that was growing in a sunny spot. Queen Saehildr accepted it with thanks, took a draught, and began to speak.

"Today we will win revenge for my daughter," she said. "I want to warn you that this enterprise will be an act of war, and Varinn will retaliate. There is no turning back now. But at this moment, we need glory, plunder, and prisoners to build our kingdom. And," she added, "I have sworn revenge, and I will do everything in my power to bring revenge. Tonight will be our first step in fulfilling my last wishes for my daughter. Fortunately for me, I learned a few things from your friend Ostryg," the Queen added quietly to Rjupa.

Rjupa nodded, hiding her puzzlement. What could the Queen have possibly learned from Ostryg? Fifty ways to braid a beard? How to drink a full tankard of ale in one swallow? Competitive swearing?

The Queen unpacked her mochilas and thrust something at Rjupa and Egill. "Here. Go change. I'll explain after you've dressed."

Rjupa gagged. The cloth smelled like rancid sweat and dirt. "Your majesty, I'm sorry, but are these clothes?"

"They are authentic. Put them on."

Rjupa went behind a tree to change, but once she was dressed, her stomach dropped. Yes, the queen was telling the truth about how authentic her outfit was.

"Come out and let me see how you look," the Queen said.

"I don't want to," she whispered. Nevertheless, Rjupa came out of hiding, head low, humiliated. She couldn't look anybody in the eye.

She was wearing the clothes of a thrall girl.

Then Egill, who had gone behind a boulder with his outfit, groaned. He came out wearing the costume of a low-ranking landowner, like some silly yokel.

"Oh, do not look at me," he groaned.

The queen came out rebraiding her hair in a simple braid, wearing the clothes of a farm wife. She looked at Egill and Rjupa and nodded at what she saw.

"We're both all going to look like this?" Egill asked, sounding almost so sad that Rjupa couldn't help but laugh. "Don't laugh at me in my plight," he added good-naturedly, looking down at himself. "I went exploring the world so I could *avoid* this lifestyle at all costs."

The queen put one hand on each of their shoulders. "We are close to victory now," she said.

"We are wearing these clothes as a disguise, because I want to see the results of last night's work."

"Last night's work? What did you do last night?" Egill asked, confused.

The Queen looked at Rjupa, who looked back, keeping her mouth shut. Satisfied, she nodded. "All shall be revealed in time. Come." She handed them a bag of supplies, as if they'd been walking a long way. "We are travelers," she said, "and we've been walking on this road all day. We are going to ask King Varinn to give us shelter for the night – but we will not stay the night," she added to the three dragons. "I will need all three of you to be alert to the sounds from his keep, because we will need your help to leave in a hurry."

The queen put her fingers under Rjupa's chin to raise her face, her dark eyes restlessly scanning her features. "Yes," she breathed. Then, softly, she began to sing under her breath so that Rjupa was not able to understand the words that she wove in through the music.

As the Queen sang, her the fingers of her other hand touched her around her face – now on her cheekbones, now on her forehead, now in the corner of her eyes. Then the Queen flicked her hand into the air with a flourish and a short phrase sung under her breath. A burst of cold broke across her face, and Rjupa flinched.

"Good," said the queen. "Now you, Egill."

Confused as to what the queen had done, Rjupa felt her face. It felt odd … as if her features were not her own, but that of a stranger's.

The queen began singing again under her breath, reaching up to touch Egill's face just as she had done for Rjupa's. When she touched her fingers to his cheekbones, they became more defined. When she touched his chin, it grew more rugged. His nose became more aquiline. His face changed, became somebody else's … that of an old beggar's.

Rjupa was amazed at the transformation. Little by little the queen turned Egill's face into the face of a man who was exhausted, who had seen better days.

But there was something else… the way they gazed at each other as the transformation took place. The way her hand lingered on his face. A grief in the queen's eyes, a need in his, as their gazes locked and held. Something trembled in the air between them, in the intensity of that moment.

But then the transformation took effect, and he winced slightly from the burst of cold … Rjupa felt it from where she stood ... and the charged moment between them was over.

How had I not noticed this before? she thought.

She turned away and faked a sneeze so her surprise wouldn't be evident. Whatever her feelings about this, they had a mission. She had to focus on that.

"We look like sister and brother, I suppose?" Egill asked Rjupa, teasingly.

"I hope not," Rjupa joked back. "You look all broken down and decrepit."

"What?" he yelped, feeling his face.

The queen laughed and pulled out the polished silver she used as a mirror. "See for yourself."

Mock indignant, he swiped the mirror from her hand and looked at himself. "What's the matter with you? I look quite svelte," as the Queen hid her smile behind her hand.

"I want to see how I look," Rjupa begged.

He put the mirror in her hand. "You have nothing to worry about," he said merrily.

Another woman looked back at her, one with blonde hair and pale blue eyes. An angry-looking woman, one she felt that she'd seen before…and here she shivered slightly without knowing why.

"Come," said the queen, accepting the mirror back from Rjupa. "We must get going if we are to accept the King's kind hospitality." With an instant, with a quick flourish of her hand, she transformed herself from a beautiful queen into a drab, exhausted hag.

"We are beggars," the queen told Egill and Rjupa in a low voice. "We will ask that man for hospitality, which he will grant us. But do not eat of his meat – only his bread and ale."

With that cryptic warning, Rjupa walked with the Queen and Egill, talking along the way, until they reached the great keep.

She gazed up at the houses and courtyards that were built into the side of the mountain, going up and up to a great keep at its summit, and above that, a dragon landing, where a small dun brown dragon came flying in, seeming almost too small for the man riding on its back.

Below them, a wide pasture and a cart road led down to a shipyard where tidy houses sat. Beyond the houses were the piers and harbors and a fleet of grand ships, their various banners fluttering. On a tower further down the coast, a dragon sat along with several guards, watching out for attacks on the sea. Other guards sat at various points over the great city in the mountain.

They arrived at the door of the keep and Rjupa said, "Let me do this."

The Queen nodded.

Rjupa could not bear to think of the Queen begging at a door like some common person. She hated being in this disguise, hated having to abase herself again, the way she had been forced to, back when she was a thrall. She used to be regularly smacked, or worse, for raising her eyes or speaking in a way that didn't please Iron Skull, or at any whim of his.

Though it had been years since she'd watched him die, every day she rejoiced that he was dead and she still walked around upon the earth that held him. His corpse could rattle around inside its barrow all it liked, but it would never walk above the earth again. She, on the other hand, still did.

With this in mind, she lowered her eyes and went to the guards at the door. "Please, sirs," she said. "My mother and father have been traveling for a long time today. Could we come in and share a crust of bread and something to drink with your people? We want to sit and eat for a while before we move on."

The law of hospitality was something that true nobility always followed without exception. Rjupa know that only the worst people would turn away a tired traveler at night.

"Get on with you, whelp," the guard said, disgusted. "No beggars here."

"Please, sire, just a little food." Just then, Rjupa saw the queen sway where she stood. "Mama, be careful. Are you all right?"

"That woman is playacting," the guard grumbled. "Probably does this act at every door she comes to. Get along with ye, now."

A second guard came strolling up. "What's wrong with you? Where are your manners?" he asked the first guard, then turned to Rjupa. "I apologize for my colleague. He doesn't understand that the gods smile down upon those who offer hospitality. Come, come inside and sit, and share our food."

The first guard went grumbling away while the second guard opened the door to them. "Straight on back is the great hall. You'll find much good food there. Find some victuals and be seated and eat. You must be tired from your journey."

"Thank you, sir," Rjupa said, feeling a little ashamed of herself. *What is he going to think when we poison the king's meat?*

They entered into a great hall.

The guard showed them to an out-of-the-way part of the great table, where they sat down. The food smelled delicious, several cuts of beef and veal smelling delicious and savory as if freshly off the spit on the hearth.

Rjupa put her hand out to the meat, thinking that maybe a tiny bite wouldn't hurt, but the queen swatted her hand with a frown. She reached for the bread and cheese instead. The savory smell of the beef was certainly tempting, though, and many people were partaking of the meat and telling each other how good it tasted. Rjupa's stomach grumbled.

At the high seat sat a Moor, wearing dark robes with ermine trim – King Varinn. His court had a number of Moors who had come north, or were visiting on their travels. Varinn murmured something to the singer at the front of the hall, and she struck up the harp and began singing a lovely song.

Rjupa wasn't the best about music, was never able to sing in tune, so she could never manage the song magic that Thora used to do. But despite her tin ear, she was impressed with the music and the woman's singing. She wished that Skeggi could listen to her … then shook her head. This *was* the enemy's court, after all.

The savory smell of the meat pervaded the hall. Rjupa didn't think she'd smelled anything as good in her life. Another servant brought them drinking horns with ale. She ate and drank gratefully, as did Egill.

But the Queen's eyes never moved from Varinn, who was busy talking to several of his subjects who had come forward to see him and talk to him. His meat remained untouched. His eyes were red; his face was swollen from grief. His subjects were talking to him, quietly. Somebody motioned at the food, the banquet spread before him, and he gazed blankly at it and shook his head.

The Queen made an exasperated sound from between her clenched teeth.

Egill put his hand on hers. "Patience, your … my dear. Perhaps in time he will … nourish himself."

The Queen shook her head and put aside her bread. "Come. Let us pay our respects to this great king."

Rjupa's bread turned dry in her mouth, and it took an enormous effort to swallow the bite she'd been chewing. *Let the Queen handle this,* she thought. *You don't even have to talk to that man who killed Thora.*

They made their way to the front of the room, to the high throne where Varinn sat, holding up his head. There was a second high seat beside him, but it was empty except for a small item that sat in its seat.

The Queen took one look and blanched so severely that Rjupa was afraid she'd faint.

It was a small portrait, exquisitely done, of Thora, sitting there in that seat. It was the most lifelike portrait that Rjupa had ever seen: Thora with her gentle smile, holding a book in her lap with a brilliant red rose on top of it.

To see her friend's eyes there, in the house of her murderer … Rjupa felt as if the breath had been struck out of her lungs by a blow to her chest.

MURDER

Egill, seeing their distress, murmured, "Do you need to sit down?"

"No," the Queen gasped. "No. How dare he place her picture there? How dare he?"

Rjupa seized the Queen's hand. "Your majesty," she murmured low in the Queen's ear. "Hide your feelings, and don't let your resolve weaken. Abase yourself before this murderer of your daughter, my friend. Ask him gentle questions about her. Show him kindness and draw him out in speech. Let him try and pretend how much he cares for her. Then, when you have gained his sympathy and trust, ask him to eat a little. Then the meat will do its work." As intent as the queen was about making Varinn eat, she was certain that it must have been poisoned.

The Queen gazed into Rjupa's eyes, as if drawing strength from her. "Yes. Thank you," she said softly. "Your words comfort me and show me the way. After he eats, be sure to stay close to me, for we will have to flee."

Rjupa nodded, her heart pounding at the praise and at the promise of peril ahead. But it was all for the Queen. Rjupa was glad to be here where she could encourage her and fight for her.

But the Queen paled again, looking at the picture of Thora. Her voice faltered. "I … I don't think I can do it," she said, low.

Rjupa's heart blazed. "I can," she said. "I can speak for you, if you cannot trust your voice. I will do these things that you desire."

The Queen squeezed her hand and nodded. "Do so. I give you permission."

The small group approached Varinn. Rjupa thought of all those years she'd spent abasing herself before Iron Skull. Like Varinn, he'd had the ability to make himself seem sad. She'd seen him playacting his grief to the point where she'd believed him, but then, moments later, shed his grief as if it were an old cloak and laugh about how she'd been so taken in by it.

She bowed deeply to Varinn on his high seat. "Your majesty, we approach in all humility with a sincere wish for your good health. We are travelers who were invited in by one of your generous guards, for a place to eat and rest for the night. But sire, what troubles you? Forgive my presumption, but you seem deeply grieved."

His eyes drifted to her as if realizing she was there, and he took a deep breath and seemed to pull himself together, sitting up and trying to look attentive. It was a convincing performance.

One of the women standing by his seat spoke for him. She wore the elegant robes of one of high rank.

"Perhaps he should not be bothered at this time. He's suffered a great loss."

"No," King Varinn said in a rumble of a deep voice. "No. I do not mind talking to these travelers. All are welcome at my door, and I am pleased that the guard extended my hospitality to you."

He gestured at the high seat next to him where the portrait sat. "She was to have been my queen," he said. "Her name was Thora, daughter of Queen Saehilda." Rjupa noted the mispronunciation of her name to herself, noted how his great hands, which rested on the arms of his chair, closed convulsively on the armrests. "I had so many hopes for her. She was kind and gentle, the very flower of a woman. She charmed all whom she met, and we talked about so many things. She went home, and she seemed to be healthy except for fatigue."

A sigh burst from him and he clasped his hands in his lap. "Shortly after, she took sick and died." He closed his eyes and breathed deeply, as if too shaken to continue.

"It was a terrible blow," said the high-ranking woman. "Your majesty, you don't need to speak any longer."

Scalding tears had risen to Rjupa's eyes, and she dashed them away. She couldn't cry now, but her indignation wouldn't let her stop. "I apologize, your majesty," Rjupa said, her voice breaking. "She shouldn't have died, she shouldn't have died! A young woman like that, so lovely and capable, should not have died!"

Now tears rose in his eyes. He breathed deeply again, but burst out with a sob. He buried his face in his hands and gave himself over to grief.

The woman of high rank smiled sadly. "How long we have waited for this," she said sadly. "He refused to give himself over to tears for all this time. This will do him do him much good. He's been dried up for days."

I'm sure he was, Rjupa thought, wiping away her own tears.

When the storm had passed, the King shakily said, "I apologize. Your sympathy undid me. I do not wish to marry anybody else, for she was …" he shook his head. "I am glad I had that portrait of her made before she left, for now her face keeps fading in my mind, as if she'd never existed, and I cannot bear to …" He cleared his throat again, shaking his head, and changed the subject. "Young lady, fellow traveler – for we are all travelers in life – can I repay you for your kindness and patience in my time of trial?"

"There is one thing you can do," Rjupa said. "I ask you to think of your health for the sake of your subjects. Eat a little bit if you can. It is not good for a man of your rank with so many responsibilities to your people and nation, to sit before all this food and ignore it. The fragrance of your meats has made my stomach grumble from a long way off while we were still walking on the road."

He chuckled a little then, a smile appearing, then vanishing. "You are very kind. You are very kind," he said so sadly that tears rose again in her eyes, so heartfelt.

He is playacting, she reminded herself sternly.

"I suppose I should eat a little," he added.

The woman in robes of high rank nodded vigorously. "You cannot lead if you wear yourself down to a skeleton," she said gently.

"Fine," he said affectionately. "Your word is law, my friend." He picked up a little meat and ate it.

"Should I codify that into the books, sire?" she asked dryly.

"By the gods, no," he said. "You law people are nothing but trouble and vexation."

"And we are paid well for it," she replied as he ate another piece of meat.

"Get along with you," he said fondly. "What cut of meat is this? It is tough but tastes good."

The queen's eyes never left the king's plate.

"We sacrificed a bull to Thora, remember? You called for the sacrifice and you watched to make sure it met with the favor of the gods."

"I guess I did." Slowly he ate another bite. "Doesn't taste like beef, though nothing tastes right anymore. It's hard to take pleasure or joy in anything," he added softly, as if to himself.

Queen Saehildr's voice rang out from behind Rjupa. "It's heart."

Varinn looked up from his food as if half awakened from his thoughts. “What’s that? Madame?”

“It’s heart,” the Queen said. “You are eating a heart.”

Varinn glanced at Rjupa, and she was sure the confusion on his face matched the confusion on hers. The he turned back to the Queen. “I beg your pardon?”

“The cut of meat you are eating is heart,” she said, more loudly.

A trickle of fear traveled down Rjupa’s spine.

“Your voice,” he said in an odd tone. “Your voice sounds so much like hers. Like Thora’s.”

“Yes.” And in a twinkling Queen Saehildr flung off her rags. With a flourish of her hand, the beggar woman vanished, and the Queen stood in her place with a burst of cold and glitter.

Oddly, his first reaction was to pick the portrait of Thora up out of the other chair and place it in his lap. He looked as if he were trying to say something, but confusion was still on his face. “Queen Saehilda. Why were you in disguise? Why are you here?” he said, his voice now cold.

“It’s an old dish, an old recipe,” the queen said, her voice ringing out against the high rafters of the hall.

The whole hall turned their heads toward them trying to understand what was happening. Their conversation quieted.

And now she stepped forward, her voice like a trumpet. "I am Queen Saehildr of Skala, and my daughter is dead because of you."

Gasps rose from all around the great banquet hall. Heads swiveled.

King Varinn's mouth dropped open as he stared at her for a long moment. "Dead! I loved Thora," he said. "The two of us were going to combine our kingdoms. To kill her would mean that I get nothing, and lose her gentle, loving self as well. Are you insane? How can you say this to me?"

"Because Thora's draugr told us so," the queen said.

"Her *draugr*?" he cried. "Woman, what is this? I don't understand."

"I am saying that you murdered my daughter," the Queen said. "Her revenant came back out of the sea and told me."

"Thora came back as a revenant?" he cried, as if horrified.

"Yes, as murdered people who cannot rest tend to do," the Queen cried.

"Your majesty, slow down. I am shocked," said the high-ranking woman. "Are you saying that he killed your daughter? How can you accuse King Varinn of these lies?"

"That, along with your other questionable behavior, made me believe it," said the queen.

Varinn's face had gone stiff and furious as the queen spoke. "Slow down, Queen Saehildr," he said, his voice deep and resonant in its anger. "You are going too fast. You seem to be accusing me of crimes before I have had a chance to respond."

"More than accusing," the queen said.

"I was sympathetic to you after your great loss, but to have you come in like this and accuse me of those things, without evidence, is trying my patience. Guards, remove this woman, queen though she may be, and we can talk like civilized people, without accusations."

"Your guards will do no such thing," Queen Saehildr cried. "My revenge has been taken. You poisoned and killed my daughter, but now I have killed your son. That dish you have eaten contains your son's heart."

Everything in the King's face and body came to life. "What?" he roared. "What?"

"You have eaten your son's heart," said Queen Saehildr. "Do you understand now?"

Rjupa felt as if everything were spinning madly and now it all came flying apart.

Varinn uprooted himself, rising from his seat like a mountain, choking, retching, trying to scream. "Find my son!" he shrieked to the guards. "Find my son and tell me if this woman's words are true! And capture that bitch who is spouting these lies!"

In a twinkling the Queen's sword was in her hand. "And now we must fight our way out," she said, almost merry, as swords and axes sprang out all over the mead hall.

Rjupa, panicked, saw Varinn stagger down out of his high seat, his portrait of Thora still clutched against his chest, even as he shouted, "I will *kill* you with my bare hands if you have touched a single hair of my son!"

The Queen grabbed Rjupa and pulled her behind her. Then she and Egill sang out their song-magic in defense, a powerful music sung in tandem that twisted the sinews of the air, flinging back the attackers that stood between them and the wall, hurling the king back against his high seat.

"Come!" shouted the Queen, and they dashed for the door.

One of the guards knew this song-magic, for she was singing against them. A wall of magic struck Rjupa across the back, slamming her against the floor.

The queen immediately turned and swept her sword up and around, drawing lines of light in the air around her and her two friends. "Freyja, protect us!" she sang, and created a glowing shield over their bodies. "Now, up, friend," she called to Rjupa. "This protection will not hold long."

Guards who ran up to attack were flung back by the magic that shielded the Queen and her friends; arrows that struck the shield bounced straight up into the rafters. Thrown axes rebounded into the crowd of angry Norsemen and Moors. Screams arose.

"King Varinn!" somebody cried from the doors to the rest of the keep, their voice thick with grief. "Your Majesty, I'm sorry, but he is dead! Your son was murdered!"

Rjupa ran at the Queen's heels, making straight for the door, their magical shield bowling over their attackers. A sudden cry that broke over them nearly made her fall over in her tracks.

King Varinn went staggering from his throne and collapsed on the ground, and the cry that broke from him was grief beyond expression.

"She killed his son!" And now the furious crowd was flinging everything at them. Chairs, bread, tables, shoes, tankards, and platters glanced off the magical guard and went flying. The screams and yells of their attackers were horrifying, and Rjupa couldn't help but cringe before them.

All while thinking, *His son? His son?? Murdered?* She remembered the Queen walking out of the camp in the darkness with her bare dagger, and felt sick to her stomach.

They burst through the door – and nearly crashed into Shriken's face, because she had been trying to peek into the hall through the tiny door. Behind her crowded Krekkaq and Tandryss, their wings open.

"What did you do to these people in there?" shouted Krekkaq at Egill, his wings wide open, ready to fly. "Climb aboard, quickly!"

The Queen and Rjupa and Egill wasted no time leaping aboard their dragons, just as Varinn's angry subjects poured out through the doors. A well-aimed shoe struck Rjupa in the back of the head, rattling her teeth together, as she flung herself up on Shriken's back.

"Hold on, my dear," Shriken said as she made a powerful leap into the air. An axe narrowly missed Rjupa's leg and went skidding across her dragon's scales, throwing sparks.

"His son?" Rjupa shouted at the Queen as they went airborne, as she dodged a axe that shot past her head. "You killed his *son?*"

A horrifying cry rose from behind them – King Varinn's voice, a roar of grief, the kind that took her straight back to that night when her city burned …

Rjupa's breaths came fast, and Shriken noticed.

"I've got you. You're safe," the little silver dragon said, darting into the air like a falcon, her sharp wings striking the air, nearly overtaking the Queen's dragon.

The dragons dashed over the treetops and over fields to escape. Egill turned in the saddle to fire arrows behind him at their attackers as they flew.

"Egill, let it go!" the queen called. "Dragons, bear to the north, quickly. We have business there."

"His son?" Rjupa demanded again.

The Queen looked up at Rjupa, her eyes flashing. "His son was a cruel man, about your age, a cruel and hateful man," she said. "Thora told me all about him. He was valued only because he was due to take Varinn's throne – or would have, if Varinn had decided not to marry."

"Oh," Rjupa said. It still didn't make sense.

"That young man didn't want Varinn to marry because he would lose all claim to the throne," said the queen. "It was a plot against my daughter. And now I am revenged."

But that cry of grief that Varinn had made … it pierced her heart, even if he had killed Thora. "But…"

Egill looked at her over his shoulder. And just like that, Rjupa fell silent.

Who had given her the dragonrider's position? Egill had.

And who could take it away just as quickly?

Rjupa faced front, thankful for the darkening night that hid how red she was becoming. She could feel the heat coming out of her face.

She couldn't question this decision. They knew what was going on more than she did. And maybe Thora told them something – or maybe they knew something – that neither she nor Thora knew.

And now we are at war, Rjupa thought as they flew.

They swiftly set forth for home. The dragons ranged silently in the air, casting about them for any oncoming danger as quickly flew away under cover of darkness.

Rjupa looked back over her shoulder to see King Varinn's keep. Now a signal fire blazed on the dragon landing, and his dragons were circling like hornets when their nest had been kicked. A small group of dragons broke out of the circle, heading in their direction.

"We've been spotted," Rjupa called.

"Fly low and swiftly," the queen said. "We need to make it home. We have a war to fight." And she sounded so satisfied that Rjupa couldn't help but note how pleased the queen was by this.

Those bastards shouldn't have killed Thora if they didn't want one of their own to be killed in return, Rjupa thought.

"Come," the Queen called as they flew. "We will stop at our friends' keeps in various places along the way and see how well their mustering for this battle is going. I believe that we will need all the help we can get to defend ourselves against this kingdom's fury."

EGILL'S LETTER

The next morning, Dyrfinna was up early as usual, helping Mama and with breakfast. They worked around the hearth, built in the middle of their house, the smoke hole in the ceiling above letting in a little light, the sky above them milk-white with hazy clouds, and a brisk breeze from the ocean to draw the smoke out.

Mama was making bannocks, a recipe from her old country. "They had to take the draugr out and the dragons had to burn her, this time to ash," Mama told Dyrfinna as she laid the bread into the pan. "It was terrible. Terrible."

"Where were you during the burning?" her mama asked. "Your friends were worried about you, and we kept looking for you."

Dyrfinna looked down at the eggs she was cooking to the side of the main fire. *I was turning into a monster that wanted to devour the flesh of my loved ones,* she thought, and shuddered. "I was … overcome by what had happened to Thora. I had to get away for a while." This, technically, was true.

At that moment, Aesa came shuffling up to the fire in her long shift, yawning widely. She sat down next to Dyrfinna and leaned in for a sideways hug, resting her head on her older sister's shoulder and shutting her eyes.

"And both of my little girls were getting themselves in trouble trying to stop the draugr," their mother said, turning a dark gaze on Dyrfinna and Aesa. "How do you think I felt, seeing both of you acting recklessly, risking their lives, not even a year after Eirik died? Losing one child is almost unbearable. How much worse it would be if I'd lost both of you, too?"

Dyrfinna lowered her face before her mother's gaze. And she had come so close to making her mother's worst fear come true. "To be honest, I only wanted to protect Aesa ..."

"... who should not have been out past the barricades in the first place!" her mother said, turning on her little sister. "Child, do you think your powers are greater than those of some of your elders, who have been practicing these arts for longer than both of you have been alive?"

Aesa, instead of pitying her mother, just looked affronted. "They were using spells to block and hold her, but they weren't working. None of them heard what Sissy said – to bring Thora back to her own mind. So that's what I did."

"Chickybug," Dyrfinna said softly, putting an arm around her sister's shoulders. "Mama is upset. She loves you, but didn't you hear the fear in her voice last night when you put yourself in danger?"

Aesa tried to keep looking affronted, but her mouth trembled, and then she looked down, too. "I'm sorry," she said in a small voice. "I was just trying to help."

Dyrfinna hugged her little sister, and Mama came over and embraced them both, her eyes starting to turn red-rimmed as the tears came again.

"It's been a year," Mama said quietly, "and it never stops hurting, never goes away."

"I don't want to talk about it. I don't want to be sad anymore," Aesa said.

Dyrfinna's eyes closed. "I'm sorry, Mama," she said again. Her throat hurt.

"I know you are. It was an accident."

It didn't feel like an accident.

Everybody became very quiet.

Her mother took a deep, shaking breath. "Let that go," she said, laying her hands on her knees. "We've been over this too much in the last year. But … after your young friend's death, I've been remembering Eirik again. I can't unwrap my mind from everything that happened … I keep wondering if, somehow, I could have changed any of it."

Dyrfinna wrapped her arms around her mama and rested her head on her shoulder. "It wasn't your fault."

"It wasn't yours, either. Despite what *some* people keep saying."

They leaned in on each other, quiet. Dyrfinna hated that her mama and sister had to deal with all the heartache she'd inflicted. They were her whole world. When her heart was low, they sympathized; when she was sullen with anger toward herself, they still loved her.

Their bond had been tight, even when her papa gradually spent more and more time at the Queen's castle in his royal duties, taking Eirik with him to learn all about how to be a good chieftain. In Papa's eyes, Eirik could do no wrong.

When Eirik had died, her papa had simply left Mama and Aesa and went to live in a house in the royal grounds, giving up even the mere pretense of being a husband and father.

Mama had merely put her wings around Dyrfinna and Aesa, like a mother hen, and together, the three of them had gotten each other through the worst year of their lives.

Just then Grandmama Jelena came in, pushing the door wide. "I have news," she said dramatically, her tiny, fur-swathed form barely making a shadow in the doorway.

Mama, Dyrfinna, and Aesa released each other, Mama wiping her eyes and going back to make more bannocks. "What kind of news do you have today?" she asked.

Grandmama Jelena sat down in her chair next to the fire, wrapped in her furs as usual. She had been born in Dalmatia, and though she had chosen to settle in Skala, she'd never been able to get used to the cold, and always wore furs even on the warmest days.

She scooted her chair a little closer to the fire. "They're all three off on a secret mission," she proclaimed, leaning toward the flames and warming her small hands. "Left early this morning on their dragons before the sun rose, and went flying south."

"Who?" Dyrfinna asked as a spark of jealousy popped into life in her heart.

"The queen, my degenerate son ..." Grandmama turned her eyes on Dyrfinna. "And your friend Rjupa, riding Shriken."

Dyrfinna's eyes nearly popped out of her head. "Rjupa? The queen chose Rjupa over some of the senior riders?"

Grandmama nodded. "I was awake in the middle of the night, as usual, so I saw them fly out, all three together, taking their own dragons and talking among each other – I recognized their voices, though I couldn't understand what they were saying. They flew south."

"Do you think they were flying to King Varinn's?" Dyrfinna asked.

"The bearing was right for that destination, so it's likely."

"Huh."

"Oh, yes. But, chicklet, the Queen might have had a reason why she chose Rjupa specifically," Mama said, patting her arm, trying to soothe her. "Maybe the queen needed somebody who she knew she could lead easily. Or maybe Rjupa has some quality from all her time with Thora that she wanted to take advantage of. I mean," Mama quickly added, "...some quality that she knew would help the queen on the mission."

"No," Grandmama Jelena said, accepting a hot cup of reindeer milk from Aesa. "No, sweet girl, it's because my son has a swelled head." She took out a scrap of rough paper and unfolded it. "This was pinned to my door when I stepped outside this morning."

Dyrfinna's eyebrows went up. Her grandmama had brought the idea of paper to Skala, having learned papermaking from some Roman prisoners she captured on board ship. Not many Skalans were interested in paper or writing, but she knew only one other besides Grandmama and Thora who used paper to send messages.

"What did Egill write?" Dyrfinna said, sitting down suddenly, her heart suddenly heavy as stone.

Grandmama frowned at the paper. "I want you to know that I think this is all nonsense," she told Dyrfinna, and began to read.

Mama, by the time you read this, I will be gone on an important mission. I am not sure when I will be back – we might be gone for about two moons, as we will have many people to contact and urge them to pledge their support to us, the Queen.

My daughter Dyrfinna must not be allowed to join the current effort. When I come back, I will begin talks with Rulf of Ilusalv to combine her fortunes to his son. It's what's best for all of us, even her. To have her involved in the upcoming war will be a disaster.

Rein her in. If I come back and she is on one of those warships, I will personally make her sorry she ever did so.

Your son, Egill.

Dyrfinna felt as if a bucket of freezing water was thrown in her face.

Nobody spoke.

Rein her in.

Dyrfinna picked up her warm cloak and sat down next to the fire to pull on her soft caribou boots with shaking hands.

"Stay here, Sissy," Aesa pleaded. "Breakfast is almost done."

"I'm going out to train," Dyrfinna said.

"You don't need to train." Aesa, trying to cheer her up, grabbed her arm and squeezing it. "Look at those muscles! They're hard as rocks!" Then a puzzled look came over her face, and she squeezed Dyrfinna's arm again, then her bicep. "Sissy, how'd your arms get to be so thick? They weren't like this yesterday."

Dyrfinna gave her a mock-disappointed gaze. "Are you kidding me? Arms don't bulk out overnight." *Well, not usually*, she thought, running her hand over her arm.

So how much of the draugr's strength did she still have? Now she was itching to find out.

Rein her in, he'd said.

Rein her in, my ass, she thought.

"I'll be back in a little while." Dyrfinna kissed the top of Aesa's head, her mama's cheek, and gave Grandmama a little peck on the lips. "I'm going to climb Mount Pyrr again. I won't be gone for long. But … I've gotta clear my head."

She picked up two bannocks to eat on the way and was out the door in a flash.

THE FLAME OF VENGEANCE

Dyrfinna ran up the long, stone steps, which had been darkened with time and occasionally by fire, to the dragon stables at the top of the mountain. She always ran up the stairs as far as she could for endurance training. A chilly wind blew down from the peaks of Mount Pyrr, the air crisp and bracing. Dyrfinna breathed it in deeply, thankful for the coolness.

She reached the top and took a moment to catch her breath, sweat dripping from her face, her legs feeling like jelly. As often as she ran to the top of those stairs, it annoyed her to be still panting for breath at the top. She had to be better. She had to be stronger.

The Queen's guards, seeing her, opened the gate to the stables and let her in. One of the guards, a friend of her father's, glared at her. He'd probably pass on to Egill, when he returned, how his wayward daughter was visiting the stables in defiance of his orders.

Dyrfinna swanned past Egill's friend, nose in the air.

The air of the stables smelled like manure, hay, and wood smoke from the many fires that burned here to keep the dragons warm, and sulfur from their breath. Over the drowsy grumbles of dragons came the sweet floating song that Skeggi was singing.

"He can't bar me from everything I love," she growled to herself.

A great platform made of black rocks stretched out before the stables, with the stables and the side of the mountain to block the wind, a warm and comfortable place for any dragons that wanted to bask in the sun on a windy day.

Her friends were there. Ostryg and Gefjun were oiling the scales of various dragons while Skeggi sang a new song he'd learned from some Balkan travelers.

And there, lying prone on the rocks with every part of their body stretched out to soak in the buttery sun, lay Serja. They raised their head to Dyrfinna as she came in, the dragon's eyes narrowed like those of a contented cat.

Dyrfinna went straight to Serja, her arms out, and hugged her around the neck.

"We've missed you, chicklet," the dragon said, and Dyrfinna rested her head against Serja's for a moment, blissfully happy.

Skeggi finished his song when the two finally drew apart. "Finna, are you going on the ships when we leave for war?" he asked. "Or has your father forbidden that, too?"

Gefjun laughed, short. "I wouldn't be surprised if he does that purely out of spite," she said scornfully.

"Guess what? He's beaten you to it," Dyrfinna said, pulling out Egill's letter.

Gefjun sat up, her mouth open. "No. Way."

Dyrfinna leaned against Serja's side as if they were the softest pillow and read the letter aloud, then she crumpled it in her hand. "He can piss up a rope," she said. "I'm not going to stay here in Skala when Thora needs revenged. I'm going with the army. I don't care how I do it, but I'm going."

"Your father might make you a servant," Ostryg said with a laugh, as if he found the idea funny, which annoyed Dyrfinna.

"I won't be his servant, but I'm almost willing to be somebody else's servant, just as long as it gets me into battle."

Dyrfinna's longing for revenge burned inside her like a flame. But she had also realized something else – something that was a long shot, but still possible.

"Are any of you familiar with the sea-road that we'll be sailing to King Varinn's keep?" she asked.

"My parents used to sail that way, long ago," Skeggi said. "A lot of rough islands and jutting rocks lie along that voyage. It's almost better to go far out to sea to avoid them, though we lose much time in doing so."

"Do you know what else lies in that direction?" Dyrfinna asked casually.

"My ass, probably," Ostryg said, vigorously rubbing oil behind a dragon's neck frills as the dragon's eyes closed in bliss.

"Your ass is always where it shouldn't be," Dyrfinna said.

"It's never close enough for me to reach," Gefjun grumbled, swatting at it with her oiling cloth but missing.

"And no, that's not the right answer. Do you know what lies in that direction?" Dyrfinna said, her eyes gleaming. "Wild dragons. There are wild dragons living in the islands out that way."

Silence fell over the dragon stables, and everybody went stock still for a moment, staring.

Serja lifted their head and broke the silence. "Tell us what you're thinking, Finna."

"It's spring. We'll be passing the islands where the wild dragons live." She paused a moment. "There might be dragon eggs."

Gefjun dropped her oiling rag, eyes blazing. "No. Are you *crazy?"*

"Yes, she is," Ostryg said, adding an ear-shattering belch.

Gefjun whacked him. "No, you can't do it. I won't let you."

"It's dangerous," Skeggi said, the concern in his brown eyes making her melt.

"But anybody who brings back a dragon egg owns that dragon," Dyrfinna said, "And if you own a dragon, then you're automatically a dragonrider. You make your own life choices then. My father can't interfere and marry me off because I've done this honorable service to the Queen."

"That's all very good," Skeggi said, "but the only drawback to that plan is that people die when they try to steal dragon eggs."

"Unless you don't," Dyrfinna added.

"You're facing wild dragons," Gefjun cried. "They don't care about your papa trying to marry you off. They'll kill you anyway."

One of the dragons that was having their scales oiled said, "Listen to her. Uncollared dragons are different than us. They can't even talk, and they see everything as potential dinner."

"But imagine a nestful of baby dragons turning their adoring eyes on you," Dyrfinna pleaded.

"Before they burn you to a crisp. They're not baby birds, Finna!"

"But if you pick up their eggs, then you'll have hatchlings. And they'll break out of their shell and turn their adoring, jeweled eyes on you, and imprint …"

Gefjun turned dewy-eyed and melted for a moment, but then she shook her head. "Don't do that! Have you ever had to deal with somebody who's been burned by a dragon?"

Dyrfinna frowned. "Well, yes, but when you work with dragons you sometimes get burned …"

Gefjun's eyes were wide. "I'm not talking about just a patch on your arm or even a spark in your hair. I'm talking about full-body burns, Finna, the kind inflicted by very pissed-off wild dragons when they catch you trying to steal their eggs!"

Serja raised their head, bumping it gently against Dyrfinna's side. "I'd like a baby dragon to imprint on me. Mine or somebody else's ... it doesn't matter whose."

"Serja, don't say that," the other dragon said.

But Dyrfinna felt Serja's longing, so painful it nearly broke her own heart.

She could see Serja with baby dragons skipping around their feet, playing games of hide-and-seek around their legs. Could see Serja lying there at night with dragon babies piled on their side, sleeping in a heap like puppies, filled with bliss. She saw the dragon's memories – teaching the young dragons how to fly, drawing their wings over them during storms, teaching them to fight.

They wanted this.

Serja and the other dragons could help raise the dragons that would grow up to fly Finna and her friends into battle.

Dyrfinna had wanted to find and bring back dragon eggs so she could have her own dragon, one that Egill couldn't take away, so she could choose her own husband, her own destiny. She wanted those dragon eggs so her friends could always be by her side.

But now she wanted those dragon eggs for Serja – to ease her friend's heartache.

"Why don't you choose a mate and lay some eggs, then?" Ostryg asked Serja, busily working the oiled chamois over Serja's wings.

"That would be rather difficult for me to do," Serja chuckled, "because I am not an egg-layer." They looked around the stables at the other dragons. "I would go on a mating flight, but…"

Just then, the carnelians on Serja's collar gleamed. "But it's just not enjoyable when your heart's not in it," they added sadly.

Dyrfinna frowned at the gleaming carnelians. "Is it because somehow a mating flight would be an act of disobedience? Is that why the carnelians are glowing when you say that?"

"Yes, partly. But there are other issues at play. That … we …" The carnelians gleamed slightly, and Serja stuttered and quit.

"Well, we need to ask the völva what is going on with this," Dyrfinna said.

"Others have asked her, time and again," Serja reminded her. "Many magicians have changed the bindings on our collars, with no success. Our best idea is to take the collars off and try that way."

"Oh, no," Ostryg said, nearly falling off Serja's wing. "No, no, no. I'd rather not see myself and the rest of the queendom as burnt and shriveled corpses, thank you very much."

"It would be for just a little while," Serja suggested.

"Death is not 'just a little while' for us," Gefjun said, laying a hand on Serja's face.

Serja twitched their wings irritably, accidentally conking Ostryg on the head. "I wouldn't hurt any of you if I were uncollared. I wouldn't!"

The dragon's carnelians glowed, and they subsided, but turned their head away.

Dyrfinna came close. "I'm sorry, Serja. Look," she said, holding up the golden carnelian ring. "I'm bound, too. And I let myself be bound because … whatever monstrous thing I have inside of me needs to be trapped. I do not want to hurt anybody in this way again." She met Serja's eyes, and her voice shook when she spoke. "I wouldn't wish this on anybody – especially you, my brilliant flier. I don't want you to have to live with this kind of pain on your heart."

Her sword-friends all around were silent, their eyes sympathetic.

But Serja sighed.

"But I do," she said. "I do live with this pain. And now you have willingly bound the richest and most powerful part of yourself – just as they have done to us."

THE PIRATE QUEEN

In Skala, over the next couple of weeks, the levies came pouring in as more fighters answered the Queen's summons. Ships came flying into the Skalan harbor bearing hard and wiry warriors, with many veterans among them.

They brought weapons and armor they'd gathered from around the world, much of it gained from plundering other nations. Many Vikings gathered on the shore and docks around the ships, showing off crossbows and pikes they'd "liberated" from other people all over the world, as excited as children with new toys, and trading went on feverishly between them.

Dyrfinna tried not to be jealous of those who had enough money to own their own ship and pick their own crew. She had no dragon. No ship. Maybe if she did well in the war, her Papa would change his mind about her and everything would be all right again.

In the meanwhile, she and her sword-friends had joined the crew of one of Skeggi's nautical friends.

"But you're dragonriders," Skeggi's friend said, confused. "Aren't you flying instead of sailing?"

An uncomfortable moment of silence between the friends. Finally Dyrfinna blurted, "My father decided to visit my sins upon the heads of my friends."

Then everything got really uncomfortable, and none of her friends could look at each other.

Finally Skeggi spoke. "Listen. We have to find our own destiny. If we can't have our dragons, then we can at least have a ship."

"We are going on this voyage to revenge Thora," Gefjun reminded them. "I don't care how we get there. But she will be revenged – on her bones."

"On her bones," the rest of the Corae Guard said, including Dyrfinna, and Skeggi's friend nodded.

"And which is better?" Ostryg said, lazily flipping his knife, one handed. "Going out into the world and doing a little damage and revenging Thora, or staying home and sulking because Egill took away our dragons?"

"Then welcome to my ship," Skeggi's friend said.

Better than nothing, Dyrfinna thought. *The fighters on this ship aren't the best, but they can learn.*

To add insult to injury, before he'd left, Egill had assigned all the dragons in the stables to his friends – a bunch of old men. Even Serja had been assigned to Egill's closest friend, just like that, an older man with no connection to Thora.

"We'll go on the ship with you," Gefjun grumbled. "Those old farts will twist an ankle getting out of bed and be out of service for six weeks – and then we'll get our chance."

I won't, Dyrfinna thought, but kept her mouth shut. Now she was seeing a new way out. She could win glory in battle, maybe find some dragon eggs, and finally earn her position. And if that didn't happen, she'd be far enough from home to allow her to go into the world and run away to a new place.

At the same time, there was a little part of her hoping ... hoping that maybe her papa would see her in battle, and maybe he would soften against her and be proud of her at last.

But Dyrfinna was dismayed at the discipline in the ranks of the squadron she was fighting in with the rest of the sword-friends. Skeggi had talked to his friend, who owned the ship, and tried to get him to restore order, but the rest of the Vikings on the ship didn't seem interested in training for battle.

They wanted to talk about how many places they'd raid while they were sailing, and how many pretty girls they'd bring back to marry. They wanted to go down to the beach and drink, where they'd howl for no reason, or fight clumsily like a pack of puppies. Dyrfinna would jump into their fights with her sword to try to show them a real fighting style, but they'd only jump back and complain, "Stop it. We know what we're doing."

Other times she would insert herself into the conversation to give them fighting tips, but they'd call her names and stalk away, affronted by the gall of a girl who dared to tell them how to fight.

One morning she was training with the rest of her sword-friends and those few of the ship that were interested in training, when some of the heavy drinkers came staggering past, coming home from their fun on the beach, stinking of ale.

"Hey, Finna baby," one of them said, and the rest of his group laughed.

Dyrfinna gritted her teeth and kept practicing with her sword.

"Hey, look at me. Look at me, Finna." He made kissing noises at her.

"She's not looking at you. What a bitch."

"Hey, bitch, bend over for me. You know you want…"

His sentence was cut off by the rock that Dyrfinna scooped off the ground and flung into his face. Blood sprayed, a chip of tooth flew, and he fell backwards hard into the ground and knocked himself out.

The rest of his drunken friends stood staring at his prone body, open-mouthed, taking a little longer than average to process what had just happened.

"Nah," said Dyrfinna, already hefting a second rock in her hand. "I have standards, and they're a lot higher than that."

Finally the realization of what just happened sank into the ale-dampened sponges of their brains, and they all shouted with indignation.

"You dog-bitch!"

"You … bitchy dog!"

One of them drew his sword. "I'm going to smack you around the way you deserve. You think you're so much better than us. I'll show you who's stronger!"

"You can't best your opponents in glorious battle if you're spending every night vomiting ale on the beach," Dyrfinna replied, her sword in a casual guard position. "Not to mention you dishonor good ale by wasting it like that. How dare you."

"Get her!"

The drunkards moved in tight battle formation – or what would have been considered a tight formation if it had been viewed from a couple of leagues in the air. Rolling, stumbling, reeling, on they came like the forces of Hel, if the forces of Hel were overweight and sloppy drunk.

The first attacker was taken down with Dyrfinna's second stone. The second attacker smashed into Ostryg's outstretched arm, which he stuck out at neck level, and the drunkard's eyes bugged out as he went down, effectively clotheslined.

The third and fourth attackers came rolling up to Dyrfinna, swords out. She parried the first sword, then spun and slammed her sword hilt into the back of the third one's head.

"Ouch, fuck," he said, and collapsed.

The fourth one held his sword up from his crotch, waggling it at Dyrfinna with his tongue hanging out. "You want some of this? You want some of this?"

"Sure," Dyrfinna said, and kicked him hard enough in the crotch to bring him off the ground.

He dropped the sword with a scream, clutched his junk, fell over sideways, and pissed himself.

The fifth one had not even approached her. "You bitch, I'm gonna fuck you up," he said from a distance. He put his hands on his knees. "I mean you're gonna feel it." He started sweating, slowly turning red. "You're gonna be hurt when I beat you up. Hurt really bad." He gagged and swallowed, looking positively green. "I'll make you sorry you were … ever born …" Then he doubled over, retched, and vomited a bucketful of bile and ale.

"He's actually not wrong," Dyrfinna said. "I am very sorry I was ever born to see that."

"Shit," said Skeggi's friend, the captain of the ship, surveying the carnage as the retching and vomiting continued behind Dyrfinna. "That was, like, half my crew."

"I'd rather go into battle alone than with this outfit, to be quite honest," Dyrfinna said scornfully.

"That was mean," said Skeggi's friend sadly as the drunkards groaned and tried to get to their feet.

Skeggi put an arm around his friend's shoulder. "What Finna *meant* to say is that it might be better for all of us to get fighters who we can depend on in the heat of battle."

Skeggi's friend shrugged helplessly. "We're running short on good soldiers," he said. "All the biggest men and most skillful fighters have been taken. We just have people with missing limbs, some shieldmaidens, a bunch of grey old men, and drunkards."

Dyrfinna's eyes narrowed. "A raft of old, feeble men would be far better than this." She made a scornful wave at the drunkards.

"You mean shieldmaidens." One of them tried to throw a punch at her ankle but missed, hitting himself in the face. "Ow."

"Shieldmaidens?" Skeggi's friend said. "With fighting men? On a *ship*? They'd have sex with everybody."

"Oh wolf shit," Gefjun growled. "Maybe your boys should keep their dicks to themselves."

"Yeah, I really don't think that's going to be a concern," Dyrfinna said, astonished.

"No, I don't think so, either," came a new voice. "Not anymore."

Everybody turned. To Dyrfinna's surprise the one who had spoken was her Grandmama Jelena, sailing up to the group. Her head poked out of the top of a gigantic coat of furs, and she wore a darling fur cap over her brown and grey hair to cover her perpetually chilly ears.

"The Pirate Queen!" Skeggi's friend gasped.

"Watch where you walk, Grandmama," Dyrfinna said. "There's been random vomiting here."

"Not *that* much, bitch," said the vomiting guy next to his lake of barf.

Grandmama Jelena surveyed the field of battle with one eyebrow raised. "I'd kick you for that remark, insolent boy, but I don't want to smell up my boots. Finna, I need you to come with me for a little while, if you don't mind."

"Take her permanently, for all I care," said Skeggi's friend. "She is not welcome on my ship, ever again."

"Well, then," Gefjun said, sheathing her sword. "I am finished here. Good luck finding a crew."

"I go where they go, man," said Ostryg. "Sorry."

Skeggi's friend turned to Skeggi. "You're not going to leave me, too, are you? For her?"

Skeggi slapped a hand on his friend's shoulder. "I always cast my lot with these fellows," he said. "We go way back."

They all followed Dyrfinna and her grandmama away.

"You didn't have to leave," Dyrfinna told her friends, now a little worried. "Not on my account."

"Pff! Think nothing of it," Gefjun said, walking at Dyrfinna's other side. "The crew was bad enough, but after what he said about shieldmaidens? Fuck him. See if he can find a crew now."

"And you should never settle for whatever crew can take you," Skeggi said.

"Though you did settle when you chose to join up with that crumbburglar," Ostryg pointed out.

"Well…" Skeggi merely shrugged.

"You joined that ship, too," Grandma Jelena pointed out to Ostryg.

"Where he goes, I go," Ostryg said, pointing to Skeggi.

They paused in their conversation as a fleet ship came flying in over the waves. The Viking ship was driven up on shore, high enough on the sand so the tide wouldn't pick it up and carry it off.

While the swordfriends were watching it, Grandmama Jelena excused herself and led Dyrfinna away for a private conversation.

"Now how did you end up with that crew?" Grandmama asked, snuggling down into her furs when a light breeze came nosing around. "Didn't you say your standards were higher than that?"

"I go where my friends go," Dyrfinna said. "And … a lot of people didn't want me on their ship because they've seen how Papa disapproves of me," she added in a lower voice.

Grandmama made a raspberry noise with her tongue. "Nonsense," she said. "They didn't want you to join them because they're all fools, afraid you'd steal their thunder."

I wish, thought Dyrfinna.

"You're old enough and wise enough to have a ship of your own."

"It would be lovely, but you know Papa will not let me have anything of the sort," Dyrfinna said stuffily.

"That's enough, Finna. He can't do anything of the sort to you."

But Grandmama. He already has been.

"At any rate, you deserve better. Therefore, I will give you a ship that you can bring into the service of the queen."

Dyrfinna stopped in her tracks. "Wait. What? A *ship*?"

"I am giving you my ship that you can command and take into battle." Grandmama smiled. "It is wholly yours."

Dyrfinna began to shake. "But Grandmama, you don't have a ship. You sold them all after Grandpapa died."

"Well, I did, except for one. I went into partnership with an old friend of mine with my favorite ship, which he sails. I earn a portion of his proceeds, and soften his losses when times are bad. It's kept him afloat, no pun intended, and gives me a decent pittance to live on."

Dyrfinna knew exactly which ship Grandmama was talking about. "You mean that Hakr's ship is still partly owned by you? I didn't know that!"

Grandmama smiled. "Yes, that's the one. Saebrandur."

Dyrfinna's eyes widened. Sea Flame was a beautiful little craft that she'd known since she was little, and Hakr was its steersman.

"And that's going to be okay with Hakr?"

Grandmama threw her head back and laughed. "Only if he can be your steersman."

Dyrfinna clutched her head in disbelief. Hakr was an old steersman who had been all over the world and fought in many naval battles, a warrior overflowing with good sense and knowledge. "Only if…! Grandmama, good grief, of course I do!"

It was all she'd really wanted, but she'd pushed that thought out of her mind so many times, knowing how her papa would react if he knew she had a ship.

But to have his own mother give her a ship? Maybe she had a chance.

Her grandmama's shaking hands held Dyrfinna's firmly. "I've already been talking this over with Hakr, believe it or not. We both want to send you into war, the way you should be going. And we want you to personally get revenge for the Queen's poor daughter."

"But what about Papa?"

Grandmama frowned. "How dare he write that letter. If he were smaller I'd put him over my knee and swat him. He has no right telling you that – you, the girl who could be the jewel of the queen's army!"

Dyrfinna's heart felt as if it would burst with joy. She gently squeezed her grandmama's hands back. "I will, Grandmother. I will. I swear it on the bones of our ancestors."

"Now you go and strike down many hundreds in magnificent battle, there's a good girl." And Dyrfinna kissed her grandma on the forehead, and her grandmama blessed her.

Dyrfinna immediately asked Skeggi, Gefjun, and Ostryg to join her crew, and naturally they accepted and they all went out together to recruit warriors for her ship.

Skeggi's friend was right – the pickings were slim.

So Dyrfinna went to the person who could help.

"I want you to help me choose my crew," she said to her grandmama while they waited for Hakr to bring the ship back from its current mission. "You did me the great honor of giving me your ship. But you've also spent years in battle on the high seas, and you've had to choose crewmates for your own ships, in Dalmatia and here in Skala. Let me learn from you."

Grandmama was something of a hard woman. But at these words, her eyes sparkled, and she placed a gnarled hand over her mouth for a moment.

"You honor me, granddaughter, more than you'll ever know," she said at last. "Here I have been, feeling sorry for myself at not being able to contribute to this grand expedition, when you come to me and give me the greatest gift I could have received, outside of my youth given back to me again. I would be happy to help you."

Dyrfinna chose a few warriors she'd had her eye on for a while. Ragnarok was her first choice, a mountain of a man. She picked several women who were skillful archers, who had been passed over by the other battle leaders. One of the women could fire a blunted arrow through an ox hide, while another of them were so skilled that she could split an arrow on a target.

With Grandmama's approval, Dyrfinna brought in a few assassin friends of Ostryg's, much to his satisfaction. "Assassins are useful for those little troublesome missions when you *really* need somebody to die," Grandmama pointed out.

Most of the fighters in town had already been snapped up by this time. However, Grandmama spent much of her time sitting near the Queen's keep and watching the battle games, or watching everybody in Skala drill for battle, so she was familiar with many of the fighters' strengths and weaknesses.

She found a few younger fighters who had great potential that needed to be developed. She found some older veterans who were missing limbs, or others who had slowed down through the years. However, these old warriors were hard to scare and would stay clear-headed and steady when a battle suddenly turned bad. "And it invariably does," she said. "These fighters will hold your band together under heavy fire, I guarantee it."

There were a few warriors who were odd sorts, some misfits, and several berserkers who were something of a handful outside of battle as well. Grandmama brought in some magic-workers that had been overlooked or avoided outright for various reasons. Some of them were a little loopy, to be honest.

Her grandmama even brought in a few thieves. "Their ethics are good enough for this voyage," she said breezily when Dyrfinna expressed her misgivings. "Just watch your knives and jewels, and you'll be fine."

Dyrfinna trusted her grandmama in all things. All the same, she couldn't help but feel a little skeptical at this motley collection of talent that she was going to embark with upon her first naval mission.

MALICE-STRIKER

Early the next morning, before the sun came up, Dyrfinna went outside and started up the side of Mount Pyrr for her daily exercise. She always used a different trail than the one she'd staggered up when she'd been transforming into a draugr, as she never wanted to stand in that place again in her life.

But Serja had healed her – had saved her life.

Serja! A dragon had healed her arm, had spoken to her within her mind, had helped to protect her. Now as she climbed, Dyrfinna touched her wounded shoulder, looking down at where Serja had licked the wound. It looked almost completely healed.

And now she wanted to try her new ability. Dyrfinna visualized the garnet dragon in her mind. Now that she was actually doing this, she felt a little stupid, as if she were playing the game that she used to play when she was a child – pretending to be a great dragonrider who could speak to dragons with her mind.

Meet me at the peak of Mount Pyrr, she told Serja.

Then, feeling stupid, she began climbing again.

After a moment, Dyrfinna heard Serja's voice, as warm and deep as if they were standing right next to her. *Well, well, my chicklet,* they said. *It's good to hear you speak to me.*

Not a child's game after all. Dyrfinna stopped and laughed aloud.

Dyrfinna clambered over a series of gigantic basalt boulders. *I wasn't sure if speaking to you like this was going to work,* she thought sheepishly to the dragon. *But I'm glad it does.*

Serja chuckled. *I will go for a little flight. When nobody is looking, I'll meet you at the top of Mount Pyrr.*

About an hour later, Dyrfinna reached the top of the mountain. Serja came sailing in and landed in a flurry of snow, and Dyrfinna shut her eyes against the stinging flakes.

Dyrfinna had climbed up on the south face of the mountain, from which she could see the city of Skala down below. Serja had flown in from the north, out of their sight. This place on the peak was out of sight of the city, and from all the prying eyes far below.

Dyrfinna ran to Serja and threw her arms around their neck. Serja pressed their head against Dyrfinna, careful because of the various horns at the back of her head, which were sharp. The dragon hummed a contented song.

"Do you want to fly?" Serja asked.

"Oh, yes, always," Dyrfinna said as she vaulted onto her friend's back. "Also, I need to talk to you about several things."

Dyrfinna swiftly buckled herself in. With a bound, the dragon galloped directly at a sheer cliff and hurtled off the side into thin air. Dyrfinna gripped her dragon's side every time Serja did this, and their wings buoyed them up. They sailed over an eagle, and Dyrfinna thrilled to see the majestic bird from above, rather than from far below.

Serja sang a dragon song under their breath as their wings carried them up between the low clouds. Dyrfinna breathed deeply of the freezing, thin air, so crisp at this altitude, as the wrinkled sea crawled beneath them and split the moon's light into millions of dazzling sparks.

They sailed higher and higher, and soon Dyrfinna began to shiver as the air grew thin, despite her warm clothes and the dragon's heat.

"What do you need to talk to me about?" Serja asked, looking over her shoulder. They leveled out above the clouds, and glided along over their gleaming white backs.

"Serja, what do you know about necromancy? About draugrs? Can a draugr be made to walk, even if it's not … you know, evil?"

"Compelled to walk, certainly," Serja said. "This kind of magic works on the dead. It doesn't investigate their moral status beforehand."

Dyrfinna thought about this. "Serja, listen. I took the völva out to look at the rock with the sigils carved on it just yesterday."

"What happened, then?" Serja asked.

So Dyrfinna told her all about what had happened with the völva and what they'd seen.

The signs were faint but the völva was just as confused by the strange signs as Dyrfinna was.

"I have not seen this type of writing before," she said slowly, crouched on her hands and knees. First she looked at the signs so closely that her nose nearly touched, them, then sitting up. "This disturbs me more than I'd like the rest of the city to know."

"How's that?" Dyrfinna had asked.

"The way this spell is structured gives me pause indeed." The völva moved her hand first over a set of interlinked circles, then following an arc that had been scraped into the rock to join another jumble of circles and odd symbols.

"This is a spell I have seen only one other time. A complex of spells, if you will," she said, spreading her fingers wide over the several different areas of markings joined by open arcs. "You see these smaller spells, here?" the völva said, waving her hand over several clumps of symbols written closely together. "The individual components of these spells have been used alone, in different forms, in raising the dead, in animating corpses."

"Creating draugrs," Dyrfinna said in a low voice.

"Correct. But these smaller spells are joined together by symbols I don't recognize." The völva walked, barefoot, to another section. "This one baffles me." She crouched next to a more carefully written area, thick with symbols. "The only part of the spell I can recognize is part of a spell used to set cheese, though clearly it is being used for some other diabolical purpose."

"Devil cheese," Dyrfinna murmured.

The völva looked up, smiled, then looked back at the spell. "I wish that it was devil cheese only that this spell was for. I could vanquish a whole wheel of devil cheese, though it's likely that I would never shit again."

"Um...okay..."

"But ... wait, I recognize this." Now the völva stooped suddenly, brow furrowed, brushing her hand over a carefully-drawn sigil that was larger than all the others. "Is ... is this correct?"

"What is it?" Dyrfinna crouched next to her. The scratches in the rock meant nothing to her, since she'd never learned how to read any language.

"If I'm reading it aright, it's a name." the völva lifted her eyes to Dyrfinna. "Nithoggr."

And now, as Dyrfinna repeated this word to Serja, the dragon stiffened – bristled – looked suddenly back at Dyrfinna.

"She said that?" the dragon said, as if on the verge of panic. "You are certain that she said that word correctly."

"Well ... yes." Dyrfinna had never seen Serja react like this.

"Say nothing else." And with that, Serja flapped hard with her wings and they rose swiftly into the air, Dyrfinna holding on tightly. In an instant, the world grew colder and the air thinner and thinner. Dyrfinna thumped Serja's side twice to let her know they were too high to breathe, and Serja lowered the altitude enough for Dyrfinna to suck in some air.

"I cannot tell you this too close to the ground, for Nithoggr lives under the earth, at the root of the World Ash," they said softly. "It is the name of the cruel one, who once bore the corpses of men under its wings.

"It was bound long ago by the Aesir during one of the wars between the gods and the monsters, and Nithoggr led the monsters, the great dragon. It was a terrible battle, but in the end, they were forced down below the earth, and the Ash took him in one of its roots and pinned him down, never to rise again. Now in his anguish he gnaws the root, but it will never let him go."

"Well then, if the Ash never releases him, then what is there to worry about?" Dyrfinna asked.

"The Ash won't let him go," Serja said. "but other entities could break him free. What frightens me about this is a story I've heard. The time will come, and it will come soon, that somebody will try and help this dragon escape, bringing forth the fires of the deep, and all its long-cherished schemes of vengeance, and the world will be overturned in molten rock and fire when that dragon is brought to the surface."

"Is this related to the dragon wars you've told me about?"

"It could be," Serja said, weighing their words. "Come. We will speak no more of it once we are back on the ground. But I need to teach you these magic things."

"I hope you don't regret trying," Dyrfinna said.

Once they were back on the mountaintop, out of sight of Skala, Serja carefully walked Dyrfinna through the magic, but when Dyrfinna removed her ring, the magic wound out of control. She would have blown a mass of rock to bits had she not quickly jammed the ring back on her finger.

Unfortunately, she had no chance to disperse the magic before her ring went back on. She immediately fell to her knees and was sick everywhere, and her body hurt so badly that she couldn't see for a moment.

"I expected that to go better," Serja said, snuffling at Dyrfinna, still hunched over on the snowy ground.

"I never want to tell a dragon that they're wrong," Dyrfinna groaned into the snowy ground, flecks of light dancing in her vision. "But this is the exception."

THE QUEEN'S RETURN

A few days later when the sword-friends were visiting the dragons, the call came from the city below.

"The Queen's dragon!" shouted one of the guardian dragons of Skala.

Gefjun jumped to her feet. "She's come back!"

The four sword-friends ran to the wall that overlooked the ocean beyond the fjords to see what was happening. Serja, who they'd been talking to, leisurely joined them, the hairs of their feathery beard drooping into Dyrfinna's face and making her sneeze.

The dragon stables sat high on the mountain's side that sloped down to the water's edge. They had an excellent view of the harbor where swift ships pulled up to the shore. The mountains crowded the edge of the inlet. The wide sea shimmered in the distance.

"There she is!" Dyrfinna cried, pointing to where the golden dragon curled in the air above the sea. At this distance, the dragon looked like a gigantic bird, until a spout of flame flashed into the air.

Skeggi jittered, staring out at sea, about to burst for waiting for his ladylove. "Only one dragon?" he said, worried. "Where are the others?"

"Right there," Dyrfinna said, pointing toward the horizon. "Shriken just blends in with the rest of the sky because she's silver."

And now the Queen's dragon flew toward their town, shimmering golden, gleaming like an ember deep in the fire.

Dyrfinna fixed her gaze on the dragons, tension building in her heart, resting her left hand on the pommel of her sword for comfort.

If the Queen is returning, then so is my father.

The realization went through her like an icicle. What would he do when he saw that his own mother, Grandmama Jelena, had given Dyrfinna control of her ship? She could almost hear him say *There will be consequences.* Dread settled in the nightmarish pit that opened in her stomach.

"Do you see Egill's dragon?" Dyrfinna asked in a low voice to Serja.

"I do not," they said, scanning the sky. "It might be that he is tarrying, though."

"Hurry," Gefjun added over her shoulder, heading for the stairs to the shore. "I want to know what happened with King Varinn."

"I know a few people who might kill him," Ostryg suggested as he and Skeggi followed. "I don't know why the Queen didn't ask me." His family was full of assassins and roughs. Some of them had assembled a levy of men and a ship in the harbor, though Dyrfinna was sure they were more interested in plundering and pillaging than in defending the Queen.

"And I want to see my beautiful lady." Skeggi was already halfway down the stairs to meet the dragons.

Now the Queen's dragon swooped onto the shoreline, and its back-beating wings kicked up sand and brought the smell of burning sulfur to Dyrfinna as she hurried through the streets of Skala toward the shore, joined by other villagers who all left their work and came running when a high-ranking dragon arrived. Even the stablers and some of the dragons were flying down from the stables to gather on the shoreline.

And the Queen's landing on her golden dragon was always a beautiful sight to see. Her breath always caught when Tandryss landed, with the grand sweep of those glorious, mailed wings.

The sword-friends joined the crowd as they rolled back from the Queen's dragon. Dyrfinna let the crowd push her against Skeggi's side to feel his heat and the skin of his arm against hers. He didn't seem to notice, because now Rjupa's dragon was landing. She came in at full speed like a silver dart, then flung her wings wide and skidded spectacularly across the sand to a stop, Rjupa laughing and protesting.

The sword-friends cheered as she hopped down and ran straight to Skeggi. He caught her and spun her around and they kissed for so long that the rest of the Vikings cheered and groaned.

Dyrfinna looked off into the distance, her heart crushed like a grape. Gefjun patted her arm.

Now Queen Saehildr's golden dragon peered around with a glittering, green-eyed gaze. This was Tandryss, the calmest dragon of the bunch. The air shimmered with heat around her. She lowered her wings, and the great expanses fell shut and tucked into its sides, neat as any bird – a fifty-cubit long bird that could kill with fire. Her collar glimmered with smooth carnelians gleaming dark red, each mounted beautifully and framed with a rope of gold.

The queen dismounted. She wore a black riding cloak, spun from triple-thick felt and fur, because her mount sailed into the highest regions of the sky, where the air was thin, and the winds were cold and brutal. The heat off the dragon helped their riders stay warm at that high altitude, though some dragonriders had gotten frostbite in their ears or fingertips from the awful cold up there.

Queen Saehildr gathered her many skirts and leapt up onto a great boulder so she could be heard. Rjupa and Skeggi stopped kissing, and the crowd grew silent. No one stirred, no one spoke, except for a little baby fussing, and its papa whispering, "Shh shh shh" under his breath.

"Skala citizens," the queen addressed them in a vibrant voice that carried well over the crowd. "Our mission has been a success. I left a couple of weeks ago with Egill and Rjupa to carry out our first step of vengeance. It was successful. Egill stayed behind to talk to some of our allies, but he will be home again later."

Dyrfinna let out her breath. Good.

"We cannot celebrate yet," the queen called, and all went quiet again. "We still have much to do."

She told the story of what happened: how she had killed the king's no-good, lazy son and mixed his heart in with the evening meal – Ostryg whistled under his breath at that – and how the king had eaten his son's heart. Thus had the queen gotten her revenge.

The older Vikings approved. "Aye, now *that's* how ye revenge yerself for the wee miss," one growled happily.

"I'd do the same if he killed me little girl."

"That's a true Queen!"

"So we escaped them as they tried to capture and kill us in the King's hall. And we had the start of them," the queen told her listeners as she stood on the rock by the sea, with her golden dragon behind her. "A good start. But King Varinn will be on the move, for we saw his dragons flying, helter-skelter, around his keep as we made our escape. There is no doubt that he will be sending his ships to our small queendom.

"Skalans, the time has come to sail. I see you have mustered fighters and commanders while I was gone. Now we must make our final preparations, and stop him with warfare and fire, and make him feel sorry for having killed my lovely daughter."

The Skalans cheered. "We'll do it for you, Queenie!" somebody shouted, and they all laughed.

The Queen inclined her head to them. "All Vikings who want to fight for me and for Skala—and for the love of my lost daughter—must come to the aid of their country," Queen Saehildr called in a thrilling voice. "I am raising the levy of Skala now, to meet the enemy and drive them far from our shores, and take revenge for my daughter. I have struck back against her murderer, but more remains to be done."

Everybody cheered again.

An excited Dyrfinna turned to her sword-friends. "Are you ready to go to war?"

"I am," said Gefjun, offering a wide grin which warmed Dyrfinna down to her toes.

"Tell me who to kill," Ostryg said, "and I'll be happy to comply."

"Rjupa," Skeggi said, "what's wrong? Why aren't you happy?"

All turned to her. Dyrfinna was shocked to see tears in her eyes.

"Did something happen while you were gone?" she asked.

"I can't talk about it here," Rjupa said, rubbing her eyes. She tipped her head slightly toward the Queen, who was still talking to her people on the shore.

A pause. Then Shriken opened her silvery wings as if stretching – just enough to hide the little group from the eyes of the Queen – and said, "I'm really tired. Can we talk more up at the dragon stables?" She folded her wings and gave a huge, toothy yawn.

"Sure we can," Gefjun said briskly. She waved Shriken toward the stables, and she and Rjupa flew up the side of the mountain. Gefjun waved at the Queen, and the rest of the sword friends followed Rjupa up on foot.

The dragon stables, fortunately, were mostly empty, for most of the stablers had gone to hear what the Queen had to say, as well as some of the dragons. Rjupa was busy unsaddling Shriken, but as soon as her friends joined her, she turned toward them.

"Is anybody else here?" she whispered, first thing.

Ostryg immediately cased out the place with his assassin's eye, moving from stable to stable and looking inside each. "Doesn't seem to be."

The rest of the sword-friends were looking around as well. As upset as Rjupa was, it was clear that something was amiss – and the fewer people who overheard, the better.

Skeggi began unsaddling Shriken. "Sit down and talk to us. I've got this."

Rjupa did not sit down. "Something's wrong with the Queen," she said in a low voice. "I approve of her taking her revenge on Varinn. He deserved it for killing Thora. But the way she did it…"

Ostryg flipped a knife. "He killed her daughter. She killed his son. I'd say that's fair."

"Fair isn't always right." Rjupa looked around at each of them. "I can't explain it. And I know she's lost Thora, and she … she feels that loss more profoundly than any of us could. She's her mother. But she was gloating over King Varinn's son in a way that made me uncomfortable."

"But he was older than Thora, wasn't he?" Dyrfinna said, trying to understand. "It wasn't like the queen killed a little child or anything."

"Yes, he was an adult." Rjupa put her head in her hands. "This doesn't sound like it makes any sense. That I'm being soft-hearted. And it broke my heart to see the Queen's grief over Thora, because I feel that loss, too. But then I saw Varinn's grief for his son, when the Queen told him that he'd eaten his son's heart … and it's not right for her to add to all the misery in the world. It doesn't bring Thora back."

Ostryg quirked his mouth. "I can't see what the problem is. We can't have people coming in and killing the best person in Skala without consequences."

"I'm telling you, she's not acting right."

Shriken leaned her silver head against Rjupa's. "I saw it too. She was not acting like herself."

Dyrfinna nodded. "Guys, I believe Rjupa. She's never led us astray once. Just because we don't understand doesn't mean anything – it just means we need to look into it."

"Thank you, Finna," Rjupa said. Though now something that sounded like … guilt? … crept into her voice. But Dyrfinna shrugged it off.

"You've just come home from a long flight," Dyrfinna continued. "You should eat and rest. We can join you, if you like, so you can tell us more about what you saw. Maybe there's something we need to do about the Queen…"

Just then, as those words were coming out of Dyrfinna's mouth, Tandryss, the golden dragon, came flying up from the shoreline with Queen Saehildr on her back, and came in for a magnificent landing next to the sword-friends.

Rjupa immediately led Shriken to her stable, leaving the others standing there.

The Queen's dark eyes were full on Dyrfinna as she dismounted. "Take care of Tandryss, please – if it's not below your old station of the Corae Guard."

Dyrfinna, though astonished, went at once to Tandryss and began to undo the saddle, though the buckles nearly burned her fingers.

Tandryss brought her head around and gazed, unspeaking, at Dyrfinna with eyes like glowing yellow glass.

"I wasn't aware you were given leave to be in the stables, Dyrfinna," the Queen said without looking over her shoulder as she walked toward her longhouse. "I advise you to leave once Tandryss has been tended to."

The rest of the sword-friends watched the Queen go as Dyrfinna fumbled stupidly with Tandryss's buckles – then gave up and bent her head against the dragon's burning side.

"If you please, Dyrfinna," the dragon scolded. "The Queen is speaking the truth. You are not allowed to be here."

Gefjun gently led her away from the dragon's saddle, then turned on Tandryss. "Oh, give it a rest. We'll all be out of your hair soon enough, once we set sail tomorrow. Ostryg, get over here and help me with this saddle."

"I don't have hair," the dragon said as the saddle was removed. "I don't understand."

"Don't explain idioms to a dragon," Gefjun said as Skeggi began speaking. "I'll make you so sorry if you try."

By now the rest of the stablers were coming back, and Dyrfinna was walking out of the stables, looking at the ground so they wouldn't see her tears. Behind her, Gefjun was bossing the stablers around to take care of the newly-arrived dragons, and then the sword-friends came running to join her.

"Okay, Rjupa was right," Ostryg said.

"I could have told you that," Skeggi replied.

"Don't let the Queen get to you," Gefjun said, putting an arm around Dyrfinna's shoulder. "This was only your favorite place in the world before your dad shat on everything. Don't be sad. You're still in charge of our ship. They can't take that away from you."

VICTORIOUS

Now that the Queen had returned, preparations began in earnest.

Dyrfinna had gotten her armor refitted, and Gefjun helped her bring it home.

She brought extra provisions, knowing that it would be possible that they would be cut off from supplies. Losing access to provisions constantly happened in Grandmama's stories about war life.

Dyrfinna found the short-handled spade that Papa had made long ago after coming back from the Erikson expedition and put that in her bag. She found her old leather canteen and her well-balanced, sharp dagger. It was plain, but it fought true.

Once she returned home, her mother insisted that Dyrfinna put on her armor and show her, along with Grandmama and Aesa, how it looked.

"Oh, Mother," Dyrfinna complained.

"Don't 'oh Mother' me! I am here to see you model that armor!"

Gefjun laughed. "Come on, Finna, give them a show."

So she put on a padded shirt and then the leather armor. Her armor consisted of a loose gorget around her neck, attached to protective plates for her shoulders and upper arms. She wore a leather cap on her head and gauntlets tied to her arms and upper legs. She looped a leather belt around her waist and hung her swords from it, and that completed the outfit.

"You look dashing," said Grandmama. "The boys will all fight over you, and then you'll have to fight them off."

Dyrfinna made a face. "I hope not."

"Your armor looks wonderful," Mama said, her hand on her chin, "but it's missing something."

Grandmama nodded. "You're right. Why don't you fix that?" she asked, fluttering her fingers at Mama.

Her mother went to the back of the house and came out with … Dyrfinna squinted. What was this?

Mama handed a great bundle of black wool into Dyrfinna's arms.

Her mouth dropped open. "Mama!" she cried. "What is this?"

"Open it and find out," Mama said, stepping back.

Dyrfinna unrolled it … and gasped. It was a massive cloak of black wool edged by the pelts of the wolves that Dyrfinna had killed, complete with a wide, warm collar of wolf pelt that covered her shoulders. Dyrfinna, eyes wide, stroked the soft furs of the wolves.

"Put it on!" Aesa cried, nearly beside herself with excitement.

Dyrfinna put it over her shoulders and looked down at herself with amazement. "Mama, this is incredible."

"This should keep the swords and snowfall at bay," her mother said, pinning it on with a lovely broach.

Her hand went to her mouth as she lifted the edges of her cloak, turning it this way and that, stroking the fur that trimmed it. "Oh, Mama. This is beautiful." It was more than beautiful. It made her feel amazingly confident, like a goddess.

"And you look so good in it," she said.

"Wolf snuffer," her grandmama said, and Dyrfinna liked the name so much that she couldn't help but apply it to herself constantly – in secret, of course.

"And look," Mama said. Now she got another bundle and handed it to Aesa. "We had to use the cloak you already had," she explained, "because we didn't have time to make you a new one. But we wanted you to look like your sister when she sails out."

Aesa squealed. Her cloak, too, had wolf fur around her shoulders. She put it on. "We look like twins!" she cried, hugging Dyrfinna around the waist.

"My little battle bird," Dyrfinna said fondly.

"I have something else for you," her mama said.

"Something else?" Dyrfinna cried, amazed. "After this beautiful cloak? After this armor? What else could I possibly need?"

Mama smiled, her black eyes crinkling. "Close your eyes."

Dyrfinna did.

Aesa said, "They're not closed!"

"They are too," she said mock-indignantly.

Aesa stretched up on her tiptoes to cover Dyrfinna's eyes with her own hands.

"Now hold out your hands, Finna."

She reached around Aesa, who was giggling, and held them out. Something heavy, made of leather, was set upon her palms. Her heart jumped, realizing what it was.

"Open them."

Dyrfinna sucked in a breath. It was a scabbard, made of finely wrought leather, and a solid-looking hilt sticking out of it. Aesa wiggled out of the way, and she took the scabbard in one hand and drew out a flash of silver.

"Oh, Sissy!" Aesa cried, her hands on her cheeks. "Sissy, it's so pretty!"

"Sweet Freyja," Dyrfinna breathed, staring at the sword that gleamed in her hand, its blade a brilliant silver like the moon. "Mother. How? Where did you get this?"

"It was a gift to me from your father, back when he still loved me," Mama said, gazing sadly at the brilliant sword. "Back when I thought that I would be allowed to fight at his side in all the battles. That didn't happen. But it's a beautiful sword, exquisitely made. It's not the sword's fault that the man was trash."

Dyrfinna stepped away from her little sister and made a few experimental slashes in the air with the sword. It was so finely balanced that it didn't feel like a sword – it felt like an extension of her arm.

Runes were written down the blade of the sword, runes that said NONE SHALL GET THROUGH ME.

"I've had this sword stored away for a long time," Mama continued sadly, looking down at the gleaming blade. "After he left us, I wanted nothing to do with him or his gifts, so I locked them all away, including the cloak you're wearing, and this sword. But no longer. I give it to you, so you can forge your own destiny. The cloak I modified so you can proudly wear the furs of the wolves you killed for all to see. This sword has a long and storied history, a fine lineage. I don't know of a more worthy person to wield this blade than you."

"Mama, I'm just … I don't have the words," Dyrfinna stammered, gazing at the sword, unable to get over its sleek beauty.

"Her name is Signe – the one who is victorious," her mother said. "I know with her in your hands, that you will be victorious."

Dyrfinna leaned against her mother. "This … this is so much. I'm humbled and grateful for these rich gifts from both of you. Grandmama gave me a whole ship, and now you've given me a beautiful wolf-cloak and this sword … if I could only forget how you received the sword, it would be perfect."

Mama brushed Dyrfinna's hair out of her eyes. "That's why I'm giving it to you," she said. "A gift automatically belongs to the one it's given to. This has been my sword all these years. Now I'm giving my sword to you, so it will protect my little girl out in the world. And I hope," she said, turning the blade so the runes NONE SHALL GET THROUGH ME gleamed, "I hope that every time my girl draws this sword, she'll remember me, even in the heat of battle, protecting her."

She and her mother embraced for a long time, both of them with tears in their eyes.

"You will go into the world and revenge our dear Thora," her mother said into her shoulder. "Then you will come back home to us. Alive."

THE BLACK DRAGON

A great bustle and movement surrounded the long stone piers by the waterside where the great black ships lay. Warriors and servants worked hard, carrying provisions and weapons to the ships. Here and there in the crowd was a bright cloak or a gilded helm to show a person of rank. The sun gleamed on helmets and coats of mail, and the noise of preparation filled the air.

Dyrfinna's sleek, dark ship sat in the harbor below. Her crew was placing a dragon's head on the prow. The workmen greeted her as she stepped into the hollow ship with its reddened ribs and tarred oar-blades. She had already loaded her gear on the ship, little by little, as she'd recruited warriors for her crew. She inhaled deeply the smell of old wood, tar, bilgewater, and sea air – the smell of her ship.

"Thank you, Grandmama," she murmured, her heart full.

My ship and my crew, she thought, almost giddy with possibility.

It was a smart little longship made all of dark oak that her grandmother had ordered built, long ago – a snekkja with a sail and rowing benches that carried a crew of about thirty-five. It was named Saebrandur, or Sea Flame, and it darted through the waves like an otter.

She had loved this ship since she was a little girl, loved how friendly it seemed to be, nudging up to her on the waves like a cat as she stood on the docks. And now Saebrandur would be the first step to the future that she desired above all others.

"Hello, little Finna!" cried the exuberant old steersman, Hakr, as he joined her on the deck. "Ye dogs and little fishes, it is a pleasure to see you again here on the wide waves."

Dyrfinna leaned in for his embrace. "It's good to see you, too."

Old steersman that he was, Hakr looked the part, in his old oilskin, cheery eyes that were permanently squinted against the wind, his sunburned face, his white beard and hair making the man look as if he were permanently rimed with salt. He had sailed for years for Dyrfinna's grandparents, and he knew the seas like the palm of his hand. He'd fought pirates and Vikings alongside Dyrfinna's grandparents, and he feared nothing in or over the wide salt seas.

"Ah," the old steersman said, "I used to help you toddle around on deck when you were a teeny lass. You'd hold my finger with your wee hand and stump around, so serious. Little did I dream that someday I would sail my ship in your service."

"I need your expertise," she said, resting her arms on the side of the ship. "You've voyaged all over the watery part of the world; you've fought many battles alongside my grandparents. I welcome your help." She didn't mean to get grandiloquent. She loved Hakr's exuberant way of speaking, and she found herself echoing it whenever she was around him.

"I am at your service," he said. "Any time you need help, I will be there. You have my word."

Warmed through with happiness, she turned to look at her crew as they clambered aboard, greeting her. They were mainly older men and women. For an instant she felt young and uncertain, but then pulled herself up. She had to act equal to the task until she actually was.

Indeed, her crew greeted her with respect as they came aboard or as they left. "Our commander," they kept saying. It felt incredible.

"Hakr, I am looking forward to this so much," she said to her old friend.

From the corner of her eye, she could see one of their black dragons circling, looking to the left and right. Her heart always leapt at those wings. How she longed to fly! Perhaps her time on this ship would be the beginning of her rise … she could prove herself as commander of her crew, and perhaps eventually the Queen would be impressed enough to allow her to become a dragonrider, despite her father.

The dragon's burning body roared straight over her ship, and Dyrfinna threw her head back in wonder. The sun shone through those gigantic wings, as if shining through thick, black smoke. She exulted in the storming of the wind against its wings, and she felt the heat from the dragon's body even far below on the ship, and its great shadow fell over her.

Except ... now she recognized the dragon, and her heart froze inside its shadow.

It was Egill's dragon.

He had returned at last.

A TALK BECOMES A FIGHT

Dyrfinna leaned over to Hakr. "Have you ever had one of those days when you think everything is going great and then suddenly you get bitten in the ass?"

"I've had years like that," he said mildly. "So, I take it that you've noticed the arrival of your esteemed father."

"Something like that, yes."

They watched his great mica dragon landing with a glittering sweep of its enormous wings. Egill's dragon was long as the Queen's *dreki* ship, possibly longer. He wore his bright sword, his black woolen cloak, his fine clothes, and a pair of expensive boots of the best leather. On his muscular biceps, he wore glittering golden armrings, given to him by the Queen due to her high esteem for him.

And here was Hakr, an old man with his white hair and beard, wearing an old oilcloth, his calloused hands marked with tar and pitch, smelling like sweat and the briny sea.

But if she could have chosen, she would have asked Hakr to be her father in Egill's place. She would have chosen him in a heartbeat.

Hakr went back to his work around the ship, preparing her for the long voyage, and Dyrfinna assisted him, but as she worked, she couldn't help but dread that voice she knew she would hear.

She had been working long enough with Hakr to finally get lost in the work when that voice finally appeared.

"Dyrfinna!"

Here it comes. She finished rolling her barrel of salt pork into its storage place before she looked up.

Egill stood in the front of her ship, his black cloak luffing in the ocean breeze, his right side toward her and hands on hips as if he were modeling for a portrait of Thor.

"We need some help moving this salt pork," Dyrfinna scolded. "Get over here and put those soft hands of yours to work."

"That is enough out of you, daughter," he said, striding toward her, his footsteps sounding hollow in the bottom of the ship. "I forbid you from doing this."

Dyrfinna straightened her back and stretched. "Well, if you forbid me from moving these barrels of salt pork, I'll stop, but I sure don't want Hakr doing all this work by himself."

"No." Egill swung his hand around. "This ship. This crew. I knew you'd pull a trick like this while I was gone."

"Are you calling these hardworking people a trick?" she asked, furrowing her brow.

He towered over her. "Answer the question, Dyrfinna."

"I answered the Queen's call for soldiers," she said sharply. "I was following her orders. That's not a trick, that's doing my duty."

"That's enough sass out of you." Egill caught her collar with one strong hand and yanked her toward him. "I'm giving you an order, now, as the chieftain of Skala and the Queen's second-in-command."

"Way to show your authority, by yanking me around like a rag doll," Dyrfinna snapped.

He flung her aside. "This is not your ship, Dyrfinna. You are not in command of anything. As of now you have no command, no crew."

She glared into her father's eyes with undisguised fury. "Why?" Her sharp voice came out loudly enough for everybody to hear. Heads turned in her ship as well as on the shore. "Would you kindly tell me exactly why you're stripping my command from me?"

He laughed. "I don't need to tell you anything."

She blurted, "Or is this part of your long-simmering revenge against me for accidentally killing your only son? Is that it?"

Dyrfinna was bluffing as never before as she said this. She choked back her guilt, her unworthiness. What, was she going to bare her heart and ask her papa for forgiveness? Was she going to ask him to treat him the way he used to when she was his little girl and he called her his little Valkyrie?

No.

If he hated her this much after his son had died, had he ever truly loved her before his son was born?

Egill's voice was a snarl. "I am stripping you of your command because you are unworthy. You are filled with delusions as to your own greatness, when you are actually soured and filled with deceit."

Dyrfinna wrenched herself free from his grip. Her voice rang out. "Don't talk to me about deceit. After all, you lied to my mother and then left her alone for two years."

Egill shoved aside a barrel of salt pork as if it weighed nothing. "I'm not sure why you see fit to bring up a lie that has been thoroughly debunked. I was on a mission for the Queen. You were too young to remember any of it."

Dyrfinna selected a shield off the side of the ship and buckled it onto her arm as she spoke. "I was not too young," she said pulling the strap tight. "I remember everything. I remember how you left and how you never came back. I remember my mama crying, day after day. But she wasn't just crying because you were gone, was she?" Dyrfinna asked. "I heard her asking herself, 'Why did he leave me? Why did he turn his back on me?'"

His ears went red, but without a change of expression, he said, "This is really not the time to lie about…"

"What mission were you *really* on?"

The people around them dropped any pretense of politely ignoring the argument at those words. Oh, yes, the gossip mill had been grinding through that story for years. The story of how Egill had left at about the same time the Queen had, as if he'd been pursuing her like a lovelorn man – never mind that King Hjalmar was her husband – and Egill had left a lovely wife and an innocent daughter at his hearthstone. Everybody knew that story. How the Queen had come back after her family visit, alone and trailing clouds of fury, to her husband, King Hjalmar. Egill stayed away for much longer, but eventually he had come trailing home, meekly going back to his wife.

Egill's eyes widened as if he'd been struck by lightning – or he was about to inflict it. He sucked in a deep breath, and as he inhaled, she felt the pull of magic from the air around him.

Magic.

And that hiss of an inhale from her father, that sound he made when he was furious beyond words, sent a shock through her as if her foot slipped at the cliff's edge.

Dyrfinna pulled the shield in front of her as his eyes darkened. She had no sword, no knife, no weapon beside this old, salt-burned shield, and he was about to unleash something on her in front of all these people…

Behind the shield, she opened her hand.

And she removed the carnelian ring that Thora had given her.

As soon as the ring slipped off her finger, a raging fire burst into being in her heart, its flames kindling within the rest of her body.

Ghostly fire burst into life upon her arms, dancing on her shoulders, tickling the sides of her face and hair.

Somebody cried out, pointing at Dyrfinna.

Her magic had awakened.

She sang now, sang so quietly, her eyes never leaving her father's.

She was singing it into life.

Finna, no! she thought, but facing Egill, she was more afraid of what he would do if she stopped.

The people on the deck of the ship around Dyrfinna cried out, scrambling back.

"Young lady, stop what you're doing this instant," Hakr commanded.

"Not until he stops," she said warily.

"Enough, Dyrfinna!" Egill cried, but instead of moving away, he took several steps toward her. "Tamp it down, Dyrfinna. Tamp it, now!"

The flames moved hypnotically up and down her arms, and the shield's armstrap began to smoke into her face. With great care, moving as if trying not to spill an overfull glass of water, she unbuckled the shield and let it fall to the deck of the ship with a clang, her blood singing with the fire.

She could only move very, very slowly, because the fire was beginning to buzz in her veins, growing louder. She took a step back, trying to get distance she needed, but Egill stepped forward and closed the gap.

"You need to leave," she told him.

"You are not going to unleash that force on the people on this ship," Egill commanded. "You wouldn't dare. Now tamp it down."

"Do not tell me what to do," she said quietly.

"I'll tell you whatever I damn well please."

This was escalating too quickly. "Do you feel this intention in the air around me?" she asked quietly. "This fire? Leave my ship now, or you'll feel everything my brother felt the night he died."

She should not have said this.

"Control yourself, Dyrfinna." Said in a low, feral voice.

Egill's words wrenched something loose within her, and everything suddenly felt out of place. Her hands came slowly up to her face as the buzzing intensified until it filled her whole world. *Control yourself.* What he said every time to her, needling her.

She could see in her mind's eye how the power would burst out of her, cutting down her father – and it would cut down her crew she'd chosen, and her mast and rowing benches and supplies.

Except at that moment, gallant Hakr stepped directly in front of her in its deadly path – unafraid.

"No, Hakr," she said, filled to the brim with deadly magic, afraid to move even an eyelash. One wrong move, and the cutting power would spill out of her in any direction. "Move away. It will kill you."

Hakr held out both empty hands. "Finna, breathe," he said quietly, as if speaking to a butterfly that he would not scare away. "Close your eyes and take in a deep breath, and then let it out, there's a good girl. Ye won't hurt anybody today. I know ye won't."

She could barely hear his words over the buzzing of magic in her blood. The flames guttered in her heart; magic shimmered around her like waves of heat rising from the desert sand.

"Hakr, get back!" Egill's voice exploded into her consciousness. The buzzing in her head grew louder at his agitation.

Hakr spoke lowly. "Peace, Egill. I am talking to Finna." His watery blue eyes never left hers, but they held a smile. "Breathe again, my girl. Listen to my voice, close your eyes, and breathe. Relax."

Dyrfinna closed her hands and pulled them close to her body to keep the magic contained. She closed her eyes, hating how vulnerable she felt when she did, and breathed, trying to release the magic as he'd asked her to. The buzzing in her veins didn't change ... even seemed to grow stronger.

"I see you trying," came Hakr's quiet voice. "Now, take a breath, then try to tamp it. Gently at first. Try."

The flames still raged inside her heart, still flickered on her arms, but Dyrfinna quieted herself, listening to his gentle voice, and pressed the flames into submission. She breathed, did it again.

The magic faded; the flames subsided, though they still flickered in her anger, because her *own father* had called her deceitful.

She slipped the ring back on … and immediately a huge weight fell on her heart. She really could have killed somebody by doing that! Dyrfinna felt sickened by the thought.

"Good girl," Hakr said quietly, and turned to her father. "Now let her alone, Egill," he said quickly. "That's quite enough. There'll be none of this unpleasantness on my ship, not out of either of you."

"This is not your ship, Hakr," Egill said, "and you can't talk to me that way."

"This is his ship," Dyrfinna said, still breathing deeply as Hakr had urged her. "Your mother gave it to me, and you can't change that."

"I will change it." Egill's voice was low, dangerous. "Get off this ship at once, Dyrfinna, or I'll have you arrested."

"Oh, you would never," Dyrfinna laughed angrily.

"Try me."

"STOP. NOW."

At the woman's voice, Egill pulled around sharply.

On the forecastle, where she'd just been deposited inside the ship by two burly shipmen, was Egill's mother – Dyrfinna's grandmama – with a stern, angry face that might have been the face of one of the Nornir, a Norn who was *this close* to swooping up her holy shears and cutting a few life-threads out of sheer exasperation.

Grandmama clutched the side of the ship with one bony hand to keep her balance. "I don't know what is happening here, but it is going to stop. Now." Her voice rang out, clear and cold.

Pure silence for a moment. Nobody moved.

Then Dyrfinna said, "Um … Egill started it."

"No wisecracks out of you." Grandmama walked carefully toward them, picking her way around rowing benches and ropes. Hakr sprang forward, moving nimbly for an old seaman, and caught her arm to keep her from tripping.

"Mother, you should not have given this ship to Dyrfinna," Egill said quietly.

Grandmama shook her head. "You have no leave to tell me what to do. This is my ship and I will do what I please, whether you like it or not."

"She is undeserving …"

"Do *not* cross me on this," Grandmama said, thumping her staff on the deck. "I gave the ship to your daughter because I can see her worth. You do her a great disservice, treating her like this. Finna is ambitious, the way I used to be when I dreamed of crossing the world. You will have no say in this, son though you are; you will not bar her from her desire."

Egill's face grew whiter and more and more furious, but his lips stayed pressed together.

Grandmama lifted her cane and shook it at him to emphasize her words. "My granddaughter is formidable. If you keep treating her like this, she will take her sword to the other side, and woe be unto you if she does."

"I wouldn't take my sword to the other side," Dyrfinna said under her voice to grandmama. "I'd never turn my back to the queen."

Grandmama patted her arm to hush her. She usually did this when "the grownups were talking."

Egill wasn't through. "The ship should go to me."

"Stop talking nonsense," Grandmama said. "Hakr is his own man, and he is more than capable of making his own choices. He is happy to throw his lot in with Finna. They will make an excellent addition to your army."

Egill went storming off.

Grandmama shook her head. "I know I raised him better than that," she grumbled.

"Thank you, Grandmama," Dyrfinna said, trying to hide how much she was shaking.

"If my son gives you any further grief, let me know," she added. "As soon as I saw his dragon appear, I left home and hurried toward this ship as quickly as I could go, because I know what he was up to." She kissed Dyrfinna on the part in her hair. "Now, my dear, go and see to your vessel. And you can put your shield away – you won't need it any more."

SLEEPWALKER

All the same, despite all that her grandmama had said on her ship, Dyrfinna was not one who put down her shield for any reason – metaphorically speaking, of course.

As soon as Egill was gone, she grabbed Gefjun's hand.

"I need you to come with me," Dyrfinna said. "The Queen's going to be superintending the sacrifices at the temple tonight, and I need to talk to her, now. Before they start." For the sun was beginning to dip toward the horizon.

"Or before Egill gets to her first," Gefjun muttered, putting away her medical kit.

The two girls hurried to the small temple site at the top of the hill. There, Queen Saehildr was standing near the temple gates, the chilly wind blowing through her hair as she gazed down at all the fighters who were preparing for battle.

"Your highness," Dyrfinna said when she joined the queen. Gefjun brushed back the tendrils of her wild red hair and bowed.

Queen Saehildr turned and smiled, the tails of her riding jacket lifting in the wind. "Well met, Dyrfinna, Gefjun."

When the queen spoke, Dyrfinna felt a prickle of dread. She didn't know why. Nevertheless, she said, "I am in command of a ship, through the generosity of my grandmama. I have chosen the warriors I wish to have by my side when it comes time for waging war and fighting. With that in mind, I have come here to ask that you see fit to not let anybody take my ship away from me."

The Queen nodded slowly, puzzled. "You have raised your people. You have gotten this ship from your grandmother. There should be no reason why anybody would take either away from you."

There shouldn't be any reason, Dyrfinna thought. *But you can be certain that he's looking for any reason, and he'll take it.*

"Of course, if you act in a way that hurts my army, that would change," the Queen said.

And there it was.

Dyrfinna schooled her expression and raised her head. "I would like a pledge that you will listen to my side of the story if such a thing does happen to me."

"Well, of course," the Queen said. "That is simple enough."

Dyrfinna cleared her throat. "And that you listen impartially."

Gefjun grimaced and shook her head slightly.

Queen Saehildr frowned. "Of course I will," she said, an edge now appearing in her voice. "I think you've known me for longer than that. I am your queen, after all."

A chill went down her spine.

Gefjun bowed and grabbed Dyrfinna's arm. "Thank you very much, your Majesty. Now, we really must…"

"Indeed, you are." Dyrfinna spoke formally, as one does in these situations. "And I have no recourse beyond your judgment. Because it is my own father who is saying that I have no business leading, even though I have mustered a crew and have been given a beautiful warship from my grandmama, who urges me to go forth and strike down your enemies – our enemies – in glorious battle."

A smile flitted across Queen Saehildr's face. "Sometimes our elders know more than we do in our youth," she said, growing serious again.

Dyrfinna felt her skepticism grow. *Which elder are you talking about – my father or my grandmama?*

Gefjun tugged on her arm, but Dyrfinna didn't move. "Yes," she said, feigning innocence. "That's why I was so happy at my grandmama's choice to give her ship to me. I wasn't sure if I was worthy, but I want to do everything in my power to make her proud of me. And you, too," she quickly added. "Everything I've done has led me to this moment."

Gefjun jumped in. "And it started so many years ago when the Danes invaded. We helped rescue Thora from the old mead hall and brought her back through the forest while pursued by our enemies."

"You got an arrow through the leg," Dyrfinna said, shaking her head.

"Skeggi passed out," Gefjun laughed. "But Finna tricked the Danish leader when we were trapped and outnumbered."

Queen Saehildr's eyes softened. "And you rescued Rjupa from Iron Skull," she said, smiling. "I've seen you in battle. You are steady in battle, afraid of nothing."

Gefjun put an arm around Dyrfinna's shoulders. She smiled inwardly. Gefjun always did this when she was sweet-talking the queen. "And that was years ago, the beginning of our time on the Corae Guard," she said. "Think of how much Finna's grown since then as a fighter and a leader. You need her leading that ship. Her grandmama thinks so."

"I wish my father thought the same," Dyrfinna said. She couldn't help that it popped out. Gefjun nudged her where the queen couldn't see.

"I'm afraid I can't give you an additional command," the queen said, as if she hadn't been questioning Dyrfinna's loyalty only a short time ago. "But prove yourself in battle, do good work. Attrition in the ranks will happen, through death or disease. Then you can move up in the ranks, if you prove yourself worthy."

"What if I found some dragon eggs along the way and brought them to you?" Dyrfinna asked. "Would that earn me a promotion?"

Gefjun grumbled low in her throat, a sound meant for only Dyrfinna. But yet, she couldn't help but think of how Queen Saehildr's eyes would light up if Dyrfinna brought home a clutch of dragon eggs and gently set them into her hands ...

The queen smiled. "It might. But I'm also ordering you not to do anything rash that is going to put you in danger."

"You know I'm probably going to disappoint you on that score."

Gefjun said, "I *promise* I'll keep her in line, your Majesty," all the while mock-glaring at Dyrfinna.

The Queen, who was familiar with Gefjun's protectiveness toward Dyrfinna, laughed. Then she became serious. "It is true that we need dragons. There is no question about that. But I forbid you from putting yourself into danger to get those eggs. We need you more. Your family needs you."

But as soon as the word *family* left her lips, Queen Saehildr winced slightly.

She didn't intend to mention my family.

Dyrfinna's grimace froze on her face. She thought of what she'd said to Egill on the ship.

The Queen would know where her father had gone for those two years. After all, when she had gone to visit her family down the coast, Egill had followed her like a lost thing, his whole soul in his eyes. So the local gossips said, even all these years later.

Tread carefully, Finna.

But now the Queen's face changed. Her eyes widened as she leaned forward slightly, flicking over Dyrfinna's face as if trying to puzzle out something. Her lips trembled, barely noticeable.

The sky seemed to darken, as if a wing had opened against the sun. Dyrfinna felt the crackle of magic suddenly at work, and she stiffened. Whose magic? It didn't seem to belong to the queen.

Dyrfinna's own magic flickered to life, as if in response to the magic already in the air.

Gefjun's eyes widened.

Not here, not now! Not with Gefjun and the queen standing so close to her!

Dyrfinna's carnelian ring lit brightly in response, and she breathed deeply as Hakr had directed her, and quelled it. But the Queen went on talking as if she hadn't even noticed.

"I've come to a realization as I've traveled over the world," she said quietly, her words seeming to travel up from the depths of her, darker than her voice had ever been. "I've seen so many young people struck down in their prime, so many young souls lost to Valhalla. Mothers who have had nothing to do with battle, having their … their babes ripped from their arms after their fighters were unable to repulse their attackers."

Dyrfinna couldn't help exchanging a horrified glance with Gefjun. "Your majesty," Dyrfinna said softly as if speaking to a sleepwalker, trying to wake the Queen up without startling her. "Your majesty, please."

Saehildr did not hear. "Your father spoke of this," she said in that deep voice. "He spoke of this when he told me how you killed your brother."

Dyrfinna went still, now unable to meet her eyes as a sickening wave of guilt washed over her. Eirik's empty eyes bobbed up before her in her memory, and there was nothing, nothing she could do to undo what she'd done.

Magic flickered to life again in her heart, now a flame of rage that guttered brightly.

She wanted to let it sweep through her like wildfire, like it had with her brother, and the queen would never speak of her father again.

A pulse of pure panic leapt through her body. *No!* She swiftly tamped the flame down, trying to make it go out. *No, no, never, not again.*

"And now I look at you," the queen continued, looking at her but not seeing her. "You, who betrayed her own family in the worst way possible. I see something there in your eyes, something that cannot be tamed, something that's dangerous … to me."

Sickened, dismayed, Dyrfinna took a step back from her queen. "Your majesty," she gasped. "How? What are you saying?"

Saehildr's cold hand gripped her arm, her eyes never leaving Dyrfinna's. "I don't know what it is – what I'm seeing, what it means – but you …" A sudden tear flashed from Saehildr's eye. "You will betray …"

"No!" Dyrfinna's face flushed. She stammered, "I would never turn my sword against you." She could hardly articulate the words. The very idea of her betraying the queen repulsed her, made her sick.

Loyalty was the bedrock on which Dyrfinna's actions and beliefs had been built. She was always loyal to those who loved her. To have these words coming out of the queen's mouth sent her reeling. "Your majesty, please. Why are you saying this?"

Saehildr subsided, now staring past Dyrfinna. "But she doesn't know," the queen murmured, as if to herself. "Nobody else does, save one other. You are safe."

Then Queen Saehildr slowly seemed to come back to herself – her eyes, which had been locked on a spot far away, now looked at Dyrfinna as if responding to her. Noticing her hand wrapped tightly around Dyrfinna's arm, the Queen startled and removed it, as if somebody else had put it there.

Something had happened. She didn't know what. But she was deeply unsettled, almost ill.

"You will have to excuse me," Dyrfinna said, stepping back slightly. "I am not … feeling myself at the moment."

"It's probably the excitement of the day," the queen said cheerfully. As if nothing had happened. As if they had only been talking of ships and commands and dragon eggs, and not … betrayal.

Dyrfinna felt her world lurch again at the thought.

"Your majesty, what did you say just now?" asked Gefjun, extra politely. "After you told Finna to not get dragon eggs."

The queen looked puzzled. "Why, I said that your family needs you. I know you want to find young dragons for our kingdom, but we need you more in our army. No adventuring," she added in a more affectionate tone. "There will be plenty of time to seek Valhalla in battle later."

Queen Saehildr glanced out at the crowds and sighed. "I wish we had time to walk in the gardens and talk, as we used to, but today it is impossible, and I must prepare for the sacrifices. Good afternoon." The queen withdrew, walking away toward the temple.

Confused, troubled, Dyrfinna turned to meet Gefjun's eyes. "What just *happened*?"

Gefjun looked just as confused as she did. "I don't know. I don't know."

THE STRAGGLER

Though Gefjun and Dyrfinna tried to talk to the völva, she was busily engaged with the sacrifices and rituals, and once the gathering was finished, all had to prepare for the voyage the next morning, and finish their good-byes.

The next morning dawned bright. It was time for the Queen's forces to leave Skala and go to war against King Varinn.

Dyrfinna walked through the crowd on the way to her ship, looking for her sword-friends, savoring her excitement among the mighty host that were ready to sail against King Varinn.

"We will further revenge ourselves for the Queen's daughter," somebody in the crowd shouted, "and then we will drive those stinking dogs out of his realm." This was greeted with a hearty cheer.

The air was filled with talk and laughter. A group of barrel-chested men with beards so thick that a flock of birds could live in them suddenly laughed, pounding each other on the back. Wiry men with skinny lances strolled along a dock. Shield-maidens with blonde hair tightly braided back were eyeing the crowd, their wide shields hanging on their backs, fierce as Valkyries.

Just then Gefjun thunked her on her shoulder, with Ostryg lurking behind. "There you are!" she said. "Are you ready to go?"

Dyrfinna nodded. "More than ready."

"Girls, this is a serious occasion," Ostryg droned into his beard, fingering the braids he'd added in at some point to doll it up.

Dyrfinna's eyebrows went up.

Gefjun laughed. "Isn't it gorgeous?" she whispered.

"Depends on your definition of gorgeous," Dyrfinna murmured.

Gefjun grinned, her eyes sliding over to Skeggi, who was sharing his goodbyes with Rjupa, with whispered words and kisses. "Spare a thought for me when you're pining away for—"

"Stop." Dyrfinna's voice was hard. Skeggi and Rjupa were too busy kissing to notice, at least.

The little group fell silent. Skeggi looked at them, his reverie about his ladylove Rjupa broken. "What happened? Did I miss something?"

"No," Gefjun said. "A Valkyrie flew overhead, I suppose."

Ostryg joined him. "Look at my shield," he said. "I painted it last night." Skeggi and Rjupa were surprised into a laugh – the shield had a cross-eyed dragon with a beard on it.

Dyrfinna stared at the ground. But Gefjun was at her side. "I'm sorry," she said. "I didn't mean for my words to cut so deep. I'm a sarcastic girl."

Dyrfinna shrugged but didn't reply.

Gefjun was quiet. Then, in a low voice, she sang a song, gentle and healing, for Dyrfinna alone.

Peace comes down
Like soft spring rain
And soothes your aching heart.

The song worked on Dyrfinna's heart, and she felt better. "Thank you."

Gefjun bumped gently against Dyrfinna's side.

"I'm sorry to be leaving you," Rjupa said apologetically. "I wish we were all flying togther."

"I do, too," Ostryg said.

"We'll get our dragons back somehow," Gefjun said, giving Rjupa a hug. "Don't worry about us. Just keep an eye on the Queen while you're up there, flying around with her."

"I've been designated as messenger," Rjupa said. "So I won't be at the battle front all the time – I'll be coming and going. But if you need me to deliver anything from home, I'll take it for you."

"I wish you could be fighting together," Dyrfinna said somberly. "It would be like old times."

"In the meantime, try and find out what is going on with the Queen," Gefjun said.

"I will."

Dyrfinna was on board when the horns for departure sounded. A great cheer and whooping arose at the sound from those on the ships and those on shore. Dyrfinna sang out with her friends as the great cheer filled the sky. The ships were ready to sail forth to war at last.

Laggards hurried to board; final kisses were bestowed; an extra keg of ale was carried down to one of the ships and hastily loaded to the additional cheers of those on board. Sails were unfurled and anchors were raised.

Dyrfinna climbed up to her favorite place next to the prow, standing on the railing with her hand on the dragon's head. There, she waved to her family on the shore. Mama was putting on a brave face and comforting Aesa. Grandmama, on the other hand, was hitching her way down the long hill toward the docks, leaning on her cane and trying to shout something to Dyrfinna.

"I love you too," Dyrfinna shouted, waving.

Just then, a small commotion from the front of her ship as an unfamiliar man climbed aboard. "Here you go," somebody called, handing a sea chest over the side of the ship to him. The man straightened, sea chest in his arms, and looked about the ship as if he belonged there.

Dyrfinna, standing on the rail at the other side of the ship, hopped down to see who was boarding her ship.

Gefjun caught Dyrfinna's arm as she went past. "Mmm! Would you look at that?"

"At what?"

"At that beautiful package, all wrapped up in a bow."

The stranger set down the sea chest and stood as he talked to some friends, crossing a perfectly matched set of muscular arms on his broad chest. One gigantic bicep sported a blue tattoo of an eagle, wings outspread. His long, blonde hair came down his broad shoulders like a waterfall, matching a long, neatly-trimmed beard. At his belt he wore two axes. He wore leather gauntlets around his forearms, which were about as wide as fence posts, and tight leather pants on his muscular legs. He was built like an ox – *and has the brains of an ox as well,* Dyrfinna thought, *if he's not able to recognize that he had boarded the wrong ship.*

"That's all very nice," she told Gefjun, "but I don't care how much of a love hunk he is, because he needs to get on the right ship before we launch. Hold," Dyrfinna added to the man, walking across the deck toward him. "Sir, our crew is already aboard. We are not taking stragglers."

The man's handsome lips curled in scorn under his glossy beard. "I am no straggler. My name is Sinkr," he said, "and I am, as of now, officially the commander of this ship."

A stir through the men and women of Dyrfinna's crew – confusion in their faces as they looked at each other. "The commander?"

Gefjun was extremely impressed, chewing on a fingernail as she looked the muscular hunk up and down. "Oh, yes, he can be my commander any time," she purred.

Ostryg frowned and began sharpening his knife.

A great spike of anger cut through Dyrfinna, and she strode forward. "You? Commander of my ship, of my crew that I picked out myself? That is wolf shit. Get off my ship at once."

Sinkr smirked. "Not so fast, doll," he said in a smarmy voice.

"Doll?" Dyrfinna's hand dropped to her sword. "I'm sorry, are maggots eating your brain?

"Show some respect for your commander, Dyrfinna," came Egill's voice. "If you are even capable of this."

Dyrfinna's stomach tumbled to the bottom of her guts. "Odin's *eye*, you can't be serious," she muttered.

Egill came flying in on his mica dragon, landing on the shore right next to the ship, behind Sinkr. "Oh, yes, I am serious," he said. "As your army's commander, I hereby revoke Dyrfinna's command and bestow it on Sinkr."

"What!" Dyrfinna cried.

His mica dragon puffed itself up. "Yeah, he does," the dragon replied, as if it had any bearing on this case.

Egill went on. "And if anybody wants to argue with me about it, they will be thrown bodily off this ship and replaced by people who *do* want to fight for the Queen – people who can follow orders. Do you understand me?"

"This is wolf shit," Dyrfinna said.

"That includes you," Egill said. "I'll throw you off the ship right now for sassing me like a child. Try me."

Furious, Dyrfinna shot a look at Hakr, hoping for help, but he shook his head. "Let it go for now," the steersman said, for now the ships were beginning to set sail. A great cheer rose from the shore as the oars came rattling out and the ships cut into the waves.

Furious, Dyrfinna said, "But I do not want to let it go."

Hakr placed his calloused hand on her shoulder. "Never let a commander know you're angry," he said in a low voice. "They take satisfaction in that – and you must never let them have the satisfaction."

"He's not a commander," she said.

"Egill says he is, unfortunately."

"Launch the ship!" Egill cried, watching the whole scene with a smug look on his face. Dyrfinna wanted to break that face in half.

Her father watched their ship move out into the harbor. Now she realized that her grandmama was hobbling toward the shore where Egill sat on his dragon, but his dragon lifted off lazily before she could get near him, pretending not to notice her.

"So that's how he honors his mother," Dyrfinna said bitterly. "By disregarding her choices, right in front of her, when she's unable to do anything about it."

They rowed their way out to the mouth of the fjord, leaving behind the crowd on shore. Dyrfinna turned to wave to Aesa, who she'd left crying in Mama's arms, but by now they were well down the inlet of the fjord.

"I'll come home for you," she said quietly as the village of Skala shrank into the hills and mountains behind her. "I swear it."

And I am going to come home with my command restored, Dyrfinna swore. *By Thora's grave, I'm going to overcome all this and get my revenge for her as well.*

Beyond the high headlands that lay before them, the whitecaps of the waves gleamed in the sunshine. The rhythm of the oarsmen picked up when they saw the open sea. Soon the ships rolled out of the fjord, and the boom of the sea breaking on the rocks lifted Dyrfinna's heart, despite everything that had happened.

Now that they'd reached the open water, the fresh breeze blew. "Up sail!" called the exuberant steersman. "Ship oars!"

The rowers brought the oars in with a great clatter, water flying everywhere. Dyrfinna got up and joined the crew, heaving on the ropes to raise the sail.

The great sail consisted of a huge length of straight pine, wider than the full span of a man's hand, which had enough heavy-woven cloth hung from it to cover part of the village. Dyrfinna wiped the sweat from her brow as she finished.

The sail caught the deep sea-wind and billowed out. The ship leaned. Slowly at first, then more quickly, the boat cut the open water, leaping over the waves. The rest of the fleet around them were rushing over the water like birds in flight. Before long, they were flying before the wind gloriously, and Dyrfinna could catch her breath in the cool breeze.

The wind was smart, thrilling in the ropes and in her ears. "That's good fortune for us all, an auspicious start," Hakr told her, his eyes traveling over the ropes, watching the sail.

Dyrfinna leaned over the side with the other warriors, watching the water and telling wild stories. Gefjun, Ostryg, and Skeggi were with her, enjoying the wind. Several brothers who had each ended up on different ships shouted at each other across the water and brandished their swords whenever their ship took the lead. The other Vikings cheered.

Theirs was a tidy fleet of twenty ships, each bearing about fifty people. Many of these were soldiers to fight for the queen, while some were nurses, or laundresses, or sailors, as well as sundry folk like blacksmiths and cooks, who would be needed to fix weapons or feed the rest of the crew.

Sinkr had claimed Dyrfinna's favorite spot on the prow, though he didn't stand on the edge of the ship the way she liked to. His long blonde hair floated in the winds, and every time somebody came over, he flexed slightly, enough to make his muscles pop under his tight shirt.

For the first time, Dyrfinna noticed that his fine cloak was clasped with a golden brooch that depicted a hound killing a deer. A very familiar brooch she'd seen since her childhood.

Dyrfinna's eyes narrowed. "Wait. I recognize that brooch you're wearing," she said. "You stole that from my father, didn't you? Nobody has a brooch like that."

Sinkr caressed the golden brooch. "I didn't *steal* it," he said in a silky voice. "He gave it to me, along with this arm ring." He displayed a beautiful golden armring that Dyrfinna recognized as one that a jarl had given to her father long ago. "Your father gave me these golden gifts as a sign of his esteem for me. Egill even said that I was as dear to him as a son." He inclined his head slightly toward Dyrfinna.

"I'm sorry, what?"

Sinkr gazed off into the distance as if bringing back to mind a fond memory. "I'll never forget his words to me. He told me that, since he did not have a son any more, that perhaps I will come to fill the gap in his heart left by his son's death."

Dyrfinna felt as stunned as if he'd physically clubbed her across the head.

So Egill had given Sinkr his valuable jewelry as if … she swallowed.

As if Sinkr were his own son. Or a replacement for him. And then, with that knowledge, had set him over her on her own ship.

"Sinkr is a little bitch snitch," Dyrfinna observed to her friends.

"But he's also kind of hot," Gefjun said.

"I'm hotter." Ostryg leaned in from behind her.

"How can you be interested in Sinkr?" Dyrfinna asked. "Just because he has muscles doesn't make him a good lover."

"Yeah, listen to Dyrfinna," Ostryg said.

"But that body." Gefjun leaned against the side of the ship, looking it over. "Mm. Dyrfinna, if you want to get your command back, all you need to do is seduce him …"

Dyrfinna pretended to vomit over the side of the ship.

"No, listen. You lead him away somewhere for a little fun – not right now, obviously, you have to wait until we're on land—"

Dyrfinna put up both hands. "Not interested."

"—and then you break him in half with so much sex that he is incapable of walking afterwards."

"Has the heat dried up your brains?" Dyrfinna sputtered.

"Then you're in charge of the ship, and he'll be groveling at your feet all day long."

Dyrfinna clutched her stomach, making a face. “I’m good. I am not going to debase myself to a walking bag of muscles to be in charge of this ship.”

“I’m willing to debase myself if you don’t.” Gefjun licked her lips.

Ostryg walked away.

“Hey, you broke your man’s heart,” Dyrfinna said, pointing after him.

Gefjun watched him go. “It’s not broken.”

“You can’t talk like that about other men in front of him. Ostryg is not exactly my favorite person to be around, but even so, you shouldn’t disrespect him like that.”

“Pfft.” Gefjun rolled her eyes. “This how I keep him in line. Don’t worry your godlike temperament about it.”

“Listen to me,” Dyrfinna said. “I’ll tell you what my godlike temperament is worried about. I’ve been humiliated in front of my entire crew by my so-called father, who happens to be in command of this whole damndable army – and, what’s worse, I’ve had my command stolen by a pair of buttcheeks in tight pants. That boy is sashaying around my ship as if he owns the place. Which he doesn’t. No, I have no interest in the little bastard, beyond killing him dead, or at least covering him in honey and throwing him on an anthill. Do I make myself clear?”

"Well, well, is this the esteemed Dyerfinna I've heard so much about?" said a man's voice from behind her.

She didn't turn around. "You know perfectly well how to pronounce my name, Sinkr. Don't pretend to be stupider than you really are."

Now she did turn around, and there was the little turd, Sinkr, pouting at her with full, luscious lips, and one muscular fist on his hip. "You can't call me stupid, miss. I heard you plotting to kill me dead by throwing me on an ant hill."

"I was joking before, but now I'm beginning to take the idea seriously," Dyrfinna said. "You have no right to my command, and before we reach King Varinn's, I intend to get this sorted out and get your ass off my ship."

"His very well-formed ass," Gefjun whispered to Dyrfinna with a wink.

Dyrfinna pressed her fingers against her eyelids. "Do not do this right now."

"You are not going to send my ass anywhere," Sinkr said, flicking his golden hair over his shoulder. "Egill said that if you try to do anything to me, he is going to kick you out of this army so fast, it will make your head spin, and he'll send you back home to be locked up for the duration of the war."

"Pff," Dyrfinna said. "You're full of it." She didn't actually mean that – she knew her father fully intended to do that – but she was too annoyed by this strutting rooster and not inclined to agree with him.

"He told me that he doesn't care how long this war takes, but you can stay down there until you rot if you touch a single hair on my head. You got that, honey?"

Before he could say more, a hand shot out and gripped Sinkr's face, crushing his handsome cheeks and squeezing his perfect mouth into a pucker.

But it wasn't Dyrfinna's hand. It was Gefjun's. And her other hand was holding the dagger she'd pulled from Sinkr's scabbard.

"You … don't … *ever* … call … her … honey." With each word, Sinkr's dagger drifted closer to his face. "And you can cool it with the threats. You hear? You're a good-looking young buck, but you won't be for long if you're going to be a total dick to my friend."

Sinkr was standing there in complete astonishment, staring at his dagger, which had drifted dangerously close to his face, seeming to indicate that it was interested in exploring his right nostril. A little squeak came out of his mouth.

Gefjun released him, flipped the dagger in her hand, and handed it back to him, hilt-first. "Dyrfinna taught me something important over the years. If you're a commander, you treat all the people in your command with respect. Otherwise, you aren't worth shit. Now get out of my sight."

He took his dagger, sheathed it, and left without a word.

Dyrfinna got her breath back. "Weren't you saying, just five seconds ago, what a hot man he is?" she asked, puzzled. "So where'd all the watchdog stuff coming from? Don't get me wrong, I thought it was amazing, but I ... did not expect that."

Gefjun shrugged, gazing back out at the ocean. "The world is overflowing with hot men, but true friends are rarer than gold."

They leaned together, shoulders touching. "Thank you," Dyrfinna said. "You're the best."

Ostryg appeared. "I'm a hot man, by the way."

"You certainly are," Gefjun said appreciatively, looking him over. "Come on, let's go somewhere and make out."

"You two have fun," Dyrfinna said affectionately, still boggled by what had happened.

Gefjun leaned in. "See? Now I have him eating out of the palm of my hand." They traipsed away, leaving Dyrfinna reviewing the scene with Gefjun and Sinkr over and over with much delight – which soon turned into disgust. Because, for all that, he was still set over her on her own ship.

RUNNING BEFORE THE STORM

The day had started out as being bright and warm, but later, as the afternoon grew later, clouds began gathering low and the wind picked up.

"I don't like the looks of this," Gefjun said, and Ostryg nodded. "Looks like dirty weather."

The wind gusted and snorted, and the waves grew taller and broke over the cutwater, and an alarming amount of seawater poured into the ship each time. The men at the rudder fought to keep the ship on course, for the wind kept pushing them in different directions.

"All hands, reef the sails!" Hakr cried. "We're taking on water."

Everybody leapt to the ropes and mast and followed Hakr's commands to reduce the sail so they could keep going without being overpowered by the wind.

The other Viking ships in the fleet – what ships they could see through the thick spray of the wild waves that hurtled themselves this way and that – turned for shore.

"Set course for land!" Hakr called. "Bring her about!"

But Sinkr, who happened to be leaning over the side of the ship, green around the gills, heard.

"Belay that order!" he shouted, and the crew looked at him with some confusion. "I command this ship, not you, old man."

There had to be some new category for that level of audacity – that seasick boy saying this to the old steersman who had sailed to the edges of the watery world and back.

"We are going to go further," Sinkr said, throwing back his hair and crossing his arms. "There's a good place to camp up ahead—a place where we can watch for King Varinn's army, and they can't sneak up on us while we cook a big meal over fine fires."

"The rest of our fleet is going to shelter." Skeggi pointed at the other ships behind them, which were quickly making for shore.

Hakr, the old steersman, joined them. "We must land," he said. "There is no question. This wind is treacherous, and our landing will be dangerous if we go farther."

The sail, which had been neatly bellied out, full of wind, now had winds gusting on both sides. The ropes and pullies rattled as the sail snapped and burst full of wind, then deflated. The sea looked like a sheet of white foam, rising and falling in great waves and troughs. A huge wave dashed against the gunwales, swamping the deck and nearly carrying away four men.

"That doesn't matter," said Sinkr, ignoring the rescue efforts going on in the front of the ship. "Like it or not, I am the commander. We will continue on, as Vikings who fear nothing."

"We will not continue on. I will not sacrifice my crew to your foolish notions of courage!" the old steersman said. "Stand down. Or by Odin I'll make you *sit* down, with one swing of my fist." Hakr rolled up his sleeves, exposing arms as big as oak trees.

The commander's face lost color, and he retreated.

"Change course!" Hakr cried to the man at the steering oar. "To shore, swiftly! Crew, bring down the sail!"

But by now the wind was too strong to bring down the rest of the sail, as they found when a corner of the sail snapped so hard that it nearly flung a man overboard.

"We'll do our best with the sail up. Out oars!" the steersman cried.

The oars came rattling out of the oarlocks as the nearest rowers leapt to their benches. Dyrfinna joined them swiftly, sloshing through the bilgewater at the bottom of the ship, and grabbed the middle of a smooth oar along with two other men.

"Row! Make for shore, swiftly! Bend the tiller thither!" the steersman cried.

Dyrfinna bent her back into the rowing, following the rhythm of a small drum in the front of the ship, ignoring the burning pain in her injured arm. The busy ocean was full of a hundred splashes of the oars dipping in, pulling, and popping up out of the water.

The ship skimmed forward, plunging up and down through the high waves.

The Vikings ran before the wind with oars and sail, aiming for the shelter of the land. But as the steersman predicted, a dark line of cliffs stretched before them as far as the eye could see. White flashes of waves broke along the rocks that crowded along the cliff walls. They had traveled far beyond the safe point to land, where the rest of the fleet had been going. Their ship would be torn to pieces by the rocks and waves if they attempted to land.

"Change course again!" Hakr said, pointing out the direction for the man at the steering oar, and the boat swung until it was flying parallel to the cliffs.

A heavy squall struck the boat, and every rope screamed in the wind as a stiff gale ripped across the deck. The wind shrieked and a deluge of cold rain and hail tore down from the sky, drenching Dyrfinna and her crewmates. They clung to their oars. She felt as if the wind were trying to rip the oar from their hands, and the hard rain smacked the backs of her arms and her face.

She could not even see the land any more through the thick rain – could not even see the end of the ship from where she sat, pulling on the oar with her comrades.

"Hold steady, oarsmen! Hold steady!" Hakr cried, bellowing over the roar of waves and rain and wind.

The man at the steering oar was joined by two others, to hold the straining oar.

The huge waves rose higher, breaking over the sides of the ship. Hakr stood at the helm, bearing the brunt of the tempest, keeping his ship's prow pointing into the towering waves. A gigantic wave rose over him, and as the seawater crashed down, Dyrfinna cried out, certain that he had been washed overboard and drowned – pulled down to the house of the goddess Ran, who feasted on the bones of the dead.

But when the wave was gone, swamping the ship, there Hakr was, clutching the helm and pulling himself to his feet, sputtering and shaking the brine out of his eyes. He spat over the side and called, "Keep rowing. We are not dead yet. Where there's life, there's hope!"

Dyrfinna glanced wildly across the wild seas, but the falling rain was so thick that she could see nothing through it. No sight of land, or islands, not even the sea itself. Rain roared on the ship's deck and sail, the ship pitching wildly on the choppy waves. The wind screamed down from the sky, driving the rain hard against them, and the ship ran like a mad thing before the gale.

A rogue wave pitched the ship hard to the left. Dyrfinna went tumbling, slammed against the ship's side, and nearly fell into the ocean with several other warriors.

Skeggi appeared out of the storm, grabbed her arms, and pulled her away from the side. It was a miracle that he could keep his feet in this storm, and yet there he was, saving her life as if it was no big deal.

"Isn't this great?" he shouted over the raging tempest, leading her away from the side of the ship as another wave dashed them with ice-cold salt water.

"I'm afraid not!" she shouted.

She crawled to the middle of the ship and climbed back onto a rowing bench as the cold water in the bottom of the boat rolled and sloshed over her. The flat-bottomed ship continued taking on water, riding lower and lower. Many Vikings simply held on for dear life, except for the hardy sailors who leaned hard on the tiller to hold it steady. Their actions alone kept the ship from yawing all over the ocean, a grim and desperate task.

"We don't even know which way we're going," somebody shouted over the screaming wind.

"We're sinking!"

"Nobody is sinking," Hakr roared over the sea and deluge. "Never give up hope!"

Dyrfinna looked into the skies … and her heart stopped.

Through the mists of the raging rain, she could see nine Valkyries riding through the skies, the shadows of their maddened horses plunging on their wild courses through the air. Their helmets gleamed, and they cut through the storm with their lances as they galloped through the air before their ship.

Did anybody else see them? Nobody seemed to.

"Have mercy on my ship and crew!" Dyrfinna cried to the Valkyries. "Drive this storm away from us. Protect my people from sea monsters and the daughters of Ran, and allow us to sail safely to land."

One Valkyrie seemed to pause, one who wore dark blue, like the midnight sky, and her black hair streamed across the sky as she gazed at Dyrfinna, as if wondering why she should help them.

"We sail to revenge my friend Thora, the queen's daughter," she called to the Valkyrie, shivering to be speaking to one of the eternal ones. "Allow us to escape this cruel storm alive, so we may revenge her murder against the man who killed her. May it be so!"

The horses and goddesses faded away in the rain. As they did, the rain softened. The wind died down.

Vikings who had taken their weapons in hand, preparing to go to Valhalla if the ship sank, now looked forward with sudden hope.

From out of the raging storm came peace as the worst of the wind died down.

Now the rain was easing, and the hail stopped falling. The Vikings cheered.

"Look at Sinkr," Dyrfinna muttered, seeing him slumped over the side of the ship, vomiting.

"A fine look for a brave commander," Skeggi said.

"He doesn't even look that hot anymore," Gefjun said.

The storm had settled at last, and though the seas were still rough and choppy, they were able to advance – but slowly, because the crew, weary with fighting the storm for hours, had little strength left for rowing. A weak sunset gleamed beyond the thick, low clouds, but Hakr was glad of it, for now he had something to guide the ship's course.

A chill settled in Dyrfinna's bones, but thankfully the wind had died. Exhausted men and women fell asleep on the rowing benches.

But then, the Hakr cried out. "Ah! The stars!" A small space of sky cleared, and some stars gleamed through.

"The Sword," Dyrfinna said, recognizing a bit of the constellation that peeped through the clouds.

"That it is, my dear," said the old steersman. "Oarsman, adjust to starboard." He called out directions, recalibrating the ship's course, until he was satisfied. "My directions will be truer once we find the land so we can guide off that. Until then, this will do."

Dizzy and exhausted, Dyrfinna clambered to her feet, dripping from her sodden clothes, and walked toward the steering oar for a spell. Skeggi was at the steering oar, and she wanted to talk to him—wanted to have him all to herself.

As she passed between the rowing benches, all lined with sleeping Vikings, she looked at Sinkr asleep on the bench, where he'd gone as soon as the ship was out of danger. She hadn't seen him while the ship was almost underwater, but knew for a fact that he hadn't been helping Hakr during the storm, which was what a commander worth his salt would have been doing.

Sinkr took up the whole bench. Apparently he thought his muscles needed a whole bench to themselves while other Vikings shared benches so everybody else was out of the bilgewater that sloshed over the bottom of the ship. His golden hair was wet, his hard muscles gleamed in the starlight, and his wet clothes clung to every inch of his body, leaving nothing to the imagination. He could probably crack a walnut with those butt cheeks, to be honest.

Just because a man was hot did not mean that he was worth a tumble.

But some men were worth a different kind of tumble.

Dyrfinna put her foot against the small of Sinkr's back and waited for the waves to swell beneath them. When the ship began to climb up a wave, she gave him a little push downhill.

Helped by gravity, Sinkr tumbled off the bench into the bilgewater with a splash that brought much joy to her heart. She took a quick step over to a different rowing bench and lay down on it, curling up behind a burly Viking, who kept snoring on, indifferent.

Sinkr thrashed around in the water and sat up, sputtering. Just as he did, the ship slid down the other side of the wave, and the bilgewater came back and splashed him in the face.

Swearing, blubbering, he looked around him in the dark to see if anybody had noticed. But, seeing no one, he finally lay back down on his bench, muttering and grumbling, and settled himself to go back to sleep.

It's the small things that bring the most satisfaction, Dyrfinna thought. She waited until he was snoring, then got up again and continued down the ship to join Skeggi at the steering oar.

THE SELKIE

She climbed up on the raised deck in the stern of the ship, where Skeggi sat with the oar. Many of her friends, as well as strangers, slept on the raised portion of the deck, out of the water. Everybody was drenched. Dyrfinna could hear snores and shivers both from the sleepers.

Vikings snored from underneath the sailcloth in the middle of the boat as well. Dyrfinna had dry clothes in a wooden case onboard ship—at least, she hoped they were dry. She'd get to find out how waterproof her case was in the morning.

Skeggi nodded a greeting, holding the steering oar steady. "I think we should be fine. The sea's much calmer now, so we can steer the Saebrandur in one direction, and now she'll go where we ask. She's a good ship."

"That's a blessing. Would you like me to help hold the oar so you can get some rest?"

Skeggi shook his head. "It's fine."

Dyrfinna eyed him a moment. "Are you all right? Do you want company to keep you awake?"

"If you need to sleep, I don't mind."

"I don't need to sleep." It was true. Sitting here with him, alone, there was no way she could have slept. Now the thin clouds were clearing away, allowing small patches of stars to shine through. A mild breeze blew over the waves, but that was not the reason she shivered. It was from the starlight on Skeggi's face, and how deep his eyes looked when he cast them toward the heavens.

The problem with love, she thought, *is that it softens you. It doesn't matter how much of a warrior you are, because when you look at the eyes of the man you love, you are instantly undone, and there's no help in the world for it.*

She glanced behind them, trying to get her mind off that particular subject. "Hey, look at that," she said, pointing atop the stern, which was shaped as the end of the dragon's tail.

Skeggi looked behind him where Dyrfinna pointed. A seagull slept while standing on the dragon's tail. He opened an eye partly at them, then shut it again.

"I miss my owl," he said.

"I miss him, too," Dyrfinna said, and flopped down beside him. "I've never been through a storm like that on a longboat before."

"I've been through a few," he said. "Don't worry. Every storm is different. You figure things out as you go, mostly."

Generally she hated small talk, wanting only to discuss deep subjects of the heart. But at the same time, it was so good to talk to him, to hear the sweet rumble of his voice, to meet his dark eyes as they flicked to hers, to return his smile.

"Yeah, unless you happen to sink the ship," she said.

He nodded musingly. "That would put an end to figuring things out."

"May it never be," she said, flicking her fingers so fate wouldn't decide to carry out her words. "Were you ever in charge of your parents' ships, when they were still alive?"

"No. I was a passenger, and I'd also go out fishing with my grandfather and his crew."

She nodded, remembering how his grandmother would take orders for the fish, and they'd both deliver. "So you've got a lot of experience on the sea. Do you like it?"

Skeggi laughed. "I do. I do. Not so much the storms … though they offer a kind of wild glory, when you're standing on a deck awash with water, holding on to the mast, and the power of the storm is breaking around you. It's awe-inspiring. But you also feel alive. Alive!" His eyes lit, looking at her, and she thrilled with it. "There's nothing like it.

"I enjoy the mundane things, too. I always liked looking at the different kinds of fish that Grandfather would pull out of the sea, and helping him throw back the ones that he wouldn't be able to sell. You get such a variety of creatures from out of the deep. Little fish like jewels. Strange shrimps and jellyfish of incredible shapes. Huge fish the size of dogs, and they would look at you with those strange eyes. You can't imagine all the animals living in the sea, and every time we went out, we'd find something new and exciting we'd never seen before. The seas are so alive, Dyrfinna. I wish there was some way we could go into the water and explore the deeps. There are worlds down there we've never dreamed of."

She listened in fascination. "Have you ever seen any selkies?"

Skeggi's eyes went wide. "I did, once. It was floating in the water like a seal. You know how seals will bob out there, when they're standing up out of the water and looking around? But this one was the wrong shape to be a seal. And … it was singing." He looked at her. "I swear by Odin she was singing. I was ten years old and went to the rail of the ship to listen. Grandfather came running across the deck and grabbed me and hauled me away. He ordered his crew to tack away from the selkie, though we hadn't the wind for it. He was so mad at me."

"What was she singing?" Dyrfinna wondered if maybe Gefjun could use a selkie song with her song magic somehow.

Skeggi grinned. "Here's the thing. You know how selkies are supposed to have beautiful voices and lure you to your doom? This one had an awful voice. Awful! The only reason I went to the rail to listen was that I couldn't believe what I was hearing. She sounded like she was hooting."

"Are you serious?" Dyrfinna laughed.

"Yes! It sounded like a little owl with hiccups."

They laughed.

Dyrfinna said, "I hope the selkie isn't out there right now, listening to us."

"Ooh," said Skeggi, covering his mouth.

"Sorry, selkie," Dyrfinna called out to the ocean. "You sing beautifully. Maybe you had a cold that day."

Somebody who was lying on the deck grumbled, "The selkie won't curse you, if you stop talking so she can go back to sleep."

Dyrfinna and Skeggi looked at each other, stifling their laughter. "Sorry, fair selkie," Dyrfinna whispered in a carrying voice.

"The fair selkie says, kiss my ass," said the sleeper, who then subsided into a grumble. Then a snore.

All was peaceful again.

They were quiet for a moment. Dyrfinna liked how pleasant their silences were, how natural. She didn't have to rush to come up with something to say. They'd always been like that, from back in the days when they were neighbors and played together with their friends under the plum tree in her yard. As they got older, they'd gone from chess matches and her battle strategy game, which she always trounced him in, to swordfights.

She rolled her shoulder, trying to take the stiffness out of the injury. It hurt, but not as bad as she'd have expected. "This morning seems forever ago."

"Doesn't it?" he asked. "Apparently you love more adventure than I can take, wolf-snuffer."

She snorted. "I'm sure you'd save your brothers from a wolf, if one attacked you."

"I don't know," he said quietly. "I don't know that I'd succeed quite as well as you did. My gift isn't in sword fighting as yours is."

This was true, for she'd actually seen Skeggi taken out by a training dummy. It had taken him months to live it down.

"I know you'd do it for Rjupa," she said. She wasn't being jealous, because it was the truth. He was a big-hearted man, and she loved him for it.

He smiled and shrugged a little. "You've got it backwards. She'd be the one saving my hide."

They laughed. Dyrfinna really did like Rjupa. She kind of wished she were here now, even when she wished Skeggi could be wholly hers. Dyrfinna half-wanted to ask him if he and Rjupa were going to be betrothed, but that thought did make her jealous. She didn't like the feeling. It made her squirm.

Dyrfinna's eyelids grew heavy. All of a sudden, the exhaustion of the whole day sank its weight on her, and her body pulled her to lie down in blissful sleep. Her head drooped.

"Why don't you sleep here?" Skeggi said.

"No …" she mumbled. "I'll just …. " She tried to get up, but now she was too weary; it wasn't happening.

"You can stay with me," he said, laying one hand on her shoulder. "It's all right. Get some rest. I'll be here when you wake up."

His hand warmed her through and through. She smiled at him, her heart filled with love, and she lay down on the deck with the other Vikings in the little space against his legs. She felt him arrange her sea cloak over her to cover her better as she drifted into sweet, delicious sleep.

She longed so much to tell him what he meant to her. How deeply she loved him.

EIRIK

Eirik was alive again. Except now, inexplicably, he was somehow Dyrfinna's age, and had grown a great blonde beard halfway down his chest.

"How ... how are you alive?" she gasped, running up to him in open-eyed astonishment.

He gave a disdainful half-shrug. "I've been here all this time, dummy. You just never noticed."

But now that he was back, he seemed so disappointed with everything. "Aesa is growing up. Mom's only a shell of her old self. And Dad just ... left," he said, opening his hands, annoyed. "Seriously, Finna, can't you do anything right?"

"But I'm the master of all these ships," she said, stretching her arm out over the harbor. There were no ships there, unfortunately – just a fat little puffin standing on the dock, eyeing her suspiciously.

Eirik blew air out through his cheeks. "Anyway," he said, feigning boredom, and turned away.

The scene changed, as it so often does in dreams. Now Dyrfinna was a wild dragon, flying with her great, fiery wings. She blazed across the town, blasting it with flames, getting revenge.

In her rage, her wings and body had turned into fire. Houses below exploded into flames. She roared through the sky, a cataclysm of fury. People she'd known all her life fled their homes, screaming, and she poured fire down over their heads.

Then she saw how everything in the town looked afterward. The fire was gone, and smoke hung low over the ruins. People stood unmoving in the streets and pathways, looking untouched and safe. *I didn't kill them after all,* Dyrfinna thought. *They are not dead.*

A tree leaned in a soft breeze that came blowing in. As the breeze passed over the silent town, a dusting of ash blew off the people. Then more and more ash as the wind blew. The lines in their faces and bodies blurred. Their faces crumbled and collapsed, their heads and chests caving in. Arms sloughed off and collapsed into powder on the ground. Her flames had burned everybody so quickly that in an instant they had become wholly ashes, too fragile to stand up to even the softest kiss of the breeze. All through the town, people she thought had survived merely crumbled into powder as soon as she turned her eyes on them.

Eirik had been caught in the split branches of a low tree, as if he'd tried to climb out of the conflagration, but, too late, had been caught in the flash of fire. Her little brother was staring at her, despair in his eyes, his mouth hanging open as if he'd cried out to her in his last moment. Then his head dropped from his body and collapsed into a flume of ash with the quietest of sighs.

Dyrfinna sat straight up with a gasp, wide awake at last, her arm stretched out, hand open as if reaching for him.

She was disoriented for a blink of time, then realized that she had just been dreaming, and was now awake. She was sitting up, her heart thudding fast, next to the brazier where she'd nodded off some time ago.

Ragnarok passed by, a mountain of a man, carrying a barrel of salt pork on his shoulder as easily as if it had been filled with feathers. He stopped as Dyrfinna caught her breath.

"You all right, Finna?" he rumbled through his gigantic beard.

"Yeah. I'm … I'm fine," she said, befuddled, and lay back against the side of the ship as Ragnarok went on his way.

Dyrfinna shut her eyes to squeeze back the tears. That look on her little brother's face in the dream was the same expression he'd had when he'd died. When she'd killed him.

It had been over a year. There were times when she thought she was over it, but then she instantly felt guilty for being able to go on with her life when he couldn't.

She looked at her hands, at the red gleam of Thora's carnelian ring.

She could feel her powers twisting in the her heart like snakes. She kept having to bury them, kept hiding them, ignoring them, praying they'd go away. Just like this memory.

Dyrfinna still couldn't look at what she'd done that awful night.

But she still could remember when her brother had fallen back against the ground, hard, too hard. Air burst out of his mouth, like the wind was knocked out of him. He lay there like a discarded rag doll, unmoving.

He had to have been playing a joke. "Stop it," she said, still dizzy from the aftereffects of her magic. "Stop it." He had to have been fooling. He had to be playing a trick. "It's not funny," but her voice wobbled. Part of her *knew* what happened. Part of her knew that this was truly the end; there was no coming back from it. But this was not supposed to happen. Eirik was supposed to get up and be mad at her for knocking him down like some jackass. They were supposed to fight about it, the way they always fought. That was what was supposed to happen.

The air had been knocked out of him – but he wasn't sucking in any breaths.

"Brother," she'd said, but now her voice cracked.

Now she knelt at his side, desperate, trying to lift him, but he was leaden, dead weight. His eyes were fixed and lopsided, the eyelids stuck halfway open. His head lolled back and his mouth dropped open. A scorched smell came out of his open mouth. Scorched, as if he'd somehow been burnt from the inside.

Dyrfinna shook him, slapped his face. He didn't stir. She breathed into his mouth as if trying to revive a drowned person, but the breath she blew into his lungs puffed back into her face with the stink of burning and rot.

"Oh, Allfather!" she breathed. What had happened? What had killed him? What had come out of her? She wasn't even a magic-doer, not a witch, not a seer. It was impossible! She pulled his body up to hers, his arms dangling, not even fitting into her arms the way he used to when he had been a little boy and had curled close to her chest like a baby kitten.

The ship sailed on. Day fled before them. Soon night came on.

Dyrfinna had kept to herself as much as possible all that long day, pleading fatigue. Sinkr strutted about, sneering down at her, bossing her crew around. She merely turned her head away.

The arrival of night was a relief. Though she was exhausted again, she could not sleep, so she took the first watch. Her fellow Vikings wrapped themselves in their sea-blankets or sailcloth and lay down on the after deck.

It must have been close to midnight, though the red glow of the sunset, which had never really gone away, still lingered in the north. This far north, the sun didn't really set in the summer months.

She paced the deck by that otherworldly light, thinking of all that had happened, and what was to come. What future waited for her? Thora was dead. The command of her grandmother's ship, which her own grandmother had given to her, had been stolen from her by a pompous ass who didn't know shit about commanding, with the blessing of her own father.

All of this was because she'd failed to keep her own brother alive.

She took a deep breath, and looked at those shameful things, and hardened her heart in order to bear them.

Not even Serja's voice reached her here. She could still feel that bond she shared with the dragon, but she had not heard Serja's voice ever since they left home, though she desperately longed to hear it again.

She could only rely on herself.

She sat down on the starboard side on the deck. The sea was quiet now, and a light mist curled up from the waves as the air cooled.

Besides … I'm broken.

She closed her eyes against that pain. She didn't deserve to be loved. Anymore. Not after what she did.

THE BURNED ISLE

A little before dawn – long enough for Dyrfinna to get a little bit of sleep, but not much – the steersman called, "Up! To oars! We've found land."

Groggy Vikings, both men and women, dragged themselves to their feet and went to the rowing benches, sloshing through the dirty water that filled the bottom of the ship.

"We've found a hole in the side of the ship that we've got to fill," Hakr said from the prow as the oars came rattling out. "During the storm we must have met some submerged ice. We need to stop and fix the ship, because she keeps taking on water, despite the efforts of our valiant bailers. I don't think it'll take more than a day or two to fix it."

Sinkr tossed his head to arrange his golden hair around his shoulders, then stepped on top of a rowing bench, flexing subtly in order to show off his muscles to best effect. "We can't take any more time," he proclaimed. "We are going to be late to the meeting point for the attack."

Hakr held up a hand. "If we don't fix this ship, we won't be meeting or attacking anything, I guarantee it. Now, if our dragons find us and bring us news of the rest of the fleet, we might be able to arrange a different scheme to attack King Varinn's crew."

In the morning sun, mountains appeared out of the mist.

"Ah! We are actually well on our way toward King Varinn's," Hakr said. "As you can see from the placement of that central peak, we are near the town of Eidem." The old Viking steersmen had an encyclopedic knowledge of how every chain of mountains and every landmark looked from the ocean, so even if they were blown off course, he was able to look at the mountains around him and how far away they were, and instantly know his location.

"We have traveled well up the coast," Hakr continued. "Last night's wind flung us far—and I'll wager that this same wind has blown King Varinn's fleet backwards. So don't give in to despair. Row to land. We'll patch the hole, find the rest of our army, and then we'll go after that scalawag."

The crew cheered. They went to their rowing places, slid out the oars, and made the ship fly through the water. Hakr expertly guided them through a motley collection of islands and standing rocks until they reached the foot of a mountain that was a great spar of rock that jutted into the air from the ocean. At the foot of the mountain was a wide beach where they were able run the longboat up onto dry land.

Everybody splashed out of the ship, Dyrfinna included, her legs wobbly on the land. All together they pushed the old ship higher up on the sand, well out of the water, exposing the hole that had caused so much trouble. Some quick-thinking person had plugged it with an old boot and a quantity of moss.

Sinkr got out and tried to boss everybody around, while Hakr, behind his back, assigned some people to gather supplies and to various important tasks. Soon the blacksmith and some craftsmen prepared a fire and began to mix some tar, while two woodsmen went into the forest to find a pine tree.

Everybody scattered to make camp. Many people wanted a chance to kill some meat and make a hot fire and eat. Others wanted to wash the brine from their skin and hair.

Dyrfinna and her friends came down from the ship all together. She carried some clothes from her chest, which had turned out to be waterproof after all.

"I'll shoot some game," Ostryg said, putting his bow over his shoulder.

"I'll shoot more game," Dyrfinna said before she could stop herself.

"I'm sitting with whoever catches enough food for tonight," Skeggi said, waggling his eyebrows at Dyrfinna.

The next moment, shouting came from downstream. "Look out! Hide!"

Certain that King Varinn's ships had found them, Dyrfinna's hand went to her sword and she crouched in a defensive position, looking for the danger.

Then a dragon flew low over the spruce trees that crowded the sky.

A wild dragon!

Brilliant as an ember blown to orange flame, shining like a topaz, the wild emberdragon shot past overhead, the blast of heat from its body rushing over her like that of a miniature sun.

Dyrfinna crouched on the bank of the stream, praying it didn't see her, prepared to plunge back into the water if it decided to lay down a line of fire. Wild dragons were quick and mean. No human could approach them. These dragons would whip around and burn them to a crisp. Like hornets, they were always pissed off and didn't care what they hurt.

The emberdragon flew on, clearing the top of the mountain and vanishing from view.

Dyrfinna pulled on her boots, checked for landmarks – she wanted to find her clothes and return to the ships later – then rushed to the other side of the mountain. She aimed her steps toward a tall group of rocks standing in the direction the dragon had flown.

She left the shelter of the low trees around the stream, hurrying through the tall grass growing from the rocky soil. It took a while to climb through the grass, then up through the rocks and moss where the grass couldn't grow. She kept the mountain on her right side, and it rose up between her and the sun. But ahead, she could hear the sea smashing against the rocks far below – the far side of the island, where the dragon had gone.

When she finally reached the sheer cliffs at the island's edge, and she could look out over the sea, her legs felt like jelly. She stopped and rested, sucking down air, trying to catch her breath after that long climb.

Shading her eyes from the bright sun, she could look behind her and see their longship at the shore, far below. She could barely make out a tiny stirring from the people around the ship. Her clothes in the forest were too far below to spy, but she could see the glint of the creek where she'd been washing.

The other side of the mountain, where she now stood, looked over the sea. The view was stunning. Far across the ocean sat other mountains, other lands, clearly visible.

But much closer to her, not far away from the cliffs on which Dyrfinna stood, was the burned island.

It was charred black as if it had been through a wildfire. But even after a wildfire, a light scrim of green on the land would show where grass was growing back. Not on that isle. There were no trees, no bushes, nothing green. Nothing but barren soil, ash-filled pools of brackish water, blackened rocks and boulders, and hardscrabble hills made almost entirely of stone.

No sign of life on that island… except for one.

The wild dragon.

Against the black, scorched island, the wild dragon gleamed a brilliant orange as it circled. Then it closed its wings like a hawk and dropped to the cliffs that faced the sea on the side facing Dyrfinna's cliffs. It landed on a ledge and ducked its head low, then vanished into a cave. Mostly. For a long moment its orange tail, gleaming like embers, lay outside the cave. Then, little by little, the tail slid inside. Gone.

Usually dragons lay outside under an outcropping of rock. There was only one reason for a dragon to be roosting in a small cave.

Little flowers grew flush against the rocks of the mountain below her feet, signifying spring. And spring was when dragons laid ....

"Dragon eggs," Dyrfinna said softly.

A NEW CHALLENGE

If Dyrfinna could have rolled down the mountain to speed her descent, she would have. She hurried as fast as she could, cursing her stiff muscles, cursing how exhausted she was. She was on fire to jump in a little boat, paddle all the way around the point until she reached the scorched dragon isle, steal some dragon eggs, and sneak back out of there before the emberdragon burned her to a crisp.

"Well, that's easy enough," Dyrfinna said, mocking her own excitement. "And all you have to do is move fast enough to go to the island and come back in one piece – *and* you have to do all that before the longboat is repaired and ready to set sail. Yeah, that's not going to be any trouble at all."

She hadn't had much sleep the night before, but she knew for a fact that she was not going to sleep tonight. She could always sleep while she was dead.

She wanted those eggs.

Her mind was all awhirl. After all, how many chances would she have in her life to go to a dragon isle and try and capture a clutch of eggs?

And yes, she knew full well she was running headlong into danger. There was a reason why people didn't pick up dragon eggs in the wild—it was like pulling lion cubs out of the paws of their mothers. Only the mother lions in these instances had claws, teeth, *and* deadly fire.

It had been a long time since anybody had captured a clutch of dragon eggs. Many adventurers had gone out to find them. Only a few had returned alive, and those who had returned … she shuddered to think of them.

One had returned to Skala after an unsuccessful attempt. Dyrfinna had seen him as he was carried into town on a horse. Half of the man's face had been burned off, half of his body singed. He'd died shortly after.

Those who had gone with him said he'd done everything the way he was supposed to. He'd slipped in during the dead of night, had disguised his smell, had turned a cow loose elsewhere on the island to distract the hungry dragon. While the dragon was busy killing the cow and bolting down slippery chunks of flesh, the man had slipped into her cave to gather the eggs.

But the dragon had come back too quickly and found him, the eggs in two baskets on his back, scaling down the side of the mountain. She'd instantly let loose a blast of fire across his body. He only survived that initial blast because the fire burned the rope through and he'd tumbled down the rocky crags, all afire, onto the rocky ground. His injuries left him to die a slow, painful death. Worse, the eggs had been abandoned on the ground, and it was possible that they'd been broken during his fall.

The memory sobered her, and she slowed. *Dyrfinna, what are you thinking?* She didn't have a cow to lure the dragon away. She didn't have a rope to scale the mountain. She didn't have a clay pot or sand to pack the eggs in to keep them warm for transport. She didn't even have anything to carry the eggs away.

She did have a little fisher boat on her ship, however, that would take her to the burned island. The trip there and back, at least, would be quick.

She'd already packed all her dragon gear … just in case.

I have my old blanket, she thought. *I'll rig a carrying sling out of that. I can scale a mountain fairly easily.* She'd spent much time climbing the rock faces on Mount Pyrr near her home in order to strengthen her body. *I have an empty barrel to pack the eggs into, and hot ashes to keep them warm.*

She followed the smell of the cooking-fires to the small beach below the mountain. Their crew was settling down around the ship and cooking their supper. Some of them had found some meat, by the smell of things, and her stomach grumbled.

"Dyrfinna! Is that you?" Gefjun squinted at her, walking up from the beach to meet her.

"It's me," Dyrfinna said, because her friend's eyesight wasn't the best.

"I thought so. I saw you making for the mountaintop after that dragon went by. We were yelling for you to come back, but I don't think you heard us."

"I didn't."

"My hot man bagged a goose, Skeggi caught some lemmings, and I gathered some ground tubers, mushrooms, and herbs."

"It's all right. Skeggi was talking to us, and he's right. I shouldn't have jumped on your case."

"Skeggi said that, huh? So what else did he say?" Dyrfinna asked as they headed down the mountain.

Gefjun grinned. "He was saying how much he loved you …. "

"Stop. He did not."

"You're right, he didn't."

Dyrfinna hated how her heart always jumped with hope even when she knew full well that Gefjun was only messing with her. "You should know better than to say that to me. Remember how you felt about Olf a couple of years ago?"

Gefjun snorted and shook her head, but she was smiling. "Fine. Fine. You're right."

"So what else did Skeggi say?"

"Just to go easy on you sometimes. He said he felt like I'd take sides with Ostryg against you, and it wasn't the easiest thing for him to watch."

Huh. He'd noticed. He'd really noticed.

And for some reason Dyrfinna felt sad all of a sudden.

"Ooo! Comfrey." Gefjun kneeled next to a thick rosette of leaves growing close to the ground. "I wish I could pot this up and bring this with us. This is such a useful plant." She picked about half the leaves off the plant, leaving the rest, and looked around for other clumps of comfrey. "Here we go," she said, moving to the next one.

Dyrfinna found another comfrey plant, picking off only half of the leaves as Gefjun did, so the plant could grow back. "Gefjun. You saw me run off after that dragon today."

"A wild dragon," Gefjun grumbled, stacking the wide, flat leaves so she could carry them more easily. "You dummy, you know you could have gotten yourself killed."

"Then you're going to love my idea."

"Oh, don't you dare."

"When I got to the top of the mountain, I saw where the dragon went."

"No. We're not going." Gefjun grabbed her stack of comfrey and stuffed it in a small bag she always carried at her waist.

Dyrfinna scrambled to her feet. "Look, the visit to the dragon's den will go faster if I have your help."

"Ugh! Finna! Are you crazy? I wouldn't go to an island infested with dragons. Because, unlike you, I don't want to die."

"You have song magic," Dyrfinna pleaded. "You can bewitch the dragons."

"No! Absolutely not!" Gefjun yelped, turning to face her. "Not with these little songs. This brand of magic works for helping little kids to go to sleep or to help knit skin."

"Your power is more than that. It's stronger. You keep telling me it can only do these little things, but I know you can do more."

"Finna, stop. Just because you saw me help that whale once .... "

"That's the thing, though. You were communicating with it."

"With *her*. But that's not big magic. Coaxing away a dragon? No, thank you. And don't forget, those are wild dragons. How do you know that the baby dragons aren't going to come out of those eggs and roast you alive with their baby dragon breath?"

"They're babies."

"Babies with firepower."

"But Gefjun ...."

"Look. I can call a chipmunk. I can call puffins. Puffins will come to me, about five hundred of them, and they all want to be my special friend. Dyrfinna, I don't know if you've noticed this, but a puffin is nowhere near the size of a really pissed-off hornet dragon that can unleash enough fire to burn all of Skala and then some."

"Yeah, but..."

"Yeah, but what about the time I had to sing you out of that cave when you got stuck?"

"But…"

"That time I had to drag you out of the water when you jumped off Promontory Rock?"

"But …"

"That time the wild boar tore your kirtle off?"

Dyrfinna blinked. "Now, you have to admit, that was pretty funny."

"Not when he started to chase me!"

"It's okay, I killed it when you distracted it."

"It wasn't funny to me."

Dyrfinna frowned. Was Gefjun really this upset?

Gefjun's voice shook. "Look. I have been saving your butt in every situation because you think it's fun to have a little adventure. I'm not letting you do it this time."

"But… you love adventure."

Gefjun fixed her with a serious look. "No … *you* loved it. And I'll admit it was funny watching you fall off things on your head because you had this notion that you could beat everything. But that was back at home, Finna. Here? We're in enemy territory, and I'm a healer. I know what I am; I know it in my heart. I also understand who you are. You're a warrior, but I am not. I'm a nurse because I want to serve the queen, but, more important, I want to stay alive."

Well, damn.

Dyrfinna didn't doubt for a moment that Ostryg had been talking to her about that, too.

"Come on," she said. "I need to get this rabbit on the fire."

Gefjun looked straight at her and picked more comfrey. "This works a little bit on burns," she said. "But, may I remind you that these little leaves will not take the pain of burns away. And severe burns take a very, very, long time to heal, and the whole time, you are living in unimaginable pain. You will not like to be treated for burns. I guarantee it."

Dyrfinna merely handed Gefjun the small stack of comfrey leaves that she had picked.

"I can see that look in your eyes," Gefjun said, giving them back. "You'd better keep these handy."

They soon reached the cook fire, and Dyrfinna had to sit down because her legs were completely done with walking. Using her dagger, she ungloved the rabbit and prepared it for cooking.

"I saw you running after that dragon," Ostryg teased as he laid a large log carefully on top of the smaller, burning logs. "Did you catch it?"

"No," Dyrfinna said. "But I didn't see you grabbing that dragon in mid-flight, either."

"I wasn't going to do that. You'd yell at me for taking your dragon."

"That's right. And I saw where it lives. It's got a clutch of eggs on the other side of this mountain, on an island. I am going to try and get them."

Both Ostryg and Skeggi looked at Gefjun.

Gefjun shrugged. "I've already tried to talk her out of it. And I'm not going. Sorry."

"No need for *you* to apologize." Ostryg put an arm around her, pulled her close in a sideways embrace. "I don't want you going on a wild-dragon chase and getting burned to death. Not like some people."

Gefjun pretended to protest and push him away, then laughed and pulled him close. "Finna, don't take this the wrong way, but I think you're out of your mind."

"Maybe I am," Dyrfinna told her. "But what would happen if I did capture them? Imagine that." Because Dyrfinna, spitting her rabbit, could imagine it vividly. Dyrfinna, hatching the eggs and collaring all three of the dragons as soon as they were out of the shell. Raising the dragonlings herself, teaching them how to carry a rider and fight in battle. Having Skeggi read them books and tell them stories to expand their understanding of the world. Dyrfinna, a few years from now, riding one of the grown dragons she'd raised from the egg.

"Imagine this," Ostryg said quietly. "Imagine your burned bones lying in the sun after your attempt fails. Then imagine Aesa crying when you don't come home."

The air puffed out of Dyrfinna as if she'd been punched in the gut. She glared at him.

Gefjun broke in. "Finna. You know the danger you'd be in, doing this. You saw Emil when they brought him in."

Her glare broke and she frowned at the rabbit in her hands. "I saw. It was horrifying. But I can't be this close to a dragon isle and not try to get eggs. Obviously I'm not going to steal into a dragon's cave while the dragon is in there, but …."

"But your ambition knows no bounds," Ostryg said.

Dyrfinna shut her mouth tightly.

"Stop, Finna. You know he's right," Gefjun said.

"So yeah, okay, that's why I'm doing this," Dyrfinna said. "I'm going to be careful. But I want to try, and see what luck gives me in my attempt. Because if you don't try, you stay alive—but you don't get anything."

"And sometimes, even when you don't try, you die," Ostryg said.

"Yeah. Why wait for death when you can go out and try and catch it?" Gefjun cried.

"I said I'll be careful." Dyrfinna squeezed her shoulder. "I want to get close enough to that dragon to at least start figuring out the logistics to accomplish this. I can scout it out and maybe think of a way to trick them and keep them out long enough to swipe a clutch of eggs."

"I'll go with you," said Skeggi, looking up at her with those soulful brown eyes.

Dyrfinna's first reaction was to immediately come up with reasons why he shouldn't go with her.

Enough, she told herself. *Do you want to get those dragon eggs, or not? You need a partner—someone to back you up … or bring your body home.*

"But you can't do song magic, can you?" she asked.

"Why can't you sing yourself, madame?" Ostryg asked.

Dyrfinna shook her head and turned from him to face the fire.

He knew perfectly well why she never sang. And of course he had to call her "Madame."

"Hello?" Ostryg said. "You can vanquish your enemies from a distance with songwork, you know."

She turned her eyes on him, her anger burning. "People die when I sing. Remember?"

He turned away with a sneer. "At least you *had* a family," he said under his breath.

Gefjun nudged him hard.

"What?" he asked, annoyed.

Gefjun simply changed the subject. "So how are you going to get off this island without anybody noticing?" she said.

"I'm going to take the fisher boat," Dyrfinna said.

"Are you going to swipe that while everybody is hanging around the ship, drinking ale and getting belligerent?" Because down on the beach, next to the longship, some of the Vikings were building a bonfire. Others were walking over and joining them, slapping each other on the back and lifting their overflowing drinking horns.

One of the Vikings on the beach had started singing a song, though it was less singing and more like yelling words at the top of his lungs. Several warriors went to him and picked him up. He left off yelling music and started swearing as they carried him into the pounding waves and dumped him in the water. The bystanders roared their approval. The singing man rose from the waves like a monster from the deep and tackled the others, dragging them into the water. The bystanders roared again.

"Half of the ship is out of their sight," Dyrfinna said. "We'll have to go in carefully, but there might be enough cover to allow Skeggi and I to sneak the fisher boat out into the ocean."

"Sinkr is looking for any reason to call you out," Skeggi reminded her.

"I'm sure he is. And I have no interest in giving him any reason to do so." Dyrfinna scanned the beach and longship from where she sat, laying out in her mind a map of the area—high points, low points, what places afforded cover, and the places the Vikings would most likely gather.

"Me too," Skeggi cried. "Maybe I should stay behind."

"Nope!" Dyrfinna said. "You're stuck with me now."

Saying that shouldn't have made her heart leap. But it did.

She kicked her lovesick heart out of the way and took another bite of rabbit. One problem at a time.

"Are we throwing aside Thora's revenge for this?" Gefjun asked. "What's important here?"

It was awful, but Dyrfinna secretly valued the living over the dead.

"I can't pass up this chance, even if it is dangerous," Dyrfinna said.

"Or insane," Ostryg muttered.

GET OUT ALIVE

They ate quickly, Dyrfinna laying out what they needed to do. Then she stowed her uneaten rabbit in her rucksack, along with some of her clothes to wrap the eggs in—or to wrap burns in, if the whole operation went wrong—several bladders of water, some herbs that could work as a preliminary burn medicine until they returned, a torch with flints, and other items. She put on her sword and a small dagger, and wore a short black cloak with hood to blend in with the night.

Skeggi packed his own supplies. Gefjun went to get ready, and Ostryg made comments about everything that was going on, as he always did.

They swiped the fisher boat and rowed away.

They were quiet. Dyrfinna was thinking about Rjupa. "Where do you think she is now?" she asked.

"I hope she's home by now. And here I am …. " He looked up at the stars for a long moment. Then he noticed Dyrfinna and quickly added, "Here I am, rowing into the jaws of death where my ladylove can't see and appreciate the kind of fun I have."

Dyrfinna felt a flush of heat pass over her face and looked down. But she said, "When we get back, and when you see her again, you can tell her everything."

Their oars flew. Once they'd rounded the mountain, the island on the other side slowly slid into view. The bonfire was tiny now, a flickering light from far away. Stars lit into view as the sky, an incredibly dark blue, slowly moved nearer to black.

From the cliffs along the island's side, a glow appeared that matched the bonfire on the opposite side of the mountain. A tiny glow, no more than a sunseed at this distance.

"So why'd you decide to go hunting for dragon eggs with me?" Dyrfinna asked. "Nobody else wanted to – or dared," she added, gazing at the burned island ahead of them.

Skeggi continued to row. "I like adventure," he said. "After our parents died, I've been running the household and raising five brothers. I don't care if you're going to fight a dragon in hand-to-hand combat; I only want to go outside and live a little."

"That bad, huh?" Dyrfinna asked.

Skeggi laughed. "I wouldn't call it bad. I love my brothers, I really do, and they know I'd do anything for them. But you get stuck around the house with them. I want to go out hunting and fishing, or hop in the boat and glide down to the next village to pick up some supplies and talk to people. But I never can get away. There's always a kiddo wanting something. My older brothers, sometimes they'd help, but only after I asked them and asked them. I've tried to get my little brothers to go with me, but I could never get in a canoe without three kids wanting to go and the other two yelling at me to stay home with them. It's just easier not to go."

"At least the kids are old enough to take care of themselves now."

She sat at the front of the fisher boat, carefully studying the looming island up ahead. There were several high points on the island, but little cover on them. Finding the highest land didn't mean much when your opponent had wings and could fly over your head, zero in on you, and burn you to a crisp.

So Dyrfinna was looking for caves, hopefully one that led to the middle of the island. If a dragon tried to burn them out of a cave, they needed to be able to escape.

"The land where we'd landed the Viking ship last night was volcanic, full of pocks and holes," she said in a low voice to Skeggi. "The island is likely the same way. My other hope is that maybe, from being out in the ocean for all these years, this island would have been washed full of holes, as other islands have been. At least that would offer us some escape, even if it's only water to duck into as the dragons breathe fire down at us. Though," Dyrfinna added almost to herself, "if the water we fell into was shallow, the dragon's fire would likely steam us to death, like clams in a bucket."

"You always look on the bright side?" asked Skeggi.

"I don't want to run headlong into this," Dyrfinna told him. "What I want to do is explore this area. Find all the places where we can make a safe run from the dragons back to the shore. I want to get dragon eggs, but I also want us to survive."

"Being dead would solve a lot of ills," Skeggi said.

Dyrfinna looked at him. "Talk about looking on the bright side of life."

"It's Viking humor."

Dyrfinna nodded and looked across the island, now so close that she could hear the water washing on the rough stones of its edges. The soil and stones were nearly black, much darker than the soil of the nearby isles. Had they been that burned over the centuries of the dragons' reign here?

When they pulled the fisher boat up onto the shore, Dyrfinna saw that the black wasn't from the rocks being scorched, but a black algae attached to the rocks, which made them slippery. Definitely a problem she'd have to contend with while they were escaping.

"Be careful of these stones if we have to run out," Dyrfinna said. "I need to find a stable place to put this boat where we can be protected from dragon attacks if it comes to that." Skeggi found a sheltered cove where some ragged rocks stood. There was also an easy way up to the island among the stones from this place. They stowed the fisher boat in the darkness around the stones.

That done, they carefully walked up the shore toward the dragon cliffs. The rough rocks crunched under their feet.

"I hope they can't hear this over the noise of the waves," Skeggi whispered.

Dyrfinna hoped the same. Logically, she knew the dragons shouldn't be able to hear their feet on the shore, but the late hour and the fact that dragons were snoozing not far away was beginning to work on her. Why on earth did she think this was a good idea? "First, search for caves," she whispered.

They found one that seemed to reach well into the rock – only a narrow gap, but a cave nonetheless. Skeggi had brought a nice small torch, and once they got it sparked with a bit of flint and rock, it popped into light and they looked around them.

This was a small cave, and they could walk only while stooping.

Dyrfinna stepped forward into the cave, keeping an ear out for dragons and watching out for pools. Rocky islands like this often had puddles that looked innocent, but they were actually pits that would drop them into the ocean with no way out.

They walked farther into the darkness. The cave grew narrower and rougher.

"You stay back here and hold the torch. I'll go forward, carefully looking for holes to the surface. I don't want to alert any dragons by shining a bunch of torchlight up into their island. I'll feel my way forward in the dark."

Dyrfinna felt her way along. With the torch well behind her, every stone under her feet cast a shadow longer than death, and her body cast a shadow in front of it that blocked everything else – as if she were walking into her own shadow.

Dyrfinna watched for dangers while clambering through narrow gaps that took her breath away. She kept looking up, praying to see a little starshine from above. Moving away from the torch, letting her eyes adjust to the dark, she didn't dare turn around and look for the torch so she wouldn't ruin her night vision. She felt alone.

Finally, a faint shine gleamed ahead. She shut her eyes and turned back toward Skeggi. "I see a light up ahead," Dyrfinna whispered back to him. "Can you hear me?"

"Yes," came his warm voice out of the darkness. Their voices carried very well in here, thank Freyja.

The stones under her hands and knees were sharp through her kirtle and pants under them. She had to worm her way between two big rocks. For a moment she was trapped. She struggled, and fought the sudden urge to scream. *Stay calm. Stay in control.* She breathed for a moment, and then wormed past.

The hole widened overhead. "I'm going up," she whispered down to Skeggi. "Are you okay?"

"Yeah," he said.

With a nod, Dyrfinna turned back and climbed to the surface. She listened for a long time just below the entrance, seeing the stars burning above. The soft rush of the ocean waves reached her, but also the skirl of an ocean bird disturbed. Dyrfinna's jaw tightened. If that bird had been startled, something out there was awake and moving around.

Dyrfinna eased herself out of the hole like a gopher and looked around. A wide starry sky arched overhead. No trees or bushes to hide behind. The dragons had burned all of them off. She reached out and felt her way, but her hands met only rocks. It occurred to her that this was probably a common place for intruders to enter the island. Here in the middle of nowhere, with no cover – and the dragons probably watched this hole closely.

She lowered herself back down the tunnel and whispered, "Skeggi, come toward me a little way with the torch. I'll tell you when to stop." She looked down at the cave floor to keep from ruining her night vision, until she could see a faint light from the torch lighting up the rocks on the floor.

"Stop," she whispered, and she heard his feet scuff to a stop. That should be enough light so it wouldn't be visible from outside, but enough to guide her back to the hole.

She climbed out, ears wide open for any sound. Only the sighing of the wind and the everlasting voice of the sea. She could barely see the glow of the torch from the hole in the ground, but that was because she knew what she was looking for. Good.

She cast around for a landmark so she could find her way back. Here was a craggy rock that jutted into the air in the middle of the island. She walked to that and crouched in its shadow – the starlight was exceptionally bright tonight. But also, she listened for the sound of dragons breathing, and found the sound toward the cliffs.

She followed her ear.

Partly there, she tripped over a skeleton. She jumped back. Her heart pounded. Probably a fellow adventurer who'd been making for the hole in the ground and got caught in a blast of flame.

Now she could see a flicker of flame from the emberdragon's sleeping places.

Then from behind her came a scrape of rock.

With a silent gasp she whirled, but it was Skeggi's silhouette, climbing out of the hole in the ground. He'd left the torch behind.

"Go back!" she whispered.

No response, except for Skeggi walking silently toward her.

She loved this brave warrior, but she wanted him in the tunnels out of sight of the dragons, where at least he would have a chance to survive. Just because she was upset about her father stealing her position of command from her, didn't mean that Skeggi should face death on her behalf.

Focus on the mission, she thought, *so we can both get out alive.*

The approach to the cliffs where the dragons slept was a clear, open path. All the dragon had to do was stick her head out of her cave and spit a little fire, and poof, the end.

Dyrfinna looked at the hill that led to the top of the cliffs. No cover there, either.

Behind the hills, though, they'd have to clamber over rocks strewn across the rough ground. However, she saw gaps between the stones—hiding places to at least dodge the dragon's fire.

Suddenly the glow from the dragon's lair the other side of the cliff turned bright. Then came a rattle of scales, sounding like somebody dragging a shirt of chain mail over the rocks, ringing unnaturally loud in the silence.

"Damn those humans!" cried a metallic voice. "Damn them, every one! I'll burn them to ash!"

"I didn't know emberdragons could talk!" Skeggi hissed.

Though she was also astonished by this, Dyrfinna was not going to stand around and ask questions of a dragon that meant to kill them.

The sound stopped, and a scream broke from the other side of the cliffs. "I'll kill all of you!" it shrieked. "You slime-kissing insects, you are not going to collar my babies!"

AGAINST THE EMBERDRAGON

Dyrfinna's heart thudded. *The collars can help your babies,* she thought, but there was no way on earth she was going to argue the point.

"Run," she whispered to Skeggi – and then she ran away from him *toward* the caves, stumbling over the rocks.

She was so close. She was not about to let this opportunity pass. Even if it killed her.

She focused on a gap in the rocks near the cave, but the light from the emberdragon grew as it emerged from the cave with a blaze of fire and a roar that shook the rocks under her feet.

Dyrfinna flung herself into the gap between the rocks next to the cave and squeezed between the rocks, certain that the dragon had seen her.

It flung itself out in a blaze of fire that would have been glorious if it hadn't meant her doom.

And at that same moment she saw something that made her stomach drop even farther.

Skeggi had flung the torch into the air as he ran away. It sailed into the sky, end over end, tracing a bright spiral of light away from the cave.

He has such a good arm, she thought.

The dragon shot out with unnatural speed with a shriek and flew toward Skeggi.

Skeggi, she thought, anguished as the dragon flew toward the flying torch, which was now falling back to the ground.

But the dragon was now out of the cave, and she was not about to waste Skeggi's daring trick. She dashed inside.

The cave was unnaturally hot. Sweat popped out over her body. The stink of burned hair and shit made her gag but she swallowed and walked in. There was very little light except a few sparks floating in the air that the dragon had left behind in its fiery departure. Their fading orange light was enough for her to see the soft rounds gleam of several smooth, round objects by the edge of the cave, far in the back, lit by the dim embers in the ashes piled around them.

Dragon eggs.

A fleeting thought: That this might be the last thing she saw before the dragon appeared behind her at the cave entrance and filled this enclosed place with flame.

Yet she dashed to the dragon's nest. She could see the deep claw marks across the floor where the dragon had scraped away the loose rocks and arranged them in piles around the edge of the nest to hide them and hold the fire in. The heat here was most intense, and she almost couldn't breathe.

She lost her footing in the loose rocks around the nest's edge and fell in on her hands and knees, narrowly missing the five grey eggs that lay clustered together, half-buried in a mound of ash in the middle of the nest.

She immediately jumped back up with a hiss, her hands burned from their contact with the rocks, her heart pounding like never before.

Despite all her work with dragons, she'd never even *seen* a dragon egg up close before, much less a whole nest.

Despite the very real danger she was in, she froze for a moment, staring at the hot ashes and faded embers heaped over the ash-grey eggs. *Does the dragon bring in wood to burn around the eggs to keep them warm?* she wondered. *Does she burn the wood separately and then pile the hot ashes around her eggs?*

A shrieking cry from outside from the emberdragon. No time to waste. Hands shaking, she reached into the hot ashes and grabbed an egg. It was hot as a freshly-cooked potato, and about the same size. She juggled it slightly, hissing in pain.

Dyrfinna opened her hands and looked at the grey, ash-covered egg. The rubbery surface moved as the dragonet kicked from within, its small peeps echoing in the cave.

The shell was rubbery, like a turtle's egg. The tiny dragon inside moved, twisted inside the shell … and made a loud *peep!* noise that startled her so much she nearly dropped it.

She carefully set it inside the sturdy leather pouch at her side, then grabbed out two more, tucking them in with the first.

The dragon eggs started a constant peeping from inside the pouch that sounded like a baby chick's, a cry for help to its mama.

"Shh, shh, shh," Dyrfinna said, desperately clutching the pouch to her side. The peeping only became louder, now ringing off the stone walls of the cave.

No wonder nobody survives these excursions, she thought as she tried to hush the crying dragonets. *The mama always hears …*

Dyrfinna remembered the song that Serja had sung over Thora during the funeral. Softly, she sang it now as she swiftly crept toward the front of the cave.

The peeping stopped as she sang in some odd appropriation of dragon language, since she had been unable to understand Serja's words.

The little dragonets calmed down – though Dyrfinna sensed they were staying alert, and … it was curious, she realized with a thrill in her heart. They seemed to be *listening* to her voice, as if wondering which dragon was singing to them.

Dyrfinna's heart melted with tenderness.

This was all she'd ever wanted.

The mama dragon shrieked further down the island.

Her blood ran cold again. Shit. Skeggi was out there with a furious emberdragon, and *it was because of her*.

She went stumbling out of the cave.

A burst of flames. She tripped over a knot of stone, landing upon her elbow, but immediately clambered to her feet, the eggs still safe in the pouch. The dragon's fire, she realized, was from farther away, but still too close.

She dashed out of the cave, and now she could see the emberdragon on the other side of the island, blasting fire at something on the ground so intently that she instinctively turned her eyes away from the white-hot fires.

"Skeggi … no …" she whispered, her knees giving out under her.

"That's not me the dragon is burning," Skeggi said.

She gasped and whirled. He stood at the bottom of the cliffs, his hair and beard white with ashes, but alive.

"I threw the torch as far as I could, and then ran. She's burning that," he said as Dyrfinna climbed, one-armed, down the cliff to him.

As she climbed down the rocks, she realized her hand had been burned – how badly, she didn't have time to see. The dragon was still blasting the place where Skeggi's torch had fallen, and even from this distance she could feel the heat from its fire.

"Did you get an egg?" was the first question from Skeggi when she reached him. Even despite the danger they were in, his face lit up with curiosity.

Before he could finish his question, a new scream. Now the emberdragon suddenly turned a brilliant orange and went sailing up into the night sky, wings wide, like an emblem of doom.

"She's spotted us," Skeggi said, all color gone from his face.

"Quick," she gasped, seizing his hand. They fled, scrambling over rocks, and Dyrfinna frantically looked for someplace for both of them to fit.

She spied a bit of cliff behind a fall of stones, and a narrow gap underneath, wide enough for two bodies.

She turned, nearly pulling her arm off in trying to change Skeggi's course. As soon as he turned, he saw it too. They both made for it.

The most terrifying scream Dyrfinna had ever heard came from behind them.

"She's airborne," Dyrfinna whispered as they crammed themselves into the space below the cliff.

"I know, I know," whispered Skeggi, his voice shaking.

Dyrfinna looked wildly around. They were under cover, but with no escape route. Once the dragon found them, they would be burned alive, and nobody would know where to find them.

Dyrfinna pressed against Skeggi's body, and he wrapped his arms around her, but she was not exactly in a place where she could appreciate it right now.

From under the sill of rock, Dyrfinna saw the dragon sink into view in the middle of the island, floating down, wings open, like a windhover hawk making sure of its aim before it dropped on the mouse it prepared to kill. Red and orange chased each other over the dragon's scales, with silver lines like hot ash. The dragon was magnificent against the blackness of the starry sky. Its burning light was hypnotic, magical.

Dyrfinna couldn't help but marvel. Even the wings shimmered with orange and red burning light that moved across its surface in waves as the wind blew across it. The wings glowed like a burning log in the fire. A soft shower of sparks leapt from the wings, and shimmered on its scales.

The dragon's lithe body uncoiled as it turned in the air, its head over the cave's entrance, its body pivoting, turning to face into a small wind that blew the ash across the ground in front of Dyrfinna.

"I know those little vermin are hiding here," the emberdragon hissed, the sound of ash in the wind, its yellow eyes glaring into the darkness – as if it could *see* them.

Skeggi's breath caught – a sound that was like a knife in her heart.

Like the gasp that her brother had made just before her lightning had struck him.

"Odin's tears, what have I done?" she whispered in an anguished breath.

The brilliant wings clapped together and the dragon hurtled to the gap where Dyrfinna and Skeggi lay, skidding to a stop in the loose rocks that cluttered the ground in front of the gap. Its furious face, nostrils flaring and eyes lit, glared into the darkness at them.

Skeggi gasped again and squirmed back further, but there was nowhere else to go. Dyrfinna pressed her body against his and closed her eyes.

The emberdragon thrust its taloned foreleg into the gap under the rocks and tried to grab them. Its claws, each as long as Dyrfinna's hand, tore long grooves into the stones. She pressed closer to Skeggi, her body touching his entire length. The sharp talons were close enough to catch a few strands of Dyrfinna's hair and yank them out, and she hissed – but were unable to reach further.

"Come out, you little bastards! I want something to eat!" the emberdragon shrieked, clawing at the rocks.

"That's hardly an incentive to come out," Dyrfinna said before she could stop herself.

"Come out, and I'll keep you in my cave, alive," the dragon said. "And then I'll give you to my babies to eat when they hatch. That'll teach you to come onto my island and try to steal my babies and put collars on them!"

"They are never going to find our bodies, are they?" Skeggi asked quietly.

The emberdragon screeched, its voice painfully loud in the enclosed space. "I am sick! And tired! Of all this! Come out or die in flames, humans!"

Skeggi's frightened breathing echoed in her ears, and the dragon's eggs squirmed a little against her side.

My body will not protect either of them from the flames, she realized with the worst despair she'd ever felt.

Here she was, with the man she loved more than she loved herself, and the unhatched dragons she'd wanted more than anything else, and she was about to die with both of them – and she wasn't even putting up a fight.

So, gazing upon the end of Skeggi's life, Dyrfinna did the only thing left to do.

Taking a deep breath, she slid Thora's carnelian ring off her finger.

THE CRUCIBLE

The magic in her heart suddenly hummed into life, and Dyrfinna's body began to glow.

"Finna. No," Skeggi breathed, his dark eyes opening wide, his fearful face now illuminated by the power coming off her.

"I'm going to go out and stop it," she whispered. She took off the pouch that held the dragon eggs and carefully slid it to him with no explanation, then wriggled away from him toward the hovering emberdragon. The magic was boiling up inside her and she didn't dare say more for fear it would overflow.

But from out of nowhere, a familiar voice stopped her.

Dyrfinna! What are you doing?

She gasped.

It was Serja, speaking through their shared bond.

Dyrfinna whispered, "I've taken off my ring because we're under attack from an emberdragon! I'm trying to protect us! Help me shield Skeggi."

Serja took in her situation through Dyrfinna's eyes in an instant: The hovering emberdragon outside, Dyrfinna and Skeggi packed into a gap under the rocks, the claw marks that showed where the emberdragon had tried to pull them out of their shelter.

Dyrfinna, get back against Skeggi to shield him. Now. I'll direct your magic to shield you both.

Dyrfinna did, stretching her body as much as possible to hide him behind her, her heart thudding. She didn't question Serja – just trusted her absolutely and opened her heart to the dragon's power.

Outside their hiding place, the emberdragon's mouth opened, and it inhaled like a bellows.

Serja spoke a word in her own language – just as a gush of fire erupted with a roar like that of the smithy's forge.

Dyrfinna's light was washed out by a blast of white-hot flames, roaring, thundering into the gap with heat and pain that she had never before experienced.

It felt like the inferno at the end of the world, the flames of Ragnarok.

The fire-blast went on—and on—and on.

But they were still breathing. They were still alive.

The small alcove amplified the heat that rolled from her fiery blast. Her sweat felt like it was being pulled straight out of her pores and evaporating. Her eyes closed, she concentrated on Serja's magic, keeping her own magic steady against the relentless power of the emberdragon's fire.

Skeggi pulled in his hands to get them out of the direct heat. He whispered prayers, his voice so small against that endless roar.

But underneath the terror that filled every part of her body, Serja was speaking softly in her dragon language.

Don't leave us, Serja, she silently pleaded.

I will never leave you, the dragon whispered.

But something else was happening. The fire was devouring the very air they breathed. Dyrfinna's breath came shorter and shorter. Skeggi's too.

Dyrfinna held her breath as they met each other's eyes, desperate, and she poured her whole soul into her eyes. There wasn't even air to tell him that she loved him. She let her eyes tell him.

But now the clothes on her back burst into flames. What agony she had endured before seemed like nothing against this.

Even in her agony she stretched herself out, holding back the white-hot flames, keeping her heart strong so he and the baby dragons could live. *If I don't breathe, maybe he can have enough breath to survive* ....

A quiet exultation came then, and she gave herself up to the fire, absorbing all of it to protect him.

She gazed into his face as she felt herself going out like a candle flame. *I do this for my brother,* she thought. *I do this for you.*

Unutterable peace came over her.

She trembled on the edge of the known world, fading.

Dyrfinna! Serja cried. *No. You are not allowed to leave.*

And the dragon pulled her back.

Go check on your babies, Serja said to the emberdragon. *Please. Make sure they're all right.*

And suddenly the flames stopped.

"Who said that?" the emberdragon asked.

Air rushed back, and they gasped for breath in that superheated space. Skeggi's frightened eyes held Dyrfinna's tightly, as if she were dangling off a cliff and he was holding her tightly, trying to pull her back to safety.

The gap in the rocks darkened as the emberdragon thrust its head in with a chain-mail rattle of scales. Dyrfinna froze, not daring to move or even think. Their eyes were still locked together.

Behind her, the emberdragon snuffled vigorously. She heard the *thwp* of its tongue tasting the air.

"Dead," the emberdragon muttered. "And they smell so nicely cooked. The only good human is a roasted human. I'll come back for your corpses later. I'm glad you're dead."

Another chain-mail rattle as the emberdragon pulled her head free. Then the leathery sweep of wings and a gust of dragon-wind as she leapt into the air, flying back toward the cave, probably to check on the eggs.

From a distance came another blast of fire. "Little bastards. They'll be good for a meal or two if I can just dig them out of there," the dragon muttered, and the leathery sound of its wings faded.

Dyrfinna moved back slightly to let the cooler air in. She was shaking badly. So was Skeggi.

"How did you …" was all that Skeggi could manage to say. Every dragonrider knew a quick spell to shield against fire, but this spell would not have stood up long to the fire that the emberdragon had blasted over them for such a long period of time.

Thank you, Serja, Dyrfinna told her through their bond. *I think we're okay.* Tears sprang to her eyes at the thought.

It was fortunate that you're still within range for me to reach you, Serja said. *If you'd been farther away, I might not have sensed your fear. Be careful out there.*

I will be, she thought. *Thank you, my friend.*

She picked up the carnelian ring and slid it back on, and the glow coming from her body went out. Then she crawled out just far enough to see overhead.

Only the endless sweep of stars—no dragon in the sky, no emberdragon brooding on a nearby rock, waiting to kill them. She crawled out further. No red glow in the sky or on the mountain. Only a few licks of fire remained where the old skeleton lay. Amazing that there was anything left there to burn.

"Here's your pouch," Skeggi whispered, sliding it out to her, then rolled into view. He didn't get up, just lay upon his back, staring into the heavens, still heaving for breath.

She felt the eggs in her pouch, her hands shaking. Still intact. The baby dragons squirmed slightly inside the shells.

"Ye gods," Skeggi said, looking into the pouch. "What's in there? Is that what I think it is?"

Dyrfinna heard the mutter of the emberdragon from the cave, saw its glow from within.

After everything that had happened so far, she deeply felt the mess she'd gotten them into. Because now, she had to escape the island with a dragon watching for them, and they had to row away and get to land without being burned to death. On the open water, they'd be in clear view of the dragon's den. There was no place to hide.

"Yes," she said softly, pulling herself together. "But I still have to get you out of here. Otherwise, it's no good."

A DEEP DIVE

The only place to go was the cave that led from the center of the island. They crept out there swiftly and hurried underground and ran—or tried to—the whole way down the tunnel. Dyrfinna was convinced that the dragon would come back and start blasting the tunnel with its fire. Indeed, the tunnel was still pulsing hot and low on oxygen from the last blast, for the emberdragon had apparently blasted it before she'd blasted their hiding place. Every step was torture, with Dyrfinna and Skeggi gasping for breath the whole way through.

Finally, they reached the open air by the ocean, and a cool breeze blew into their faces. Dyrfinna gasped and all but drank the air, she was so grateful for it.

The fisher boat was still tucked in the alcove of rocks where they'd hidden it. They pushed the boat out and began rowing as quickly as possible. Neither of them spoke. False dawn was beginning, where the sky in the east brightened even though dawn was still a good way off. But any amount of light might reveal them to the dragon.

Once they were out on the water, Skeggi, who was rowing, said, "So … can I see what's in the pouch?"

Dyrfinna, who had been carefully scanning the skies around the island for the smallest sign of the emberdragon, felt her heart leap. “It’s not much,” she said quietly, opening the pouch and setting it in Skeggi’s lap so he could see it.

His eyes went wider and wider, staring at it. Then he looked up at Dyrfinna, his face alight like the sunrise.

“You did it,” he whispered, a world of joy in his words. “Finna, I can’t believe this! I’ve never even seen one of these, much less three! Can I hold one?”

“Be careful,” she said, her heart like a singing bird.

He lifted one out and held it as tenderly as he would have held a baby. The tiny dragon twisted inside the egg.

“It’s … so tiny,” Skeggi gasped. “I really thought these would be larger.”

“I know, right?”

“Finna, if anybody deserves to hatch these eggs, it’s you.”

Pride warmed her heart. But then she realized something. “My papa would disagree,” she said softly.

“He’s not here, is he?”

“No. But Sinkr is.”

Skeggi gently handed back the egg, laying it in her hand. “Then we’ll hide it from him. Find ways to keep it warm without him noticing. Then when it hatches, the first one imprints on you. And it’s yours.”

Dyrfinna cradled it in her hands, but now fear laid its cold hand on her. *My grandmama gave me a ship, with her blessing, that was mine. She gave me a group of fighters to command, which was mine. They took both away from me in a heartbeat. Who's to say they'd let me keep these baby dragons?*

They were nearly around the island, the eastern sky growing light. Dyrfinna started to think that they might be able to escape … when a chain-mail rattle echoed from the rocks behind them, bouncing off the quiet mainland.

Without a word, Skeggi dug his oars in hard and flew faster through the water, making a superhuman effort to escape.

She knelt on the bottom of the boat, her fingers fumbling with the eggs as she slid them into the pouch, wrapped it up in the protective cloth, secured the waterproof pouch, and slid it under her tunic above her belt. She needed both of her hands free. Her mind leapt ahead, and she prayed she wouldn't have to carry out the scenario she thought might be coming.

The cliffs on the island lit up with the light of the emberdragon creeping out of its cave. It stretched its neck out and screeched, and the screech bounced off the hills and crags on that side of the world in a way that went straight down Dyrfinna's spine. Then it opened its wings wide and leapt, hurtling through the air toward them. She had no idea how fast those dragons could go.

"You little shits!" the dragon screeched, blazing toward them. "I see you there! You think you're so smart!"

"Stop paddling!" Dyrfinna cried. "Breathe in deep! Let it out and take another. Get air into you!"

She pulled at the air with great, deep breaths as the dragon hurtled toward them, making herself dizzy.

She splashed in the water with Skeggi, and they held on to the side. She could hear Skeggi's deep breaths beside her.

"Get ready to dive," he said. Dyrfinna filled her lungs, a little more, a little more, watching that awful dragon come on.

The dragon inhaled, and at that sound she and Skeggi let go of the boat and dove into the water.

Both of them swam down, deeper and deeper as the water got cold and dark—

And suddenly the water behind them filled with light and grew hot.

Not again, not again, she thought frantically. But Skeggi gestured, pointing behind them, and started swimming in that direction. The water was cool and dark over here, where the dragon was not directing its flames. In the ocean, heat was slow to travel.

They clung together, slowly drifting upward. The water boiled where the dragon continued blasting it.

She pointed, and Skeggi shook his head. Their hands were clasped together, his hand warm in hers.

The flames stopped. Above, the wavery dragon circled several times, then flew away.

Slowly, they rose to the surface, broke the water, breathed.

The dragon was flying back toward its cliff, as if in a hurry to get back to its babies. "Little shits," it muttered.

Thank Freyja.

They were both gasping for breath. The top of the boat was burned black, swaying back and forth on each wave. Their bodies bumped against each other as the waves tossed.

"Oh, ye gods," Skeggi said softly, his voice cracking. "Let's never do that again."

She couldn't do anything about how her heart was pounding.

A wave nudged them together.

And suddenly they were kissing.

His mouth opened to hers, and she was pressing her body to his, feeling his heat. His arms went around her waist, and her hands rose out of the water to his face, holding him there for a moment, his thick beard rough under her palms. Her heart pounded like never before.

A long, sweet kiss.

He caught the fisher boat with one hand to keep them afloat, as she was sinking into the waves. With the other arm pulled her in, hard, against his body, and they kissed passionately.

Dyrfinna wrapped her legs around him, about to die from joy. They couldn't stop kissing, as if the dragon attack and their brushes with death, had unlocked something primal in them both.

Dyrfinna's heart pounded with what she knew would happen next, almost dizzy with the feel of his lips on her, his body against hers. The taste of him and seawater in her mouth. She only wanted more. She'd only wanted him for years.

"The eggs," Skeggi said against her lips, kissing her again and again.

But she thought of those dragon eggs in the waterproof pouch and her heart went cold.

She had nearly died for him – had kept him alive under a storm of dragon fire – she had every right to accept his kisses and all the pleasure his body could give her. All she had to do was go with the moment, the passion between them….

And though her blood pounded in her ears, and her need for him was overpowering, she gently extricated herself, gently pushed herself back from him in the water.

"I would have given my life for you," she said, her voice low and trembling from the force of her longing. "And I give my life for you again, by telling you no."

He stared at her, chest heaving, droplets of water trembling off the ends of his brown hair.

She knew that it was just their closeness to death that had suddenly set this off.

"Don't do this," she pleaded, her voice husky. "Not now. After all we've been through, so close to our moment of triumph, I can't let this endanger the Corae Guard and all that our friendship means."

She had three dragon eggs; she'd survived a dragon attack; now she wanted one more thing – one more thing for her very own. But she could survive without his love. She'd done it before.

There were more important things in the world than conquering everything she met.

They climbed back into the boat in silence. Skeggi took up the oars and began rowing.

She turned sideways on the bench so she wouldn't have to look at him, cradling her dragon egg in her hands, letting the sun warm it, watching the tiny dragon twitch inside the rubbery shell as if it were deep in quiet dragon dreams.

Then a chuckle from Skeggi. He stopped rowing for a moment, leaning on the oars, looking at her.

"You're right, Finna," he said quietly. "You did the right thing. And I thank you for it."

Dyrfinna looked up and met his smiling eyes. Her heart eased.

"Come on," he said, beginning to row. "Let's get these eggs back to our ship and show them to the rest of the Corae Guard. Upon her bones."

"Upon her bones," Dyrfinna echoed softly.

New joy sparked in her as they rounded the curve of the island and the dragon's isle fell out of sight behind them.

MEETING FUTURE FRIENDS

They managed to sneak onto shore, where Gefjun and Ostryg had been waiting for them. Gefjun took one look at their faces and said, "Let us help you get the fisher boat back to the ship. I'm just glad you both made it back alive."

"We're about to leave," Ostryg said, hoisting the fisher boat into Dyrfinna's ship.

Sure enough, when they came back to the camp, Hakr had just stood up and quieted the crew.

"I also came out here to make an announcement about the ship," Hakr said to the crowd in general. "The hole has been patched and that we should be ready to sail in a short while. So gather your possessions, finish cooking your food, and we will leave soon. Prepare to sail!" he added in a louder voice, which was taken up by others to spread the word to the rest of the crew.

Among all the relief to be moving again, Dyrfinna couldn't help but share their joy. She couldn't tell everybody – though she wished she could shout the news of their discovery.

She sat down alone next to the small brazier that burned near the prow. She opened her cloak to catch the heat to dry off her clothes, and carefully worked the pouch under her shirt to the front, so the dragon eggs inside of it could feel the heat.

The rowers took their places on the benches, and Hakr directed the ship through an obstacle course of rocky islands, making certain they did not run afoul of any rocky shoals hidden by the waves.

The dragon eggs were quiet. Her heart thudded again, and she turned away, feeling at the pouch under her shirt. Were they asleep? What if they were dying? What would she do if it were dying? How would she know?

Then felt the eggs stir inside the pouch and nearly collapsed with relief.

Soon the dragon-headed longship was underway again, crowded with Vikings talking, a couple of them guffawing at some joke that Sinkr was telling in the back of the ship.

Now Gefjun and Ostryg came to join her. Skeggi came, too, though he stood behind them, keeping a lookout.

"Skeggi said you found something," Gefjun murmured, leaning in.

Dyrfinna looked around to be sure nobody was nearby to hear. "This must be kept secret – especially from Sinkr. I don't know how long we can keep this under wraps, since we're on board ship, where there's no real privacy..."

Gefjun's eyes went wide. "What's so important that it needs to be kept secret? What did you find on that island?"

Ostryg made a rude noise with his lips. "She's messing with you. There's no way they could have found what you're thinking of."

"If you're messing with me I'll throw you overboard, I swear," Gefjun growled, but her eyes were staring at the pouch the way a dog stares at a treat in its owner's hand.

Joy awoke in Dyrfinna again as she looked around her, slowly moving the pouch into the shadow of her legs. Then she took a moment to look at Gefjun, memorizing that look on her face. She carefully opened the pouch and lifted out the eggs, and her friends leaned in.

She'd never heard Ostryg make that "Oh!" sound before. He sounded like a little boy who had been given a puppy.

Gefjun said, "I can't believe what I'm seeing," and she actually started to cry. She looked at Dyrfinna, a brilliant smile on her face, tears rolling out of her eyes.

"You did it, Finna," she whispered, looking back at the eggs. "I can't believe you did it."

"I can't believe they're so small," Ostryg said in a hushed, awe-filled voice. "Let me hold one."

"Me, too," Gefjun said, reaching out.

They cradled the eggs for a while, gazing in wonder at them like children, gasping in surprise when the little dragonets moved inside the rubbery shells.

"I'm so happy to meet you, little friend," Gefjun whispered to the egg she was holding, and Dyrfinna was overjoyed to see it twitch in response.

"Psst. Hide them," Skeggi whispered as a couple of Vikings passed. But as soon as they were gone, the eggs came out again.

"I brought a bucket for hot ashes," Dyrfinna told them in a low voice. "I'll fill it, and we can keep the eggs warm in there."

"Bring it," Gefjun whispered. "Let's get them tucked in."

Dyrfinna did, and moments later, the three eggs were quietly hidden in the hot ashes. One of the dragonets made a happy trill once its egg was lapped in warm ashes, and all four sword-friends jumped at the noise. Skeggi pretended to have been whistling, but he looked so startled that they all laughed.

"So who gets the dragons when they hatch?" Ostryg said quietly once the bucket had been loosely covered.

"Obviously Finna and Skeggi get one each," Gefjun said in a low voice, looking around to be sure she wasn't heard. "Then you and me can share one when it's old enough."

"I can get my own dragon, I bet," Ostryg said. "That dragon can be all yours."

"If Egill thinks he can stop the Corae Guard from existing, we've got other plans," Gefjun gloated. "Finna, for once I'm glad you didn't listen to my sensible words."

"Thank you."

The rowers rowed the ship into the ocean, the great red sail luffing in the fitful breeze. Once the ship was far enough out to catch the sea wind, the sail billowed out and the ship leaned. With a cheer, the rowers brought the oars rattling in, and Dyrfinna's ship was sailing once more – now with its precious cargo.

HOPE IS THE BEST REVENGE

Dyrfinna fell asleep and knew nothing more until the sun shining in her face, along with the heave of the ship on a long swell, woke her.

It was morning. A few Vikings were sitting around the ship eating oatcake or apples, polishing their swords, or fishing off the back of the ship. The ship was heeling to the wind, the sail billowing out beautifully in a way that Dyrfinna loved. The foam of the sea slid along the ship's side as she cut southward through the water, and the sun sparkled in the salt drops that flew up and spangled the air. Skeggi sat in the back of the ship, steering, while others dozed in the sun on the warm rowing benches.

She looked wildly around, and found the ash bucket next to her feet, the ashes still warm.

Dyrfinna got to her feet, groggy, refilled the bucket with hot ashes, making sure the baby dragons were okay. She was pleased and relieved to find them still wriggling, and one made a little snoring sound. Then she covered the bucket loosely and went to the front of the ship.

Hakr was shielding his eyes from the morning sun, staring out at the horizon. Dyrfinna looked too, but saw no sign of stormy weather, no dark line along the sea to warn her of an oncoming squall.

"What are you looking at out there?" she asked, standing beside him.

"I'm not sure," he replied, still staring out. "But for a moment, I saw something that looked like a sail on the edge of those islands, yonder."

Others joined them, gazing out to try and see what he saw.

"Maybe it's a bird."

"Storm cloud?"

"Gods, I hope not."

But then Dyrfinna saw the speck he meant, glimpsed between the great islands that littered their part of the world. It was a square, brown sail, following the same course their ship was. "He's right. It's a sail."

"And there's a second one," said a keen-eyed warrior woman, pointing. A few moments later, Dyrfinna was able to discern it as well, coming up alongside the first.

"A third," somebody whispered.

Her heart went cold when she saw the three ships on the water some distance off, sailing into view from behind an island.

Everybody made guesses about whose ships they were. Hakr climbed a little way up the mast, holding to the rigging and squinting across the water, while others gave their opinions on the shape of the masthead.

"They look like they're lions – King Varinn's ships."

"You blockhead, those are clearly dragons – Queen's ships."

Hakr shook his head. "No. Those ships are coming from King Varinn's holdings. Some of them, anyway."

That silenced the Vikings.

Now, as Dyrfinna watched, the low black hull and colorful sail of a fourth warship appeared from around the bend.

Then a fifth.

"Well," said Dyrfinna. "This should be fun."

The Vikings watched the strange fleet in silence. One by one, the longships turned and bore down upon them, five ships in all, their oars rhythmically churning the sea, the rampant lions on their prows creeping nearer.

"I see we've found King Varinn's fleet," muttered Skeggi.

"Or a part of it." Ostryg replied.

"Down sail! Warriors, prepare to fight! The only groaning and lamentation I want to hear is from the king's men you kill on board in glorious battle."

The mood grew somber as everyone leapt to take down the great sail.

Dyrfinna hated with all her heart that she was facing her end, but she faced it stoically. Never able to tell Aesa that she died defending her and her mama. Never able to watch her grow up, or help train her to become a great swordswoman like her big sissy. Or an artist if she wanted, that was also fine.

To never see her little sister again, to never hug her mama, was the worst pain she'd ever borne.

And the baby dragonets! She couldn't die now – she had dragon eggs!

Stop that, she scolded herself. *You are not dead yet. Where there's life, there's hope.*

So she faced her fear and she mastered it. Dyrfinna filled her mind with ways to take down as many other fighters as she could before she died.

Maybe it would be better if I died, she thought. Those same words she'd said, all unknowing, as she stood over Thora's body so long ago.

Because her death would atone for her little brother.

No. Dyrfinna gritted her teeth. She had to live. For her little sister, for her mother. For Thora, so she could take her revenge on behalf of her friend. And for the tiny dragons that would be under her care when they hatched.

"I'm staying alive," she murmured, "because a life of hope is the best revenge. Also," she added, flicking out her sword, "I'm revenging Thora – but I'm also revenging myself, for all that was taken from me."

"That's right," Gefjun said, coming to join her. "And if we keep the eggs alive, you've given the rest of the Corae Guard another chance."

"Upon her bones," Dyrfinna said solemnly, and Gefjun echoed her words as they tapped their sword hilts together.

She lowered her voice to her friends. "Quickly. Where can we put the dragon eggs so they're safe and warm? A place that's quickly accessible so we can grab them if we have to swim for our lives."

"I can hold them in my medical pouch," Gefjun said. "I will stay out of the fight to tend to the wounded. I will be wearing it at all times, and it's fairly waterproof."

"Get them," Dyrfinna said. "Ostryg, stand guard with her so nobody sees what she's doing."

Both her friends headed toward the brazier like a shot, where the dragon eggs had been tucked into the warm ashes.

Once the sail was down, she went to the side of the ship with the rest of the crew to face King Varinn's fighters and greet them with iron as they tried to come aboard. She looked at the runes on its blade – NONE SHALL GET THROUGH ME – and rolled her shoulders.

"Where is Sinkr?" she asked, trying to keep the sarcasm out of her voice. "Is he not here to put us in fighting order?"

One of the old veteran warriors, well-advanced in years and missing several fingers, jerked his thumb over his shoulder. "He's back there," he said, "in the rear of the ship, sleeping off his hangover."

Dyrfinna was aghast. "He's still sleeping? Why doesn't he rouse himself?"

The veteran shrugged. "He told us himself that we were making too much noise and that we were not to wake him."

One of the thieves that her grandmama had chosen for the crew piped up. "We're just following orders, you know."

"To be honest," the veteran added, meeting Dyrfinna's eyes, "we'd prefer to have you and Hakr lead us into this battle, over that seasick bastard who has never been seen a fight."

For a moment, Dyrfinna couldn't reply, not certain that she'd heard him correctly.

But a murmur of approval followed his words.

And now the steersman, that stout sea-rover, turned to his crew with a glint of grim humor in his eyes. "Fighters! Prepare for battle." Hakr took down the war horn from where it hung on the masts and blew a resounding blast that echoed off the far mountains across the water.

The warriors buckled on their armor and pulled their shields out of the sides of the ship, as lances, swords, and axes gleamed in their hands.

Ostryg put his arm around Gefjun. "Watch me," he said. "I'll kill all of King Varinn's people, all right? I bet that'll turn you on."

"*Not* the time," Gefjun snapped.

"Okay," Ostryg said. After a moment, he added in a hopeful voice, "But later, right?"

King Varinn's ships slowed down, oars dragging at the water. Dyrfinna, climbing into the rigging, could see the king's fighters hurriedly preparing for battle.

Well, she thought grimly, *at least they were taken aback by our presence as we sit here waiting for them.*

She hopped down and went to the prow with Hakr. Behind them stood the berserkers. Then, behind the mast stood the archers and spearmen, as well as several who were skilled with slinging stones. And well in the back, lying on a rowing bench with his arm over his eyes, was Sinkr, still sleeping through the racket. Not even the blast of the war horn had stirred him. Nobody had bothered to wake him. Dyrfinna felt a little hiccup of satisfaction as she turned her back on him.

The first ship was nearly in hailing distance.

Skeggi had been leaning over the rail, watching the ships approach. "This is odd," he said over his shoulder to his friends. "Look at the other four ships. They have the drekki heads, and if you've spent any time on the water, you know they're King Varinn's ships. You can recognize them right away. But this ship that's coming up to us, ahead of theirs – the people on it are wearing the finest armor, but they're sailing in a merchant's ship, not a warship."

Dyrfinna joined him, squinting at the ships. She'd thought that something had been off about this ship in particular, but hadn't focused on it since she had been assessing the warriors on board – trying to think of ways that her little crew could hold off all these fighters.

"Is that ship even a part of King Varinn's fleet? They're not showing it," Skeggi said, confused. "There are no banners – no shields with his emblem on them…"

A blonde woman in a red cloak came to the front of the ship and stood haughtily in the prow as they glided toward Dyrfinna and her ship. Something gleamed golden on her brow, looking out of place. Behind the woman, the forward decks were crowded with King Varinn's warriors.

"Stop rowing!" the woman called back to the rowers with an imperious gesture, and she paused as if annoyed by the amount of time it took for the oars to come out of the water and rumble in.

Her kohl-rimmed eyes like pinpricks, her blonde hair blowing in the breeze that blew in over the prow of her ship. Her armor was stained with dark patches – blood and gore from old battles that she had never bothered to clean off.

Then the woman in the red cloak turned toward Dyrfinna. "Tell me, you sorry-looking bitches, what is the name of your commander?"

Dyrfinna said, "Beg your pardon?" A flame of hatred lit in her heart and her shipmates snarled around her.

"I don't know," Ostryg growled. "Which bitch is asking?"

"Your main bitch is Sinkr," Gefjun looked over her shoulder toward the back of the ship. "But he's still on a rowing bench, sleeping off his hangover."

"Sucks to be him." Dyrfinna hopped up onto the rail on the prow, placing a hand on the dragonhead of her ship for balance. "I am Dyrfinna, the daughter of Egill, chieftain to the Queen Saehildr of Skala. And who are you, who asks my name?" Dyrfinna called defiantly, and added to herself, "because I'm a bigger bitch than you'll ever be."

The woman in the red cloak called, "I am …" but then she stopped, an odd look on her face. "Wait, what? Say that again," as if confused.

Dyrfinna exchanged puzzled looks with her friends. "Did I not enunciate enough for her liking?"

"I'd bet she's on something," Gefjun muttered.

She called again across the water, enunciating very clearly this time, "I am Dyrfinna, daughter of Egill, chieftain of Skala."

The woman in the red cloak gave a slow smile that somehow sickened Dyrfinna, though she didn't know why. Then she laughed, low, a sound that traveled across the water and made the group of Vikings behind her go quiet.

"So it's you," the woman said, smiling like a wolf. "You, who I've heard so much about. Daughter of

Egill!" And she crossed her arms, staring at Dyrfinna, smiling like a wolf.

Dyrfinna had no idea what the girl was playing at but she was not in a mood to be trifled with, especially over her so-called father's parentage. "I don't know if you might have anything of actual *interest* to say, but why don't you hurry up and introduce yourself. Unless you've forgotten your own name."

The scum on the ship behind the woman snarled and brandished their spears and swords at Dyrfinna, but the woman's smile merely twisted into a smirk as her ship drifted closer.

"I am Nauma," the woman called back. "Nauma, lover of blood. And I am the daughter of nobody."

But now the thing that had glittered on Nauma's grimy forehead earlier suddenly became clear to Dyrfinna's eyes – and a thrill of hatred burst through her body.

"Gefjun, Ostryg, Skeggi!" she shouted, hardly able to get the words out past her fury. "Look at that woman's brow. What is she wearing? Am I really seeing this?"

A sudden silence from the sword-friends, except for Gefjun's quiet song as she sang her eyesight sharper. And then hissing intakes of air – gasps – and Ostryg's guttural voice saying, "I am going to *kill* her."

"How did she get that?" Gefjun cried, close to exploding.

For on Nauma's brow gleamed a simple golden circlet with a gleaming carnelian on it.

Thora's crown. Simple and elegant, just the way she'd always liked everything.

The last time Dyrfinna and her friends had seen that crown was on the day of Thora's last rites, when they'd placed it gently on her head on her funeral ship, then sent her out to sea, all gloriously ablaze.

And now this laughing woman was wearing it.

"How did she steal that crown from Thora's head?" Gefjun asked, her voice shaking with anger.

Almost dizzy with hatred, Dyrfinna flung a prayer heavenward to Odin, the Allfather.

"I don't care if we face five ships or twenty," Dyrfinna said, her voice trembling with anger. "We are going to take Thora's crown back, and make that girl sorry she dared to touch it."

THUS ENDETH BOOK ONE.
LOOKETH THOU FOR BOOK TWO:
A BLAZE OF VALKYRIES

So what's going to happen in the next book? Let's use a Magic 8 Ball to randomly answer these questions:

How could Dyrfinna possibly pull this battle out of the fire?

BETTER NOT TELL YOU NOW

Will she see her little sister again?

DON'T COUNT ON IT

How many things are going to go wrong for her in the next book?

IT IS DECIDEDLY SO

When is Dyrfinna going to get a dragon buddy?

OUTLOOK HAZY TRY AGAIN

Will there be more undead walkers in the next book?

OUTLOOK GOOD

How about unicorns? Triceratops-es? Drunken raccoons? What about gardening geniuses? Or gnomes? Sentient trees named Ralph?

ASK AGAIN LATER

Is the author going to be a complete jerk and break the reader's heart?

IT IS CERTAIN

Or, instead of having your questions answered by a Magic 8 ball with no understanding of this story, a toy that doesn't understand how the author is absolutely *not* a complete jerk and is actually a very nice gal – just skip over here and get those questions answered by grabbing a copy of A BLAZE OF VALKYRIES, the second book in the

DRAGONRIDERS OF SKALA series. Then all your questions will be answered! … well, for the most part.

A BLAZE OF VALKYRIES, book 2 of the Dragonriders of Skala series, picks up where book 1 left off.

A FINISHED DRAGON SERIES

THE DRAGONRIDERS OF FIORENZA

Well, I am writing my way through this whole Skala series and trying to get this series finished in a timely fashion, lol. While you're waiting for my next book (I *really* hope you're waiting for my next book), why not splurge on my completed six-book series about a young dragonrider in 1200s Florence, and her fiercely loyal dragon Ryelleth. They love each other with all their hearts and they are ready to set the world on fire to keep from being separated.

The Dragonriders of Fiorenza series

Assassin's Blade
Dragon's Inferno
Guardian's Race
Witch's Plight
Warrior's Doom
Traitor's Oath

ACKNOWLEDGEMENTS

Every writer works from within a community, even if the writer happens to be a complete hermit who, at least inwardly, is quietly sidling away from any human contact whatsoever, if not galloping outright.

Big thanks to C. Dennis Moore, who got me into self-publishing in the first place, but who was also my accountability buddy for this novel and kept me writing when I was wandering off doing everything else BUT writing. If he hadn't showed up in my email when he did, back in 2016, I would be the most miserable gal in the world right now. I'm happy as a lark, all because Dennis set my feet on the road to self-publishing where I could publish all my old books plus a zillion new ones.

Anyway, now we send our daily word counts back and forth, which is our accountability thing, and it's been very helpful for keeping me on task. Thanks a million, Dennis. If you like horror, go buy his books.

I had a contest to name Dyrfinna's sword, and my newsletter folks voted and chose Signe, which means Victory, as its name. Many thanks to Tina Lonergan, who came up with this name!

Many thanks to my readers, Acrobolus, Karin Anderson, Laurie MacLaren, Arissa, Sam Stokes, MFA, and Adrienne Foo. An additional hats off to Trae McMaken, for an excellent critique that helped me fill some plot holes.

A special thank you to Ky Bateman, the editor who really helped me whip this book into shape. My sales were lousy when I first sent the updated book into the world, so I enlisted his help in the rewrite, and he gave me a thousand-page critique (it wasn't actually a thousand pages, but close enough) that helped me get this book, and its sequel, into gear.

And of course Brad, Sophie, and Stevie. You guys are my whole world.

AUTHOR'S NOTE

Here's the backstory about how I came to write the Skala books.

I had been trying to get into traditional publishing for decades. Seriously. I'd written and sent many novels on submission, revised them over and over again. I'd gotten close with various editors and agents, had some super-encouraging emails, and a number of "revise and resubmit" requests (where the agent or editor wants to look at your story after you revise it). In 2008, an agent wanted to take me on, and I was so excited because after all of these years I finally found an agent! The only problem was, she wanted me to write contemporary, realistic novels. Well, that wasn't going to work for me, and we ended up parting ways because fantasy wasn't in her wheelhouse. In the end, it didn't matter how close I could get to yes, because the agents and editors always ended by saying No.

In late 2016, I had just come off a very discouraging stint of querying. I'd finally gotten one nonfiction book traditionally published, and I had a MFA for writing for children, but even despite these victories, I was getting less interest in my stories than before. I was doing cartwheels trying to attract the attention of agents and editors who didn't give a damn. By this time, I couldn't write two words without constantly looking over my own shoulder and worrying, "Will they like this? Will they like that? Is this good enough?"

I was so discouraged that I was wondering if I really had it in me to be a writer – and that's bad, because writing is something I've done for all my life, and allegedly I'm good at it.

But it was also about that time when I started self-publishing all my old novels that I'd sent out to agents and editors over and over. I loved self-publishing, loved getting my books into the world. But I wasn't writing novels (though I was writing gardening books). I honestly didn't think I had it in me to write another novel.

Then I ran into Pauline Creeden on a YA collaboration board. She asked me to collaborate with her on a series where we mixed dragons and Vikings. I hadn't collaborated with anybody before, didn't know the first thing about it – but Pauline put her faith in me at a time when absolutely nobody else would. So I was determined to do the best job I possibly could for her to repay her trust, even though I was secretly wondering if I really had it in me to pull this off.

She gave me a deadline of a couple months to write an 80,000-word novel – and this was during the busiest time of the year for me at work, during overtime city! I cranked out the words, even when I didn't think I could do it, even when I didn't think I had anything to write about, even when I was sure my writing well was dry.

When I was finished with the first book, I'd written 90,000 words in those two months, and I was blown away. It felt like I'd leapfrogged over Mt. Everest! I'd never even written so many words on any of my other books in my life!!

When people put their faith in you, it's a game-changer. It is an absolute game-changer.

Anyway, I wrote the rest of the original Skala series for her, plus an additional book, and it's been a good partnership. Now I'm doing my own thing with the books and taking the series in a slightly different direction.

Since then, I've written a new dragon series set in the same universe, except all the action takes place in Italia in the bustling city of Fiorenza, where a girl and her dragon fight to keep from being separated – the DRAGONRIDERS OF FIORENZA series. I kept wanting to return to Skala now and then, and when I finished the Fiorenza series, I was happy to jump back to Skala, up in western Norway, and dig into this world again, and revisit all my old friends again.

At first, my plan was to simply rewrite the Skala series, but as I revised, I kept seeing so many missed opportunities that I wanted to build upon this time around, and I really wanted to dig deeply into this world. So I did, and it's really paid off. Now the Queen's daughter has a ton of backstory, Rjupa plays a bigger role. I've been able to explore the difficult relationship between Dyrfinna and her father, and oh yes, now the dragons TALK, which they didn't do in the original version of THE FLAME OF BATTLE. This book is just about brand new, with only a smidgeon of the original book remaining – and even that, too, has been revised and hammered into a different form.

But hats off to Pauline, for believing in me during a dark time, and giving me the boost that I so badly needed. I believe in myself and my abilities again, and after that, I took off like a rocket sled on rails. And now, instead of fretting about what some overworked agent might think about my book, I am writing and publishing my own books like crazy. And I love my work.

Sometimes, when you can't obtain a dream, you end up pursuing a better dream. And that makes all the difference.

All best,
Melinda R. Cordell
Nodaway, Mo.

A Cup
o' Tea
Buy me a cup of tea on Patreon! In return, you get a behind-the-scenes look at upcoming books, new book covers, audiobooks, free reads. You'll see chapters as I write them. And I get tea. It's a win-win!
CLICK HERE TO FOLLOW
@Rosefiend on Patreon

This was me back in 1995 when I was just starting my writing career and I was a real writing hotshot. To tell the truth, I still am.

About the Author

Melinda R. Cordell has written a truckload of YA novels, including the Dragonriders of Fiorenza series (like *Game of Thrones*, with Vikings).

A former city horticulturist and a long-time garden writer, Melinda has also written 12 books in the Easy-Growing Gardening series under the name Rosefiend Cordell.

Melinda lives in northwest Missouri with her husband and two kids, the best family to walk the earth, and is writing about 24 books at once, fueled by passion and caffeine.

If you want to keep up with her, subscribe to her newsletter, to get a free book!! Or drop her a friendly note at rosefiend@gmail.com.

Follow her on Patreon to get a behind-the-scenes look at this author's world. See new book covers, read excerpts of upcoming stories before anybody else does, help her name characters, and superfans get to show up on her novels! Buy Melinda a cup of tea every month here.

Don't forget to leave a book review on your favorite retailer, or on BookBub or Goodreads!

melindacordell.com

Thanks for reading!

www.ingramcontent.com/pod-product-compliance
Lightning Source LLC
La Vergne TN
LVHW041107080826
845145LV00007B/1716